"DO YOU THINK she's really going to do it?" Emily whispered. A car slid past, brightening Toby's house.

"Nah," Spencer said, nervously twirling her diamond studs. "She's bluffing."

Aria put the tip of one of her black braids in her mouth. "Totally."

"How do we know Toby's even in there?" Hanna asked.

They fell into an edgy silence. They'd been in on their fair share of Ali pranks, but those had been innocent— sneaking into the saltwater hot tub at Fermata spa or putting droplets of black dye into Spencer's sister's shampoo. But something about this made them all just a little . . . uneasy.

Boom!

Flawless

A PRETTY LITTLE LIARS NOVEL

SARA SHEPARD

HARPERTEEN
An Imprint of HarperCollins*Publishers*

For MDS and RNS

HarperTeen is an imprint of HarperCollins Publishers.

Flawless

 Produced by Alloy Entertainment
151 West 26th Street, New York, NY 10001

Library of Congress Cataloging-in-Publication Data
Shepard, Sara, 1977–
   Flawless / Sara Shepard.— 1st ed.
      p.   cm. — (Pretty little liars)
   Summary: After their friend who has been missing for more than
three years turns up dead, four former best friends continue to receive
frightening messages from someone who knows damaging secrets about
them.
   ISBN 978-0-06-088735-3 (pbk.)
   [1. Secrets—Fiction. 2. Conduct of life—Fiction. 3. Friendship—
Fiction. 4. High schools—Fiction. 5. Schools—Fiction. 6. Mystery
and detective stories.] I. Title.
PZ7.S54324Fl 2007   2007002989
[Fic]—dc22   CIP
                                                          AC

❖
First HarperTeen paperback edition, 2008
13 CG/RRDC 40 39 38 37 36 35 34 33 32 31

An eye for an eye and the whole world goes blind.

—GANDHI

HOW IT REALLY BEGAN

You know that boy who lives a few doors down from you who's just the creepiest person alive? When you're on your front porch, about to kiss your boyfriend good night, you might glimpse him across the street, *just standing there.* He'll randomly appear when you're gossiping with your best friends—except maybe it's not so random at all. He's the black cat who seems to know your route. If he rides by your house, you think, *I'm going to fail my bio exam.* If he looks at you funny, watch your back.

Every town has a black-cat boy. In Rosewood, his name was Toby Cavanaugh.

"I think she needs more blush." Spencer Hastings leaned back and examined one of her best friends, Emily Fields. "I can still see her freckles."

"I've got some Clinique concealer." Alison DiLaurentis sprang up and ran to her blue corduroy makeup bag.

Emily looked at herself in the mirror propped up on Alison's living room coffee table. She tilted her face one way, then another, and puckered her pink lips. "My mom would kill me if she saw me with all this stuff on."

"Yeah, but we'll kill you if you take it off," warned Aria Montgomery, who was, for her own Aria reasons, prancing around the room in a pink mohair bra she'd recently knitted.

"Yeah, Em, you look awesome," Hanna Marin agreed. Hanna sat cross-legged on the floor and kept swiveling around to check that her crack wasn't sticking out of her low-rise, slightly-too-small Blue Cult jeans.

It was a Friday night in April, and Ali, Aria, Emily, Spencer, and Hanna were having one of their typical sixth-grade sleepovers: putting way too much makeup on one another, chowing on salt-and-vinegar kettle chips, and half-watching MTV *Cribs* on Ali's flat-screen TV. Tonight there was the added clutter of everyone's clothes spread out on the carpet, since they'd decided to swap clothes for the rest of their sixth-grade school year.

Spencer held up a lemon-yellow cashmere cardigan to her slender torso.

"Take it," Ali told her. "It'll look cute on you."

Hanna pulled an olive corduroy skirt of Ali's around her hips, turned to Ali, and struck a pose. "What do you think? Would Sean like it?"

Ali groaned and smacked Hanna with a pillow. Ever since they'd become friends in September, all Hanna could talk about was how much she *looooved* Sean Ackard, a boy in their class at the Rosewood Day School, where they'd all been going since kindergarten. In fifth grade, Sean had been just another short, freckled guy in their class, but over the summer, he'd grown a couple inches and lost his baby fat. Now, pretty much every girl wanted to kiss him.

It was amazing how much could change in a year.

The girls—everyone but Ali—knew *that* all too well. Last year, they were just . . . *there*. Spencer was the über-anal girl who sat at the front of the class and raised her hand at every question. Aria was the slightly freaky girl who made up dance routines instead of playing soccer like everyone else. Emily was the shy, state-ranked swimmer who had a lot going on under the surface—if you just got to know her. And Hanna might've been klutzy and bumbling, but she studied *Vogue* and *Teen Vogue*, and every once in a while she'd blurt out something totally random about fashion that no one else knew.

There was something special about all of them, sure, but they lived in Rosewood, Pennsylvania, a suburb twenty miles outside Philadelphia, and *everything* was special in Rosewood. Flowers smelled sweeter, water tasted better, houses were just plain bigger. People joked that the squirrels spent their nights cleaning up litter and weeding errant dandelions from the cobblestone sidewalks so Rosewood would look perfect for its demanding residents. In a place where everything looked so flawless, it was hard to stand out.

But somehow Ali did. With her long blond hair, heart-shaped face, and huge blue eyes, she was the most stunning girl around. After Ali united them in friendship—sometimes it felt like she'd *discovered* them—the girls were definitely more than just there. Suddenly, they had an all-access pass to do things they'd never dared to before. Like changing into short skirts in the Rosewood Day girls' bathroom after they got off the bus in the morning. Or passing boys ChapStick-kissed notes in class. Or walking down the Rosewood Day hallway in an intimidating line, ignoring all the losers.

Ali grabbed a tube of shimmery purple lipstick and smeared it all over her lips. "Who am I?" The others groaned—Ali was imitating Imogen Smith, a girl in their class who was a little bit too in love with her Nars lipstick.

"No, wait." Spencer pursed her bow-shaped lips and handed Ali a pillow. "Put this up your shirt."

"Nice." Ali stuffed it under her pink polo, and everyone giggled some more. The rumor was that Imogen had gone all the way with Jeffrey Klein, a tenth grader, and she was having his baby.

"You guys are awful." Emily blushed. She was the most demure of the group, maybe because of her super-strict upbringing—her parents thought anything fun was evil.

"What, Em?" Ali linked her arm through Emily's.

"Imogen's looking awfully fat—she should *hope* she's pregnant."

The girls laughed again, but a little uneasily. Ali had a talent for finding a girl's weakness, and even if she was right about Imogen, the girls all sometimes wondered if Ali was ever ripping on *them* when they weren't around. Sometimes it was hard to know for sure.

They settled back into sorting through one another's clothes. Aria fell in love with an ultra-preppy Fred Perry dress of Spencer's. Emily slid a denim miniskirt up her skinny legs and asked everyone if it was too short. Ali declared a pair of Hanna's Joe's jeans too bell-bottomy and slid them off, revealing her candy-pink velour boy shorts. As she walked past the window to the stereo, she froze.

"Oh my God!" she screamed, running behind the blackberry-colored velvet couch.

The girls wheeled around. At the window was Toby Cavanaugh. He was just . . . *standing there.* Staring at them.

"Ew, ew, ew!" Aria covered up her chest—she had taken off Spencer's dress and was again in her knitted bra. Spencer, who was clothed, ran up to the window. "Get away from us, perv!" she cried. Toby smirked before he turned and ran away.

When most people saw Toby, they crossed to the other side of the street. He was a year older than the girls, pale, tall, and skinny, and was always wandering around the neighborhood alone, seemingly spying on everyone. They'd heard rumors about him: that he'd been caught French-kissing his dog. That he was such a good swimmer because he had fish gills instead of lungs. That he slept in a coffin in his backyard tree house every night.

There was only one person Toby spoke to: his stepsister, Jenna, who was in their grade. Jenna was a hopeless dork as well, although far less creepy—at least she spoke in complete sentences. And she was pretty in an irksome way, with her thick, dark hair, huge, earnest green eyes, and pursed red lips.

"I feel, like, *violated*." Aria wriggled her naturally thin body as if it were covered in E. coli. They'd just learned about it in science class. "How dare he scare us?"

Ali's face blazed red with fury. "We have to get him back."

"How?" Hanna widened her light brown eyes.

Ali thought for a minute. "We should give him a taste of his own medicine."

The thing to do, she explained, was to scare Toby. When Toby wasn't skulking around the neighborhood, spying on people, he was guaranteed to be in his tree house. He spent every other waking second there, playing with his Game Boy or, who knows, building a giant robot to nuke Rosewood Day. But since the tree house was, obviously, up in a tree—and because Toby pulled up the rope ladder so no one could follow him—they couldn't just peek in and say boo. "So we

need fireworks. Luckily, we know just where they are."
Ali grinned.

Toby was obsessed with fireworks; he kept a stash of
bottle rockets at the base of the tree and often set them
off through his tree house's skylight. "We sneak over
there, steal one, and light it at his window," Ali explained.
"It'll totally freak him out."

The girls looked at the Cavanaugh house across the
street. Although most of the lights were already out,
it wasn't that late—only ten-thirty. "I don't know,"
Spencer said.

"Yeah," Aria agreed. "What if something goes wrong?"
Ali sighed dramatically. "C'mon, guys."

Everyone was quiet. Then Hanna cleared her throat.
"Sounds good to me."

"All right." Spencer caved. Emily and Aria shrugged
in agreement.

Ali clapped her hands and gestured to the couch by
the window. "I'll go do it. You can watch from here."

The girls scrambled over to the great room's big bay
window and watched Ali slip across the street. Toby's
house was kitty-corner to the DiLaurentises' and built in
the same impressive Victorian style, but neither house
was as big as Spencer's family's farm, which bordered
Ali's backyard. The Hastings compound had its own
windmill, eight bedrooms, a five-car detached garage, a
rock-lined pool, and a separate barn apartment.

Ali ran around to the Cavanaughs' side yard and right

up to Toby's tree house. It was partially obscured by tall elms and pines, but the streetlight illuminated it just enough for them to see its vague outline. A minute later, they were pretty sure they saw Ali holding a cone-shaped firework in her hands, stepping about twenty feet back, far enough so that she had a clear view into the tree house's flickering blue window.

"Do you think she's really going to do it?" Emily whispered. A car slid past, brightening Toby's house.

"Nah," Spencer said, nervously twirling the diamond studs her parents had bought her for getting straight A's on her last report card. "She's bluffing."

Aria put the tip of one of her black braids in her mouth. "Totally."

"How do we know Toby's even in there?" Hanna asked.

They fell into an edgy silence. They'd been in on their fair share of Ali's pranks, but those had been innocent— sneaking into the saltwater hot tub at Fermata spa when they didn't have appointments, putting droplets of black dye into Spencer's sister's shampoo, sending fake secret admirer letters from Principal Appleton to dorky Mona Vanderwaal in their grade. But something about this made them all just a little . . . uneasy.

Boom!

Emily and Aria jumped back. Spencer and Hanna pressed their faces against the window. It was still dark across the street. A brighter light flickered from the tree house window, but that was all.

Hanna squinted. "Maybe that wasn't the firework."

"What else could it have been?" Spencer said sarcastically. "A gun?"

Then the Cavanaughs' German shepherd started to bark. The girls grabbed one another's arms. The side patio light snapped on. There were loud voices, and Mr. Cavanaugh burst out the side door. Suddenly, little fingers of fire leapt up from the tree house window. The fire started to spread. It looked like the video Emily's parents made her watch every year at Christmas. Then came the sirens.

Aria looked at the others. "What's going on?"

"Do you think . . . ?" Spencer whispered.

"What if Ali—" Hanna started.

"Guys." A voice came from behind them. Ali stood in the great room doorway. Her arms were at her sides and her face was pale—paler than they'd ever seen it before.

"What happened?" everyone said at once.

Ali looked worried. "I don't know. But it wasn't my fault."

The siren got closer and closer . . . until an ambulance wailed into the Cavanaugh driveway. Paramedics poured out and rushed to the tree house. The rope had been lowered down.

"What happened, Ali?" Spencer turned, heading out the door. "You've got to tell us what happened."

Ali started after her. "Spence, no."

Hanna and Aria looked at each other; they were too afraid to follow. Someone might see them.

Spencer crouched behind a bush and looked across the street. That was when she saw the ugly, jagged hole in Toby's tree house window. She felt someone creeping up behind her. "It's me," Ali said.

"What—" Spencer started, but before she could finish, a paramedic began climbing back down the tree house, and he had someone in his arms. Was Toby *hurt*? Was he . . . *dead*?

All the girls, inside and out, craned to see. Their hearts began to beat faster. Then, for just a second, they stopped.

It wasn't Toby. It was Jenna.

Several minutes later, Ali and Spencer came back inside. Ali told them all what happened with an almost-eerie calmness: the firework had gone through the window and hit Jenna. No one had seen her light it, so they were safe, as long as they all kept quiet. It was, after all, Toby's firework. If the cops would blame anyone, it would be him.

All night, they cried and hugged and went in and out of sleep. Spencer was so shell-shocked, she spent hours curled in a ball, wordlessly flicking from E! to the Cartoon Network to Animal Planet. When they awoke the next day, the news was all over the neighborhood: someone had confessed.

Toby.

The girls thought it was a joke, but the local paper confirmed that Toby had admitted to playing with a lit firework in his tree house, accidentally sending one at his sister's face . . . and the firework had *blinded* her. Ali read it out loud as they all gathered around her kitchen table, holding hands. They knew they should be relieved, except . . . they knew the truth.

The few days that Jenna was in the hospital, she was hysterical—and confused. Everyone asked her what had happened, but she didn't seem to remember. She said she couldn't recall anything that happened right before the accident, either. Doctors said it was probably post-traumatic stress.

Rosewood Day held a don't-play-with-fireworks assembly in Jenna's honor, followed by a benefit dance and a bake sale. The girls, especially Spencer, participated overzealously, although of course they pretended not to know anything about what had happened. If anyone asked, they said that Jenna was a sweet girl and one of their closest pals. A lot of girls who'd never spoken to Jenna were saying the exact same thing. As for Jenna, she never came back to Rosewood Day. She went to a special school for the blind in Philadelphia, and no one saw her after that night.

Bad things in Rosewood were all eventually gently nudged out of sight, and Toby was no exception. His parents homeschooled him for the remainder of the year. The summer passed, and the next school year Toby went to a reform school in Maine. He left unceremoniously one clear day in mid-August. His father drove him to the

SEPTA station, where he took the train to the airport alone. The girls watched as his family tore down the tree house that afternoon. It was like they wanted to erase as much of Toby's existence as possible.

Two days after Toby left, Ali's parents took the girls on a camping trip to the Pocono Mountains. The five of them went white-water rafting and rock-climbing, and tanned on the banks of the lake. At night, when their conversation turned to Toby and Jenna—as it often did that summer—Ali reminded them that they could never, *ever* tell *anyone*. They'd all keep the secret forever . . . and it would bond their friendship into eternity. That night, when they zipped themselves into their five-girl tent, J. Crew cashmere hoodies up around their heads, Ali gave each of them a brightly colored string bracelet to symbolize the bond. She tied the bracelets on each of their wrists and told them to repeat after her: "I promise not to tell, until the day I die."

They went around in a circle, Spencer to Hanna to Emily to Aria, saying exactly that. Ali tied on her bracelet last. "Until the day I die," she whispered after making the knot, her hands clasped over her heart. Each of the girls squeezed hands. Despite the dreadfulness of the situation, they felt lucky to have each other.

The girls wore their bracelets through showers, spring break trips to D.C. and Colonial Williamsburg—or, in Spencer's case, to Bermuda—through grubby hockey practices and messy bouts with the flu. Ali managed to keep her bracelet the cleanest of everyone's, as if getting it dirty would cloud its purpose. Sometimes, they would touch their fingers to the bracelet and whisper, "Until the day I die," to remind themselves of how close they all were. It became their code; they all knew what it meant. In fact, Ali said it less than a year later, the very last day of seventh grade, as the girls were starting their summer-kickoff sleepover. No one knew that in just a few short hours, Ali would disappear.

Or that it would be the day she died.

1

AND WE THOUGHT
WE WERE FRIENDS

Spencer Hastings stood on the apple-green lawn of the Rosewood Abbey with her three ex–best friends, Hanna Marin, Aria Montgomery, and Emily Fields. The girls had stopped speaking more than three years ago, not long after Alison DiLaurentis mysteriously went missing, but they'd been brought back together today for Alison's memorial service. Two days ago, construction workers had found Ali's body under a concrete slab behind what used to be her house.

Spencer looked again at the text message she'd just received on her Sidekick.

I'm still here, bitches. And I know everything. —A

"Oh my God," Hanna whispered. Her BlackBerry's screen read the same thing. So did Aria's Treo and Emily's Nokia. Over the past week, each of them had gotten e-mails, texts, and IMs from someone who went by the initial *A*. The notes had mostly been about stuff from seventh grade, the year Ali went missing, but they'd also mentioned new secrets . . . stuff that was happening *now*.

Spencer thought A might have been Alison—that somehow she was back—except that was out of the question now, right? Ali's body had decayed under the concrete. She'd been . . . dead . . . for a long, long time.

"Do you think this means . . . The Jenna Thing?" Aria whispered, running her hand over her angular jaw.

Spencer slid her phone back in her tweed Kate Spade bag. "We shouldn't talk about this here. Someone might hear us." She glanced nervously at the abbey's steps, where Toby and Jenna Cavanaugh had stood just a moment before. Spencer hadn't seen Toby since before Ali even went missing, and the last time she saw Jenna was the night of her accident, limp in the arms of the paramedic who'd carried her down.

"The swings?" Aria whispered, meaning the Rosewood Day Elementary playground. It was their old special meeting place.

"Perfect," Spencer said, pushing through a crowd of mourners. "Meet you there."

It was the late afternoon on a crystal-clear fall day. The air smelled like apples and wood smoke. A hot-air balloon floated overhead. It was a fitting day for a memorial service for one of the most beautiful girls in Rosewood.

I know everything.

Spencer shivered. It had to be a bluff. Whoever this A was, A couldn't know *everything*. Not about The Jenna Thing . . . and certainly not about the secret only Spencer and Ali shared. The night of Jenna's accident, Spencer had witnessed something that her friends hadn't, but Ali had made her keep it a secret, even from Emily, Aria, and Hanna. Spencer had wanted to tell them, but when she couldn't, she pushed it aside and pretended that it hadn't happened.

But . . . it had.

That fresh, springy April night in sixth grade, just after Ali shot the firework into the tree house window, Spencer ran outside. The air smelled like burning hair. She saw the paramedics bringing Jenna down the tree house's shaky rope ladder.

Ali was next to her. "Did you do that on purpose?" Spencer demanded, terrified.

"No!" Ali clutched Spencer's arm. "It was—"

For years, Spencer had tried to block out what had come next: Toby Cavanaugh coming straight for them. His hair was matted to his head, and his goth-pale face was flushed. He walked right up to Ali.

"*I saw you.*" Toby was so angry he was shaking. He glanced toward his driveway, where a police car had pulled in. "I'm going to tell."

Spencer gasped. The ambulance doors slammed shut and its sirens screamed away from the house. Ali was calm. "Yeah, but I saw *you*, Toby," she said. "And if you tell, I'll tell, too. Your *parents*."

Toby took a step back. "No."

"*Yes*," Ali countered. Although she was only five-three, suddenly she seemed much taller. "*You* lit the firework. You hurt your sister."

Spencer grabbed her arm. What was she doing? But Ali shook her off.

"Stepsister," Toby mumbled, almost inaudibly. He glanced at his tree house and then toward the end of the street. Another police car slowly rolled up to the Cavanaugh house. "I'll get you," he growled to Ali. "You just wait."

Then he disappeared.

Spencer grabbed Ali's arm. "What are we going to do?"

"Nothing," Ali said, almost lightly. "We're fine."

"Alison . . ." Spencer blinked in disbelief. "Didn't you hear him? He said he saw what you did. He's going to tell the police right now."

"I don't think so." Ali smiled. "Not with what I've got on him." And then she leaned over and whispered what she'd seen Toby do. It was something so disgusting Ali had forgotten she was holding the lit firework until it shot out of her hands and through the tree house window.

Ali made Spencer promise not to tell the others about any of it, and warned that if Spencer *did* tell them, she'd figure out a way for Spencer—and only Spencer—to take the heat. Terrified at what Ali might do, Spencer kept her mouth shut. She worried that Jenna might say something—surely Jenna remembered that Toby hadn't done it—but Jenna had been confused and delirious . . . she'd said that night was a blank.

Then, a year later, Ali went missing.

The police questioned everyone, including Spencer, asking if there was anyone who wanted to hurt Ali. *Toby*, Spencer thought immediately. She couldn't forget the moment when he'd said: *I'll get you.* Except naming Toby meant telling the cops the truth about Jenna's accident—that she was partially responsible. That she'd known the truth all this time and hadn't told anyone. It also meant telling her friends the secret she'd been keeping for more than a year. So Spencer said nothing.

Spencer lit another Parliament and turned out of the Rosewood Abbey parking lot. *See?* A couldn't possibly know everything, like the text had said. Unless, that was, A was Toby Cavanaugh . . . But that didn't make sense. A's notes to Spencer were about a secret that only Ali knew: back in seventh grade, Spencer had kissed Ian, her sister Melissa's boyfriend. Spencer had admitted what she'd done to Ali—but no one else. And A also knew about Wren, her sister's now-ex, whom Spencer had done more than just kiss last week.

But the Cavanaughs *did* live on Spencer's street. With binoculars, Toby might be able to see in her window. And Toby *was* in Rosewood, even though it was September. Shouldn't he be at boarding school?

Spencer pulled into the brick-paved driveway of the

Rosewood Day School. Her friends were already there, huddling by the elementary school jungle gym. It was a beautiful wooden castle, complete with turrets, flags, and a dragon-shaped slide. The parking lot was deserted, the brick walkways were empty, and the practice fields were silent; the whole school had the day off in Ali's memory.

"So we all got texts from this A person?" Hanna asked as Spencer approached. Everyone had her cell phone out and was staring at the *I know everything* note.

"I got two others," Emily said tentatively. "I thought they were from Ali."

"I did too!" Hanna gasped, slapping her hand on the climbing dome. Aria and Spencer nodded as well. They all looked at one another with wide, nervous eyes.

"What did yours say?" Spencer looked at Emily.

Emily pushed a lock of blondish-red hair out of her eye. "It's . . . personal."

Spencer was so surprised, she laughed aloud. "You don't have any secrets, Em!" Emily was the purest, sweetest girl on the planet.

Emily looked offended. "Yeah, well, I do."

"Oh." Spencer plopped down on one of the slide's steps. She breathed in, expecting to smell mulch and sawdust. Instead she caught a whiff of burning hair—just like the night of Jenna's accident. "How about you, Hanna?"

Hanna wrinkled her pert little nose. "If Emily's not talking about hers, I don't want to talk about mine. It was something only Ali knew."

"Same with mine," Aria said quickly. She lowered her eyes. "Sorry."

Spencer felt her stomach clench up. "So everyone has secrets only *Ali* knew?"

Everyone nodded. Spencer snorted nastily. "I thought we were best friends."

Aria turned to Spencer and frowned. "So what did yours say, then?"

Spencer didn't feel like her Ian secret was all that juicy. It was nothing compared to what else she knew about The Jenna Thing. But now she felt too proud to tell. "It's a secret Ali knew, same as yours." She pushed her long dirty-blond hair behind her ears. "But A also e-mailed me about something that's happening now. It felt like someone was *spying* on me."

Aria's ice-blue eyes widened. "Same here."

"So there's someone watching all of us," Emily said. A ladybug landed delicately on her shoulder, and she shook it off as though it were something much scarier.

Spencer stood up. "Do you think it could be . . . Toby?"

Everyone looked surprised. "Why?" Aria asked.

"He's part of The Jenna Thing," Spencer said carefully. "What if he knows?"

Aria pointed to the text on her Treo. "You really think this is about . . . The Jenna Thing?"

Spencer licked her lips. *Tell them.* "We still don't know why Toby took the blame," she suggested, testing to see what the others would say.

Hanna thought for a moment. "The only way Toby could know what we did is if one of us told." She looked at the others distrustfully. "*I* didn't tell."

"Me neither," Aria and Emily quickly piped up.

"What if Toby found out another way?" Spencer asked.

"You mean if someone else saw Ali that night and told him?" Aria asked. "Or if he saw Ali?"

"No . . . I mean . . . I don't know," Spencer said. "I'm just throwing it out there."

Tell them, Spencer thought again, but she couldn't. Everyone seemed wary of one another, sort of like it had been right after Ali went missing, when their friendship disintegrated. If Spencer told them the truth about Toby, they'd hate her for not having told the police when Ali disappeared. Maybe they'd even blame her for Ali's death. Maybe they should. What if Toby really had . . . done it? "It was just a thought," she heard herself saying. "I'm probably wrong."

"Ali said no one knew except for us." Emily's eyes looked wet. "She *swore* to us. Remember?"

"Besides," Hanna added, "how could Toby know that much about us? I could see it being one of Ali's old hockey friends, or her brother, or someone she actually spoke to. But she hated Toby's guts. We all did."

Spencer shrugged. "You're probably right." As soon as she said it, she relaxed. She was obsessing over nothing.

Everything was quiet. Maybe too quiet. A tree branch

snapped close by, and Spencer whirled around sharply. The swings swayed back and forth, as if someone had just jumped off. A brown bird perched atop the Rosewood Day Elementary roof glared at them, as if it knew things, too.

"I think someone's just trying to mess with us," Aria whispered.

"Yeah," Emily agreed, but she sounded just as unconvinced.

"So, what if we get another note?" Hanna tugged her short black dress over her slender thighs. "We should at least figure out who it is."

"How about, if we get another note, we call each other," Spencer suggested. "We could try to put the pieces together. But I don't think we should do anything, like, crazy. We should try not to worry."

"I'm not worried," Hanna said quickly.

"Me neither," Aria and Emily said at the same time. But when a horn honked on the main road, everyone jumped.

"Hanna!" Mona Vanderwaal, Hanna's best friend, poked her pale blond head out the window of a yellow Hummer H3. She wore large, pink-tinted aviator sunglasses.

Hanna looked at the others unapologetically. "I've gotta go," she murmured, and ran up the hill.

Over the last few years, Hanna had reinvented herself into one of the most popular girls at Rosewood Day. She'd lost weight, dyed her hair a sexy dark auburn, got a whole new designer wardrobe, and now she and Mona Vanderwaal—also a transformed dork—pranced around school, too good for everyone else. Spencer wondered what Hanna's big secret could be.

"I should go too." Aria pushed her slouchy purple purse higher on her shoulder. "So . . . I'll call you guys." She headed for her Subaru.

Spencer lingered by the swings. So did Emily, whose normally cheerful face looked drawn and tired. Spencer put a hand on Emily's freckled arm. "You all right?"

Emily shook her head. "Ali. She's—"

"I know."

They awkwardly hugged, then Emily broke away for the woods, saying she was going to take the shortcut home. For years, Spencer, Emily, Aria, and Hanna hadn't spoken, even if they sat behind one another in history class or were alone together in the girls' bathroom. Yet Spencer knew things about all of them—intricate parts of their personalities only a close friend could know. Like, of course Emily was taking Ali's death the hardest. They used to call Emily "Killer" because she defended Ali like a possessive Rottweiler.

Back in her car, Spencer sank into the leather seat and turned on the radio. She spun the dial and found 610 AM, Philly's sports radio station. Something about over-testosteroned guys barking about Phillies and Sixers stats calmed her. She'd hoped talking to her old friends might clear some things up, but now things just felt even . . . *ickier*. Even with Spencer's massive SAT vocabulary, she couldn't think of a better word to describe it than that.

When her cell phone buzzed in her pocket, she pulled it out, thinking it was probably Emily or Aria. Maybe even Hanna. Spencer frowned and opened her inbox.

Spence, I don't blame you for not telling them our little secret about Toby. The truth can be dangerous—and you don't want them getting hurt, do you? —A

2

HANNA 2.0

Mona Vanderwaal put her parents' Hummer into park but left the engine running. She tossed her cell phone into her oversize, cognac-colored Lauren Merkin tote and grinned at her best friend, Hanna. "I've been trying to call you."

Hanna stood cautiously on the pavement. "Why are you here?"

"What are you talking about?"

"Well, I didn't ask you for a ride." Trembling, Hanna pointed to her Toyota Prius in the parking lot. "My car's right there. Did someone tell you I was here, or . . . ?"

Mona wound a long, white-blond strand of hair around her finger. "I'm on my way home from the church, nut job. I saw you, I pulled over." She let out a little laugh. "You take one of your mom's Valiums? You seem sort of messed up."

Hanna pulled a Camel Ultra Light out of the pack in

her black Prada hobo bag and lit up. Of course she was
messed up. Her old best friend had been murdered, and
she'd been receiving terrifying text messages from someone named A all week. Every moment of today—getting
ready for Ali's funeral, buying Diet Coke at Wawa, merg-
ing onto the highway toward the Rosewood Abbey—
she felt sure someone was watching her. "I didn't see you
at the church," she murmured.

Mona took her sunglasses off to reveal her round blue
eyes. "You looked right at me. I waved at you. Any of this
sound familiar?"

Hanna shrugged. "I . . . don't remember."

"Well, I guess you were busy with your old friends,"
Mona shot back.

Hanna bristled. Her old friends were a sticky subject
between them—back a million years ago, Mona was one
of the girls Ali, Hanna, and the others teased. She
became *the* girl to rag on, after Jenna got hurt. "Sorry. It
was crowded."

"It's not like I was hiding." Mona sounded hurt. "I
was sitting behind Sean."

Hanna inhaled sharply. *Sean.*

Sean Ackard was her now ex-boyfriend; their relationship had imploded at Noel Kahn's welcome-back-to-school
field party last Friday night. Hanna had made the deci-
sion that Friday was going to be the night she lost her
virginity, but when she started to put the moves on Sean,
he dumped her and gave her a sermon about respecting

her body. In revenge, Hanna took the Ackard family's BMW out for a joyride with Mona and wrapped it around a telephone pole in front of a Home Depot.

Mona pressed her peep-toe heel on the Hummer's gas pedal, revving the car's billion-cylinder engine. "So listen. We have an emergency—we don't have dates yet."

"To what?" Hanna blinked.

Mona raised a perfectly waxed blond eyebrow. "Hello, Hanna? To Foxy! It's this weekend. Now that you dumped Sean, you can ask someone cool."

Hanna stared at the little dandelions growing out of the cracks in the sidewalk. Foxy was the annual charity ball for "the young members of Rosewood society," sponsored by the Rosewood Foxhunting League, hence the name. A $250 donation to the league's choice of charity got you dinner, dancing, a chance to see your picture in the *Philadelphia Inquirer* and on glam-R5.com—the area's society blog—and it was a good excuse to dress up, drink up, and hook up with someone else's boyfriend. Hanna had paid for her ticket in July, thinking she'd go with Sean. "I don't know if I'm even going," she mumbled gloomily.

"Of course you're going." Mona rolled her blue eyes and heaved a sigh. "Listen, just call me when they've reversed your lobotomy." And then she put the car back into drive and zoomed off.

Hanna walked slowly back to her Prius. Her friends had gone, and her silver car looked lonely in the empty parking lot. An uneasy feeling nagged at her. Mona was her best friend, but there were tons of things Hanna wasn't telling her right now. Like about A's messages. Or how she'd gotten arrested Saturday morning for stealing Mr. Ackard's car. Or that Sean dumped *her*, and not the other way around. Sean was so diplomatic, he'd only told his friends they'd "decided to see other people." Hanna figured she could work the story to her advantage so no one would ever know the truth.

But if she told Mona any of that, it would show her that Hanna's life was spiraling out of control. Hanna and Mona had re-created themselves together, and the rule was that as co-divas of the school, they had to be perfect. That meant staying swizzle-stick thin, getting skinny Paige jeans before anyone else, and never losing control. Any cracks in their armor could send them back to unfashionable dorkdom, and they never wanted to go back there. Ever. So Hanna had to pretend none of the horror of the past week had happened, even though it definitely had.

Hanna had never known anyone who had died, much less someone who was murdered. And the fact that it was *Ali*–in combination with the notes from A–was even spookier. If someone really knew about The Jenna Thing . . . and could tell . . . *and* if that someone had something to do with Ali's death, Hanna's life was definitely not in her control.

Hanna pulled up to her house, a massive brick

Georgian that overlooked Mt. Kale. When she glanced at herself in the car's rearview mirror, she was horrified to see that her skin was blotchy and oily and her pores looked *enormous*. She leaned closer to the mirror, and then suddenly . . . her skin was clear. Hanna took a few long, ragged breaths before getting out of the car. She'd been having a lot of hallucinations like this lately.

Shaken, she slid into her house and headed for her kitchen. When she strode through the French doors, she froze.

Hanna's mother sat at the kitchen table with a plate of cheese and crackers in front of her. Her dark auburn hair was in a chignon, and her diamond-encrusted Chopard watch glinted in the afternoon sun. Her Motorola wireless headset hung from her ear.

And next to her . . . was Hanna's father.

"We've been waiting for you," her dad said.

Hanna took a step back. There was more gray in his hair, and he wore new wire-rimmed glasses, but otherwise he looked the same: tall, crinkly eyes, blue polo. His voice was the same, too—deep and calm, like an NPR commentator. Hanna hadn't seen or spoken to him in almost four years. "What are you *doing* here?" she blurted.

"I've been doing some work in Philly," Mr. Marin said, his voice squeaking nervously on *work*. He picked up his Doberman coffee cup. It was the mug her dad used faithfully when he'd lived with them; Hanna wondered if he'd rooted through the cupboard to find it.

"Your mom called and told me about Alison. I'm so sorry, Hanna."

"Yeah," Hanna sounded out. She felt dizzy.

"Do you need to talk about anything?" Her mom nibbled on a piece of cheddar.

Hanna tilted her head, confused. Ms. Marin and Hanna's relationship was more boss/intern than mother/daughter. Ashley Marin had clawed her way up the executive ladder at the Philly advertising firm McManus & Tate, and she treated everyone like her employee. Hanna couldn't remember the last time her mom had asked her a touchy-feely question. Possibly never. "Um, that's okay. But thanks," she added, a little snottily.

Could they really blame her for being a tad bitter? After her parents divorced, her dad moved to Annapolis, started dating a woman named Isabel, and inherited a gorgeous quasi-stepdaughter, Kate. Her father made his new life so unwelcoming, Hanna visited him just once. Her dad hadn't tried to call her, e-mail her, anything, in years. He didn't even send birthday presents anymore—just checks.

Her father sighed. "This probably isn't the best day to talk things over."

Hanna eyed him. "Talk what over?"

Mr. Marin cleared his throat. "Well, your mom called me for another reason, too." He lowered his eyes. "The car."

Hanna frowned. Car? What car? *Oh.*

"It's bad enough you stole Mr. Ackard's car," her father said. "But you left the scene of the accident?"

Hanna looked at her mom. "I thought this was taken care of."

"Nothing is taken care of." Ms. Marin glared at her.

Could've fooled me, Hanna wanted to say. When the cops let her go on Saturday, her mother mysteriously told Hanna she'd "worked things out" so Hanna wouldn't be in trouble. The mystery was solved when Hanna found her mom and one of the young officers, Darren Wilden, practically doing it in her kitchen the next night.

"I'm serious," Ms. Marin said, and Hanna stopped smirking. "The police have agreed to drop the case, yes, but it doesn't change what's going on with *you*, Hanna. First you steal from Tiffany, now this. I didn't know what to do. So I called your father."

Hanna stared at the plate of cheese, too weirded out to look either of them in the eye. Her mom had told her dad that she'd gotten caught shoplifting at Tiffany too?

Mr. Marin cleared his throat. "Although the case was dropped with the police, Mr. Ackard wants to settle it privately, out of court."

Hanna bit the inside of her mouth. "Doesn't insurance pay for those things?"

"That's not it exactly," Mr. Marin answered. "Mr. Ackard made your mother an offer."

"Sean's father is a plastic surgeon," her mother explained, "but his pet project is a rehabilitation clinic for burn victims. He wants you to report there at three-thirty tomorrow."

Hanna wrinkled her nose. "Why can't we just give him the money?"

Ms. Marin's tiny LG cell phone started to ring. "I think this will be a good lesson for you. To do some good for the community. To understand what you've done."

"But I *do* understand!" Hanna Marin did not want to give her free time away to a burn clinic. If she *had* to volunteer, why couldn't it be somewhere chic? Like at the UN, with Nicole and Angelina?

"It's already settled," Ms. Marin said brusquely. Then she shouted into her phone, "Carson? Did you do the mock-ups?"

Hanna sat with her fingernails pressed into her fists. Frankly, she wished she could go upstairs, change out of her funeral dress—was it making her thighs look huge, or was that just her reflection in the patio doors?—redo her makeup, lose five pounds, and do a shot of vodka. Then she would come back down and reintroduce herself.

When she glanced at her father, he gave her a very small smile. Hanna's heart jumped. His lips parted as if he were going to speak, but then his cell phone rang, too. He held up one finger to Hanna to hold on. "Kate?" he answered.

Hanna's heart sank. *Kate.* The gorgeous, perfect quasi-stepdaughter.

Her father tucked the phone under his chin. "Hey!

How was the cross-country meet?" He paused, then beamed. "Under eighteen minutes? That's *awesome*."

Hanna grabbed a hunk of cheddar from the cheese plate. When she'd visited Annapolis, Kate wouldn't look at her. She and Ali, who'd come with Hanna for moral support, had formed an insta–pretty girl bond, excluding Hanna entirely. It drove Hanna to wolf down every snack within a one-mile radius—this was back when she was chubby and ugly and ate and ate. When she clutched her stomach in binged-out agony, her father had wiggled her toe and said, "Little piggy not feeling so good?" In front of *everyone*. And then Hanna had fled to the bathroom and forced a toothbrush down her throat.

The hunk of cheddar hovered in front of Hanna's mouth. Taking a deep breath, she stuffed it into a napkin instead and threw it in the trash. All that stuff happened a long time ago . . . when she was a very different Hanna. One only Ali knew about, and one Hanna had buried.

3

IS THERE AN AMISH SIGN-UP
SHEET SOMEWHERE?

Emily Fields stood in front of the Gray Horse Inn, a
crumbling stone building that was once a Revolutionary
War hospital. The current-day innkeeper had converted
its upper floors into an inn for rich out-of-town guests
and ran an organic café in the parlor. Emily peered
through the café's windows to see some of her classmates
and their families eating smoked-salmon bagels, pressed
Italian sandwiches, and enormous Cobb salads. Everyone
must have had the same post-funeral brunch craving.

"You made it."

Emily swung around to see Maya St. Germain leaning
against a terra-cotta pot full of peonies. Maya had called
as Emily was leaving the Rosewood Day swings, asking
that she meet her here. Like Emily, Maya still had on her
funeral outfit—a short, pleated black corduroy skirt, black
boots, and a black sleeveless sweater with delicate lace

stitching around the neck. And also like Emily, it seemed that Maya had scrounged to find black and mournful-looking stuff from the back of her closet.

Emily smiled sadly. The St. Germains had moved into Ali's old house. When workers started to dig up the DiLaurentises' half-finished gazebo to make way for the St. Germains' tennis court, they uncovered Ali's decayed body underneath the concrete. Ever since then, news vans, police cars, and curiosity seekers had gathered around the property 24/7. Maya's family was taking refuge here at the inn until things died down.

"Hey." Emily looked around. "Are your folks having brunch?"

Maya shook her thick brownish-black curls. "They went to Lancaster. To get back to nature or something. Honestly, I think they've been in shock, so maybe the simple life will do them some good." Emily smiled, thinking of Maya's parents trying to commune with the Amish in the small township west of Rosewood.

"You wanna come up to my room?" Maya asked, raising an eyebrow.

Emily pulled at her skirt—her legs were looking beefy from swimming—and paused. If Maya's family wasn't here, they'd be alone. In a room. With a bed.

When Emily first met Maya, she'd been psyched. She'd been pining for a friend who could replace Ali. Ali and Maya were really similar in a lot of ways—they were both fearless and fun, and they seemed to be the only two people in the world who understood the real Emily. They had something else in common: Emily felt something *different* around them.

"C'mon." Maya turned to go inside. Emily, not sure what else to do, followed.

She trailed Maya up the creaky, twisty stairs of the inn to her 1776-themed bedroom. It smelled like wet wool. It had slanted pine floors, a shaky, queen-size four-poster bed with a giant crazy quilt on top, and a puzzling contraption in the corner that looked like a butter churn. "My parents got my brother and me separate rooms." Maya sat down on the bed with a squeak.

"That's nice," Emily answered, perching on the edge of a rickety chair that had probably once belonged to George Washington.

"So, how *are* you?" Maya leaned toward her. "God, I saw you at the funeral. You looked . . . devastated."

Emily's hazel eyes filled with tears. She *was* devastated about Ali. Emily had spent the past three-and-a-half years hoping Ali would show up on her porch one day, as healthy and glowing as ever. And when she started receiving the A notes, she was sure Ali was back. Who else could have known? But now, Emily knew for certain that Ali was really gone. Forever. On top of that, someone knew her squirmiest secret—that she'd been in love with Ali—*and* that she felt the same way about Maya. And maybe that same someone knew the truth about what they'd done to Jenna, too.

Emily felt bad, refusing to tell her old friends what her notes from A said. It was just . . . she *couldn't*. One of A's notes was written on an old love letter that she'd sent to Ali. The ironic thing was that she *could* talk to Maya about what the notes said, but she was afraid to tell Maya about A. "I think I'm still pretty shook up," she finally answered, feeling a headache coming on. "But, also . . . I'm just tired."

Maya kicked off her boots. "Why don't you take a nap? You aren't going to feel any better sitting in that torture contraption of a chair."

Emily wrapped her hands around the chair's arms. "I–"

Maya patted the bed. "You look like you need a hug."

A hug *would* feel good. Emily pushed her reddish-blond hair out of her face and sat down on the bed next to Maya. Their bodies melted into each other. Emily could feel Maya's ribs through the fabric of her shirt. She was so petite, Emily could probably pick her up and spin her around.

They pulled away, pausing a few inches from each other's faces. Maya's eyelashes were coal black, and there were tiny flecks of gold in her irises. Slowly, Maya tilted Emily's chin up. She kissed her gently at first. Then harder.

Emily felt the familiar whoosh of excitement as Maya's hand grazed the edge of Emily's skirt. Suddenly, she reached underneath it. Her hands felt cold and surprising. Emily eyes shot open and she pulled away.

The frilly white curtains in Maya's room were open wide, and Emily could see the Escalades, Mercedes wagons, and Lexus Hybrids in the parking lot. Sarah Isling and Taryn Orr, two girls in Emily's grade, sauntered out of the restaurant exit, followed by their parents. Emily ducked.

Maya sat back. "What's wrong?"

"What are you *doing?*" Emily covered her unbuttoned skirt with her hand.

"What do you think I'm doing?" Maya grinned.

Emily glanced at the window again. Sarah and Taryn were gone.

Maya jiggled up and down on the bed's creaky mattress. "Did you know there's a charity party this Saturday called Foxy?"

"Yeah." Emily's whole body throbbed.

"I think we should go," Maya continued. "It sounds fun."

Emily frowned. "The tickets are $250. You have to be invited."

"My brother scored tickets. Enough for both of us." Maya inched closer to Emily. "Will you be my date?"

Emily shot off the bed. "I . . ." She took a step backward, stumbling on the slippery hooked rug. Lots of people from Rosewood Day went to Foxy. All the popular kids, all the jocks . . . everyone. "I have to go to the bathroom."

Maya looked confused. "It's over there."

Emily shut the crooked bathroom door. She sat on

the toilet and stared at the print on the wall of an Amish woman wearing a bonnet and an ankle-length dress. Perhaps it was a sign. Emily was always looking for signs to help her make decisions—in her horoscope, in fortune cookies, in random things like this. Maybe this picture meant, *Be like the Amish.* Weren't they chaste for life? Weren't their lives maddeningly simple? Didn't they burn girls at the stake for liking other girls?

And then her cell phone rang.

Emily pulled it out of her pocket, wondering if it was her mother wanting to know where Emily was. Mrs. Fields was less than pleased that Emily and Maya had become friends—for disturbing, possibly racist reasons. Imagine if her mom knew what they were up to now.

Emily's Nokia blinked, *One new text message.* She clicked READ.

> Em! Still enjoying the same kinds of *activities* with your best friends, I see. Even though most of us have totally changed, it's nice to know you're still the same! Gonna tell everyone about your new love? Or shall I? —A

"No," Emily whispered.

There was a sudden whoosh behind her. She jumped, bumping her hip on the sink. It was only someone flushing the toilet in the next guest room. Then there was some whispering and giggling. It sounded like it was coming from the sink drain.

"Emily?" Maya called. "Everything okay?"

"Uh . . . fine." Emily croaked. She stared at herself in the mirror. Her eyes were wide and hollow, and her reddish-blonde hair was disheveled. When she finally emerged from the bathroom, the bedroom lights were off and the shades were drawn.

"*Psssst*," Maya called from the bed. She'd laid seductively on her side.

Emily looked around. She was pretty sure Maya hadn't even locked the door. All those Rosewood kids were eating brunch downstairs. . . .

"I can't do this," Emily blurted out.

"What?" Maya's dazzlingly white teeth glowed in the dimness.

"We're friends." Emily plastered herself against the wall. "I like you."

"I like you, too." Maya ran a hand over one bare arm.

"But that's all I can be right now," Emily clarified. "Friends."

Maya's smile disappeared in the dark.

"Sorry." Emily shoved on her loafers fast, putting her right shoe on her left foot.

"It doesn't mean you have to leave," Maya said quietly.

Emily looked at her as she reached for the doorknob. Her eyes were already adjusting to the dim light, and she could see that Maya looked disappointed and confused and . . . and beautiful. "I should go," Emily mumbled. "I'm late."

"Late for what?"

Emily didn't answer. She turned for the door. Just as she suspected, Maya hadn't bothered to lock it.

4

THERE'S TRUTH IN WINE . . . OR, IN ARIA'S CASE, AMSTEL

As Aria Montgomery slipped into her family's boxy, avant-garde house—which stuck out on their typical Rosewood street of neoclassical Victorians—she heard her parents talking quietly in the kitchen.

"But I don't understand," her mother, Ella—her parents liked Aria to call them by their first names—was saying. "You told me you could make it to the artists' dinner last week. It's important. I think Jason might buy some of the paintings I did in Reykjavík."

"It's just that I'm already behind on my papers," her father, Byron, answered. "I haven't gotten back into the swing of grading yet."

Ella sighed. "How is it they have papers and you've only had two days of class?"

"I gave them their first assignment before the semester

started." Byron sounded distracted. "I'll make it up to you, I promise. How about Otto's? Saturday night?"

Aria shifted her weight in the foyer. Her family had just returned from two years in Reykjavík, Iceland, where her dad had been on sabbatical from teaching at Hollis, Rosewood's liberal arts college. It had been a perfect reprieve for all of them—Aria needed the escape after Ali went missing, her brother, Mike, needed some culture and discipline, and Ella and Byron, who'd begun to go days without speaking, seemed to fall back in love in Iceland. But now that they were back home, everyone was reverting back to their dysfunctional ways.

Aria passed the kitchen. Her dad was gone, and her mom was standing over the island, her head in her hands. When she saw Aria, she brightened. "How you doing, pumpkin?" Ella asked carefully, fingering the memorial card they'd received from Ali's service.

"I'm all right," Aria mumbled.

"You want to talk about it?"

Aria shook her head. "Later, maybe." She scuttled into the living room, feeling spastic and distracted, as though she'd drunk six cans of Red Bull. And it wasn't just from Ali's funeral.

Last week A had taunted Aria about one of her darkest secrets: In seventh grade, Aria caught her father kissing one of his students, a girl named Meredith. Byron had asked Aria not to tell her mother, and Aria never had, although she always felt guilty about it. When A threatened to tell Ella the whole ugly truth, Aria had assumed A was Alison. It was Ali who'd been with Aria when she caught Bryon and Meredith together, and Aria had never told anyone else.

But now Aria knew A couldn't be Alison, but A's threat was still out there, promising to ruin Aria's family. She knew she should tell Ella before A got to her—but she couldn't make herself do it.

Aria walked to the back porch, winding her fingers through her long black hair. A flash of white zoomed by. It was her brother, Mike, racing around the yard with his lacrosse stick. "Hey," she called, getting an idea. When Mike didn't answer, she walked out onto the lawn and stood in his path. "I'm going downtown. Wanna come?"

Mike made a face. "Downtown's full of dirty hippies. Besides, I'm practicing."

Aria rolled her eyes. Mike was so obsessed with making the Rosewood Day varsity lacrosse team, he hadn't even bothered to change out of his charcoal gray funeral suit before starting drills. Her brother was so cookie-cutter Rosewood—dirty white baseball cap, obsessed with PlayStation, saving up for a hunter-green Jeep Cherokee as soon as he turned sixteen. Unfortunately, there was no question they shared the same gene pool—both Aria and her brother were tall and had blue-black hair and unforgettable angular faces.

"Well, I'm going to get bombed," she told him. "You *sure* you want to practice?"

Mike narrowed his grayish-blue eyes at her, processing this. "You're not secretly dragging me to a poetry reading?"

She shook her head. "We'll go to the skankiest college bar we can find."

Mike shrugged and laid down his lacrosse stick. "Let's go," he said.

Mike fell into a booth. "This place rocks."

They were at the Victory Brewery—indeed the skankiest bar they could find. It was flanked by a piercing parlor and a store called Hippie Gypsy that sold "hydroponic seeds"—nudge, nudge. There was a puke stain on the sidewalk out front, and a half-blind, three-hundred-pound bouncer had waved them right through, too engrossed in *Dubs* magazine to card them.

Inside, the bar was dark and grubby, with a dingy Ping-Pong table in the back. This place was pretty much like Snooker's, Hollis's other grimy student bar, but Aria had vowed to never set foot in Snooker's again. She'd met a sexy boy named Ezra at Snooker's two weeks ago, but then he wound up being less of a boy and more of an AP English teacher—*her* AP English teacher. A sent Aria taunting texts about Ezra, and when Ezra accidentally saw what A had written, he assumed that Aria was telling the whole school about them. So ended Aria's Rosewood faculty romance.

A waitress with enormous boobs and Heidi braids

came up to their booth and looked at Mike suspiciously. "Are you twenty-one?"

"Oh, yeah," Mike said, folding his hands on the table. "I'm actually twenty-five."

"We'll have a pitcher of Amstel," Aria interrupted, kicking Mike under the table.

"And," Mike added, "I want a shot. Of Jaeger."

Heidi Braids looked pained, but she came back with the pitcher and the shot. Mike downed the Jaeger and made a puckered, girlish face. He slammed the shot glass on the chipped wooden table and eyed Aria. "I think I've cracked why you've become so loco." Mike had announced last week that he thought Aria was acting even freakier than usual, and he'd vowed to figure out why.

"I'm dying to know," Aria said dryly.

Mike pushed his fingers together in a steeple, a professorly gesture their father often made. "I think you're secretly dancing at Turbulence."

Aria laughed so forcefully, beer flew up her nasal passages. Turbulence was a strip club two towns over, next to a one-strip airport.

"A couple of guys said they saw a girl going in there who looked *just* like you," Mike said. "You don't have to keep it a secret from me. I'm cool."

Aria pulled discreetly at her knitted mohair bra. She'd made one for herself, Ali, and her old friends in sixth grade, and had worn hers to Ali's memorial as a tribute. Unfortunately, in sixth grade, Aria's measurements were about a cup size smaller, and the mohair itched like hell. "You mean you don't think I'm acting strange because a) we're back in Rosewood and I hate it here, and b) my old best friend is dead?"

Mike shrugged. "I thought you didn't really like that girl."

Aria turned away. There had been moments when she really didn't like Ali, that was true. Especially when Ali didn't take her very seriously, or when she hounded Aria for details about Byron and Meredith. "That's not true," she lied.

Mike poured more beer into his glass. "Isn't it messed up that she was, like, dumped in the ground? And, like, concrete was poured on top of her?"

Aria winced and shut her eyes. Her brother had zero tact.

"So you think someone killed her?" Mike asked.

Aria shrugged. It was a question that had been haunting her—a question no one else had asked. At Ali's memorial, no one came out and said Ali had been *murdered*, only that she'd been *found*. But what else could it have been but murder? One minute, Ali was at their sleepover. The next, she was gone. Three years later, her body showed up in a hole in her backyard.

Aria wondered if A and Ali's killer were linked—and if the affair was tangled up in The Jenna Thing. When Jenna's accident happened, Aria thought she saw some-one *besides* Ali at the base of Toby's tree house. Later that night, Aria was startled awake by the vision and decided she needed to ask Ali about it. She'd found her and Spencer whispering behind the closed bathroom door, but when Aria asked to come in, Ali told her to go back to sleep. By morning, Toby had confessed.

"I bet the killer's, like, someone out of left field," Mike said. "Like . . . someone you'd never guess in a trillion years." His eyes lit up. "How about Mrs. Craycroft?"

Mrs. Craycroft was their elderly neighbor to the right. She'd once saved up $5,000 worth of coins in Poland Spring jugs and tried to redeem them for cash at a nearby Coinstar. The local news did a story on her and everything. "Yep, you cracked the case," Aria deadpanned.

"Well, someone like that." Mike drummed his knobby fingers on the table. "Now that I know what's going on with *you*, I can focus my attention on Ali D."

"Go for it." If the cops weren't adept enough to find Ali in her own backyard, Mike might as well try his hand at it.

"So I'm thinking we need to play some beer-pong," Mike said, and before Aria could answer, he had already collected some Ping-Pong balls and an empty pint glass. "This is Noel Kahn's favorite game."

Aria smirked. Noel Kahn was one of the richest kids at school and *the* quintessential Rosewood boy, which basically made him Mike's idol. And, irony of all ironies, he seemed to have a thing for Aria, which she was trying her hardest to squelch.

"Wish me luck," Mike said, holding the Ping-Pong

ball ready. He missed the glass, sending the ball rolling off the table onto the floor.

"Chug it down," Aria singsonged, and her brother wrapped his hands around his beer and poured the whole thing down his throat.

Mike tried for the second time to get the Ping-Pong ball in Aria's glass but missed again. "You suck!" Aria teased, the beer beginning to make her feel a little buzzy.

"Like you're any better," Mike shot back.

"You wanna bet?"

Mike snorted. "If you don't make it, you have to get me into Turbulence. Me *and* Noel. But not while you're working," he added hastily.

"If I make it, you have to be my slave for a week. That means *during* school, too."

"Deal," Mike said. "You're not going to make it, so it doesn't matter."

She moved the glass to Mike's side of the table and took aim. The ball careened off one of the table's many dents and landed cleanly in the glass, not even bumping its sides on the way in. "Ha!" Aria cried. "You are *so* going down!"

Mike looked stunned. "That was just a lucky shot."

"Whatever!" Aria snickered gleefully. "So, I wonder . . . should I make you crawl on all fours behind me at school? Or wear mom's *faldur*?" She giggled. Ella's *faldur* was a traditional Icelandic pointed cap that made the wearer look like a deranged elf.

"Screw you." Mike grabbed the Ping-Pong ball out of his glass. It slipped out of his hands and bounced away from them.

"I'll get it," Aria offered. She stood, feeling pleasantly tipsy. The ball had rolled all the way to the front of the bar, and Aria bent down on the floor to get it. A couple swept past her, squeezing into the discreet, partially blocked seats in the corner. Aria noticed that the girl had long dark hair and a pink spiderweb tattoo on her wrist.

That tattoo was familiar. *Very* familiar. And when she whispered something to the guy she was with, he started coughing maniacally. Aria straightened up.

It was her father. And Meredith.

Aria bolted back to Mike. "We have to go."

Mike rolled his eyes. "But I just asked for a second shot of Jaeger."

"Too bad." Aria grabbed her jacket. "We're leaving. Now." She threw forty bucks on the table and pulled on Mike's arm until he stood. He was a little wobbly, but she managed to push him toward the door.

Unfortunately, Byron chose that very moment to let out one of his very distinctive laughs, which Aria always said sounded like a dying whale. Mike froze, recognizing it too. Their father's face was turned to the side, and he was touching Meredith's hand across the table.

Aria watched Mike recognize Byron. He knitted his brow. "Wait," he squeaked, looking confusedly at Aria. She willed her face to look unworried, but instead, she felt the corners of her mouth wiggle down. She knew she was making the same face Ella did when she tried to protect Aria or Mike from things that might hurt them.

Mike narrowed his eyes at her, then looked back at their father and Meredith. He opened his mouth to say something, then closed it, taking a step toward them. Aria reached out to stop him—she didn't want this happening right now. She didn't want this happening *ever*. Then Mike steeled his jaw, turned away from their dad, and stormed out of Victory, bumping into their waitress as he went.

Aria pushed through the door after him. She squinted in the bright afternoon light of the parking lot, looking back and forth for Mike. But her brother was gone.

5

A HOUSE DIVIDED

Spencer awoke on the floor of her upstairs bathroom with no idea how she'd gotten there. The clock on the shower radio said 6:45 P.M., and out the window, the evening sun cast long shadows on their yard. It was still Monday, the day of Ali's funeral. She must have fallen asleep . . . and sleepwalked. She used to be a chronic sleepwalker—it got so bad that in seventh grade, she had to spend a night at the University of Pennsylvania Sleep Evaluation Clinic with her brain hooked up to electrodes. The doctors said it was just stress.

She stood up and ran cold water over her face, looking at herself in the mirror: long blond hair, emerald-green eyes, pointed chin. Her skin was flawless and her teeth were radiantly white. It was preposterous that she didn't look as wrecked as the felt.

She ran the equation over again in her head: A knew about Toby and The Jenna Thing. Toby was back. Therefore,

Toby *had* to be A. And he was telling Spencer to keep her mouth shut. It was the same torture from sixth grade, all over again.

She went back to her bedroom and pressed her forehead to the window. To her left was her family's own private windmill—it had long since stopped working, but her parents loved how it gave their property such a rustic, authentic look. To her right, the Do Not Cross tape was still all over the DiLaurentises' lawn. The Ali shrine, which consisted of flowers, candles, photos, and other knickknacks in Ali's honor, had grown larger, swallowing the whole cul-de-sac.

Across the street from that was the Cavanaughs' house. Two cars in the driveway, a basketball in the yard, the little red flag up on the mailbox. From the outside, everything seemed so normal. But *inside* . . .

Spencer closed her eyes, remembering May of seventh grade, a year after The Jenna Thing. She had boarded the Philadelphia-bound SEPTA train to meet Ali in the city to go shopping. She was so busy texting Ali on her spanking-new Sidekick that it was five or six stops before she noticed there was someone across the aisle. It was *Toby*. Staring.

Her hands started shaking. Toby had been at boarding school all year, so Spencer hadn't seen him in months. As usual, his hair hung over his eyes and he wore enormous headphones, but something about him that day seemed . . . stronger. *Scarier.*

All of the guilty, anxious feelings about The Jenna Thing that Spencer had tried to bury flooded back. *I'll get you.* She didn't want to be in the same train car as him. She slid one leg into the aisle, then the other, but the conductor abruptly stepped in her way. "You going to Thirtieth Street or Market East?" he boomed.

Spencer shrank back. "Thirtieth," she whispered. When the conductor passed, she glanced at Toby again. His face bloomed into a huge, sinister smile. A split second later, his mouth became impassive again, but his eyes said, *Just. You. Wait.*

Spencer shot up and moved to another car. Ali was waiting for her on the platform at Thirtieth Street, and when they glanced back at the train, Toby was looking straight at them.

"I see someone's been let out of his little prison," Ali said with a smirk.

"Yeah." Spencer tried to laugh it off. "And he's still a loser with a capital *L.*"

But a few weeks later, Ali went missing. And then it wasn't so funny.

A slide-whistle noise coming from Spencer's computer made her jump. It was her new e-mail alert. She paced over to her computer nervously and double-clicked the new message.

Hi, love. Haven't spoken to you in two days, and I'm going crazy missing you. —Wren.

Spencer sighed, a nervous sensation fluttering through her. The moment she'd laid eyes on Wren—her sister had brought him to meet their parents at a family dinner— something had happened to her. It was like . . . like he'd put a hex on her the second he sat down at Moshulu, took a sip of red wine, and met her eyes. He was British, exotic, witty, and smart, and liked the same indie bands Spencer did. He was just so wrong for her milquetoast, prim-and-perfect sister Melissa. But he was *so* right for Spencer. *She* knew it . . . and apparently he did too.

Before Melissa caught them making out Friday night, she and Wren experienced an unbelievable twenty minutes of passion. But because Melissa tattled, and because Spencer's parents *always* took her side, they banned Spencer from seeing Wren ever again. She was going crazy missing him, too, but what was she supposed to do?

Feeling groggy and unsettled, she walked down the stairs and passed the long, narrow gallery hall where her mother displayed the Thomas Cole landscapes she'd inherited from her grandfather. She stepped into her family's spacious kitchen. Her parents had restored it to look just like it had in the 1800s—except with updated countertops and state-of-the-art appliances. Her family was gathered at the kitchen table around Thai takeout containers.

Spencer hesitated in the doorway. She hadn't spoken to them since before Ali's funeral—she'd driven there alone and had barely seen them afterward on the lawn.

Actually, she hadn't spoken to her family since they reprimanded her about Wren two days ago, and now they'd shunned her again by starting dinner without her. And they had company. Ian Thomas, Melissa's old boyfriend—and the first of Melissa's exes that Spencer had kissed—was sitting in what should've been Spencer's seat.

"Oh," she squeaked.

Ian was the only one who looked up. "Hey, Spence! How are you?" he asked, as if he ate in the Hastingses' kitchen every day. It was hard enough for Spencer that Ian was coaching her field hockey team at Rosewood—but this was bizarre.

"I'm . . . fine," Spencer said, looking shiftily at the rest of her family, but no one was looking at her . . . or explaining why Ian was scarfing down Thai food in their kitchen. Spencer pulled up a chair to the corner of the table and started to spoon some lemongrass chicken onto her plate. "So, um, Ian. You're having dinner with us?"

Mrs. Hastings looked at her sharply. Spencer shut her mouth, a hot, clammy feeling coursing through her.

"We ran into each other at the, um, memorial," Ian explained. A siren interrupted him, and Ian dropped his fork. The noise was most likely coming from the DiLaurentises' house. Police cars had been there non-stop. "Pretty crazy, huh?" Ian said, running a hand through his curly blond hair. "I didn't know so many cop cars would still be here."

Melissa elbowed him lightly. "You get a big police

record, living out there in dangerous California?" Melissa and Ian had broken up because he'd moved across the country to go to college at Berkeley.

"Nah," Ian said. Before he could go on, Melissa, in typical Melissa fashion, had moved on to something else: herself. She turned to Mrs. Hastings. "So, Mom, the flowers at the service were the exact color I want to paint my living room walls."

Melissa reached for a *Martha Stewart Living* magazine and opened it to a marked page. She was constantly talking about home renovations; she was redecorating the Philadelphia town house their parents bought her as a reward for getting into U Penn's Wharton School of Business. They'd never do anything like that for Spencer.

Mrs. Hastings leaned in to see. "Lovely."

"Really nice," Ian agreed.

A disbelieving laugh escaped from Spencer's mouth. Alison DiLaurentis's *memorial service* was today, and all they could think to talk about was paint colors?

Melissa turned to Spencer. "What was that?"

"Well . . . I mean . . ." Spencer stuttered. Melissa looked offended, as if Spencer had just said something really rude. She nervously twirled her fork. "Forget it."

There was another silence. Even Ian seemed to be wary of her now. Her dad took a hearty sip of wine. "Veronica, did you see Liz there?"

"Yes, I spoke with her for a while," said Spencer's mother. "I thought she looked fantastic . . . considering." By

Liz, Spencer assumed they meant Elizabeth DiLaurentis, Ali's youngish aunt who lived in the area.

"It must be awful for her," Melissa said solemnly. "I can't imagine."

Ian made an empathetic *mmm*. Spencer felt her lower lip quiver. *Hello, what about me?* she wanted to scream. *Don't you guys remember? I was Ali's best friend!*

With every minute of silence, Spencer felt more unwelcome. She waited for someone to ask how she was holding up, offer her a piece of fried tempura, or at least to say, *Bless you*, when she sneezed. But they were still punishing her for kissing Wren. Even though today was . . . *today*.

A lump formed in her throat. She was used to being everyone's favorite: her teachers', her hockey coaches', her yearbook editor's. Even her colorist, Uri, said she was his favorite client because her hair took color so nicely. She'd won tons of school awards and had 370 MySpace friends, not counting bands. And while she might not ever be her parents' favorite—it was impossible to eclipse Melissa—she couldn't bear them hating her. Especially not now, when everything else in her life was so unstable.

When Ian got up and excused himself to make a phone call, Spencer took a deep breath. "Melissa?" Her voice cracked.

Melissa looked up, then went back to pushing her pad Thai around her plate.

Spencer cleared her throat. "Will you please talk to me?"

Melissa barely shrugged.

"I mean, I can't . . . I can't have you hate me. You were completely right. About . . . you know." Her hands shook so badly, she kept them wedged under her thighs. Apologizing made her nervous.

Melissa folded her hands over her magazines. "Sorry," she said. "I think that's out of the question." She stood and carried her plate to the sink.

"But . . ." Spencer was shocked. She looked to her parents. "I'm really sorry, guys. . . ." She felt tears brimming at her eyes.

Her father's face bore the tiniest glimmer of sympathy, but he quickly looked away. Her mother spooned the remaining lemongrass chicken into a Tupperware container. She shrugged. "You made your bed, Spencer," she said, rising and carrying the leftovers to the massive stainless-steel fridge.

"But—"

"Spencer." Mr. Hastings used his *stop talking* voice.

Spencer clamped her mouth shut. Ian loped back into the room, a big, stupid grin on his face. He sensed the tension and his smile wilted.

"Come on." Melissa stood and took his arm. "Let's go out for dessert."

"Sure." Ian clapped a hand on Spencer's shoulder. "Spence? Want to come?"

Spencer didn't really want to—and by the way Melissa nudged him, it seemed she didn't want her to, either, but she didn't have the chance to respond. Mrs. Hastings quickly said, "No, Ian, Spencer is *not* getting dessert." Her tone of voice was the same one she used when reprimanding the dogs.

"Thanks anyway," Spencer said, biting back tears. To steel herself, she shoved an enormous bite of mango curry into her mouth. But it slid down her throat before she could swallow, the thick sauce burning as it went down. Finally, after making a series of horrible noises, Spencer spit it up into her napkin. But when the tears cleared from her eyes, she saw that her parents hadn't approached to make sure she wasn't choking. They'd simply left the room.

Spencer wiped her eyes and stared at the nasty gob of chewed-up, spit-out mango in her napkin. It looked exactly the way she felt inside.

CHARITY ISN'T SO SWEET

Tuesday afternoon, Hanna adjusted the cream-colored camisole and slouchy cashmere cardigan she'd changed into after school and strolled purposefully up the steps of the William Atlantic Plastic Surgery and Burn Rehabilitation Clinic. If you were going in for burn treatment, you called it the William Atlantic. If you were having lipo, you called it Bill Beach.

The building was set back in the woods, and just the teensiest bit of blue sky peeked out from the majestic, overpowering trees. The whole world smelled like wild-flowers. It was the perfect early fall afternoon to lie out at the country club pool and watch boys play tennis. It was the perfect afternoon to take a six-mile run to work off the box of Cheez-Its she'd binged on last night, freaked out by the surprise visit from her dad. It might even be the perfect afternoon to look at an anthill or baby-sit the bratty six-year-old twins next door. Anything would be better than what she *was* doing today: volunteering at a burn clinic.

Volunteering was a four-letter word to Hanna. Her last attempt at it was at the Rosewood Day School Charity Fashion Show in seventh grade. Rosewood Day girls dressed up in designer clothes and paraded across the stage; people bid on their outfits, and the money went to charity. Ali wore a stunning Calvin Klein sheath and some size-zero dowager bid it up to $1,000. Hanna, on the other hand, got stuck with a frilly, neon-colored monstrosity by Betsey Johnson, which made her look even fatter than she was. The only person to bid on her outfit was her dad. A week later, her parents announced they were getting divorced.

And now her dad was back. Sort of.

When Hanna thought of her dad's visit yesterday, she felt giddy, anxious, and angry all at the same time. Since her transformation, she'd dreamed about the moment she'd see him again. She'd be thin, popular, and poised. In her dream he always came back with Kate, who'd gotten fat and zitty, and Hanna looked even more beautiful in comparison.

"Oof," she cried. Someone had come out the door just as she was going in.

"Watch it," the person mumbled. Then Hanna looked up. She was standing at the double-glass doors, next to a stone ashtray and a large potted primrose plant. Coming out the door was . . . Mona.

Hanna's mouth fell open. The same surprised look passed over Mona's face. They considered each other. "What are you doing here?" Hanna asked.

"Visiting a friend of my mom's. Boob job." Mona tossed her pale blond hair over her freckled shoulder. "You?"

"Um, same." Hanna eyed Mona carefully. Hanna's bullshit-radar told her that Mona might be lying. But then, maybe Mona could sense the exact same thing about her.

"Well, I'm off." Mona tugged on her burgundy tote. "I'll call you later."

"Okay," Hanna croaked. They walked in opposite directions. Hanna turned back and glanced at Mona, only to see that Mona was looking over her shoulder at her.

"Now, pay attention," said Ingrid, the portly, stoic, German head nurse. They were in an examination room, and Ingrid was teaching Hanna how to change out the trash cans. As if it was hard.

Each exam room was painted a guacamole green, and the only posters on the wall were grim pictures of skin diseases. Ingrid assigned Hanna to the outpatient check-up rooms; some day, if Hanna did well, she might be allowed to clean the inpatient rooms instead—where serious burn victims stayed. Lucky her.

Ingrid pulled out the trash bag. "This goes in the blue Dumpster out back. And you must empty the infectious waste bins, too." She gestured to an identical-looking trash can. "They need to be kept separate from the regular trash at all times. And you need to wear these." She handed Hanna a pair of latex gloves. Hanna looked at them as if *they* were covered in infectious waste.

Next, Ingrid pointed her down the hall. "There are ten other rooms here," she explained. "Clean the trash and wipe down the counters in each, then see me."

Trying not to breathe—she despised the antiseptic, sick-person way hospitals smelled—Hanna trudged to the utility closet to get more trash bags. She looked down the hall, wondering where the inpatient rooms were. Jenna had been an inpatient here. A lot of things had made her think of The Jenna Thing in the past day, although she kept trying to shove it out of her mind. The idea that someone knew—and could tell—was something she couldn't even comprehend.

Although The Jenna Thing had been an accident, Hanna sometimes felt like it wasn't *exactly*. Ali had given Jenna a nickname: Snow, as in Snow White, because Jenna had an annoying resemblance to the Disney character. Hanna thought Jenna looked like Snow White, too—but in a good way. Jenna wasn't as polished as Ali, but there was something oddly pretty about her. It had once occurred to Hanna that the only character she looked like from *Snow White* was Dopey Dwarf.

Still, Jenna was one of Ali's favorite targets, so back in sixth grade Hanna scrawled a rumor about Jenna's boobs just below the paper-towel dispenser in the girls' bathroom. She spilled water on Jenna's seat in algebra so Jenna would get a fake pee stain on her pants. She poked fun at the way Jenna put on a fake French accent in French II. . . . So when the paramedics carried Jenna out of the tree house, Hanna felt sick. She'd been the one to agree to pranking Toby first. And in her head, she'd thought, *Maybe if we prank Toby, we can prank Jenna, too.* It was like she'd willed this to happen.

The automatic doors swished open at the end of the hall, breaking Hanna out of her thoughts. She froze, heart pounding, wishing for the new arrival to be Sean, but it wasn't. Frustrated, she pulled her BlackBerry out of her cardigan pocket and dialed his number. It went to voice mail, and Hanna hung up. She redialed, thinking maybe he was just fumbling for his phone and hadn't gotten it in time, but it went to voice mail again.

"Hey, Sean," Hanna chirped after the beep, trying to sound carefree. "Hanna again. I'd really like to talk, so, um, you know where to find me!"

She'd left him three messages today saying she'd be here this afternoon, but Sean hadn't responded. She wondered if he was at a V Club meeting—he'd recently signed a virginity pledge, vowing not to have sex, like, *ever.* Maybe he'd call her when he was done. Or . . . maybe he wouldn't. Hanna swallowed, trying to shove that possibility out of her mind.

She sighed and walked to the employee closet/supply

room. Ingrid had hung Hanna's pewter Ferragamo hobo bag on a hook next to a striped vinyl thing from the Gap, and she suppressed the urge to shudder. She dropped her phone into her bag, grabbed a roll of paper towels and a spray bottle, and found an empty exam room. Maybe actually doing her job would keep her mind off stressing about Sean and A.

As she finished sponging off the sink, she accidentally bumped open a metal cabinet right next to it. Inside were shelves of cardboard containers all emblazoned with familiar names. Tylenol 3. Vicodin. Percocet. Hanna peeked inside. There were thousands of drug samples. Just . . . just sitting there. Without a lock.

Jackpot.

Hanna quickly shoved a few handfuls of Percocet into the surprisingly deep pockets of her cardigan. At least she could get a fun weekend with Mona out of this.

Then someone placed a hand on Hanna's shoulder. Hanna jumped back and whirled around, knocking the Fantastik-soaked paper towels and a jar full of cotton swabs onto the floor.

"Why are you only on room two?" Ingrid frowned. She had a face like a grumpy pug.

"I . . . I was just trying to be thorough." Hanna quickly tossed the paper towels in the trash and hoped the Percocet would stay in her pockets. Her neck burned where Ingrid had touched it.

"Well, come with me," Ingrid said. "There's something

in your bag that's making a noise. It's disturbing
the patients."

"Are you sure it's *my* bag?" Hanna asked. "I was just at
my bag, and—"

Ingrid led Hanna back into the closet. Sure enough,
there was a tinkling sound coming from her purse's
inside pocket. "It's just my cell phone." Hanna's spirits
jumped. Maybe Sean *had* called!

"Well, please make it quiet." Ingrid sighed. "And then
get back to work."

Hanna pulled out her BlackBerry to see who was
calling. She had a new text.

> Hannakins: Mopping the floors at Bill Beach won't help
> you get your life back. Not even you could clean up this
> mess. And besides, I know something about you that'll
> guarantee you'll never be Rosewood Day's it girl—
> ever again. —A

Hanna looked around the coatroom, confused. She
read the note again, her throat dry and sticky. What
could A know that could guarantee *that*?

Jenna.

If A knew that . . .

Hanna quickly typed a response on her phone's key-
pad: *You don't know anything.* She hit SEND. Within seconds, A responded:

> I know it all. I could RUIN YOU.

7

O CAPTAIN, MY CAPTAIN

Tuesday afternoon, Emily hovered in Coach Lauren's office doorway. "Can I talk to you?"

"Well, I only have a couple minutes until I have to give this to the officials," Lauren said, holding up her meet roster. Today was the Rosewood Tank, the first swim meet of the season. It was supposed to be a friendly exhibition meet—all the area prep schools were invited and there was no scoring—but Emily usually shaved down and got pre-meet jitters all the same. Except not this time. "What's up, Fieldsy?" Lauren asked.

Lauren Kinkaid was in her early thirties, had perma-chlorine-damaged blondish hair, and lived in T-shirts with motivational swimming slogans like EAT OUR BUBBLES and I PUT THE STYLE IN FREESTYLE. She had been Emily's swim coach for six years. First at Tadpole League, then at long-course, and now Rosewood Day. Not very many people knew Emily so well—not well enough to call her "Fieldsy," to know that her favorite pre-swim meet dinner was pepper steak from China Rose, or to know that when Emily's butterfly times were three-tenths of a second faster, it meant she had her period. Which made what Emily was about to say that much harder.

"I want to quit," Emily blurted out.

Lauren blinked. She looked stunned, like someone had just told her the pool was filled with electric eels. "W-Why?"

Emily stared at the checkerboard linoleum floor. "It's not fun anymore."

Lauren blew air out of her cheeks. "Well, it isn't always fun. Sometimes it's work."

"I know. But . . . I just don't want to do it anymore."

"Are you *sure*?"

Emily sighed. She thought she was sure. Last week she was sure. She'd been swimming for years, not asking herself whether she liked it or not. With Maya's help, Emily had mustered up the courage to admit to herself—and to her parents—that she wanted to quit.

Of course, that was before . . . everything. Now, she felt more like a yo-yo than ever. One minute, she wanted to quit. The next, she wanted her normal, good-girl life back, the life where she went to swimming, hung out with her sister Carolyn on the weekends, and spent hours goofing off on the bus with her teammates and reading from the birthday horoscope book. And then she wanted the freedom to pursue her own interests all over again. Except . . . what were her interests, aside from swimming?

"I feel really burnt out," Emily finally offered, attempting to explain.

Lauren propped her head up with her hand. "I was going to make you captain."

Emily gaped. "Captain?"

"Well, yeah." Lauren clicked and unclicked her pen. "I thought you deserved it. You're a real team player, you know? But if you don't want to swim, then . . ."

Not even her older siblings Jake and Beth, who had swum all four years of high school and gotten college scholarships, had been captain.

Lauren wound her whistle around her finger. "How about I go easy on you for a bit?" She took Emily's hand. "I know it's been hard. With your friend . . ."

"Yeah." Emily stared at Lauren's Michael Phelps poster, hoping she wouldn't start crying again. Every time someone mentioned Ali—which was about once every ten minutes—her nose and eyes got twitchy.

"What do you say?" Lauren coaxed.

Emily ran her tongue over the back of her teeth. Captain. Sure, she was state champion in the 100-meter butterfly, but Rosewood Day had a freakishly good swim team—Lanie Iler got fifth in the 500 freestyle at Junior Nationals, and Stanford had already promised Jenny Kestler a full ride next year. That Lauren chose Emily over Lanie or Jenny *meant* something. Maybe it was a sign that her yo-yoing life was supposed to go back to normal.

"All right," she heard herself saying.

"Awesome." Lauren patted her hand. She reached into one of her many cardboard boxes of T-shirts and handed one to Emily. "For you. A start-of-the-season present."

Emily opened it up. It said, GAY GIRLS: SLIPPERY WHEN WET. She looked at Lauren, her throat cottony dry. Lauren *knew*?

Lauren cocked her head. "It's in reference to the stroke," she said slowly. "You know, butterfly?"

Emily looked at the shirt again. It didn't say *gay* girls. It said *fly* girls. "Oh," she croaked, folding the T-shirt. "Thanks."

She left Lauren's office and walked through the natatorium lobby on shaky legs. The room was crammed full of swimmers, all here for the Tank. Then she paused, suddenly aware that someone was looking at her. Across the room, she saw Ben, her ex-boyfriend, leaning up against the trophy case. His stare was so intense, he didn't blink. Emily's skin prickled and heat rose to her cheeks. Ben smirked and turned to whisper something to his best friend, Seth Cardiff. Seth laughed, glanced again at Emily, and whispered something back to Ben. Then they both snickered.

Emily hid behind a crowd of kids from St. Anthony's.

This was another reason why she wanted to quit swimming—so she wouldn't have to spend every day after school with her ex-boyfriend, who *did* know. He'd caught Maya and Emily in a more-than-just-friends moment at Noel's party on Friday.

She pushed into the empty hallway that led to the girls' and boys' locker rooms, thinking again about A's latest note. It was weird, but when Emily read the text in Maya's hotel bathroom, it was almost like she could *hear* Ali's voice. Except that was impossible, right? Besides, Ben was the only person who knew about Maya. Maybe he'd somehow found out that Emily had tried to kiss Ali. Could . . . could Ben be A?

"Where are you going?"

Emily whirled around. Ben had followed her into the hall. "Hey." Emily tried to smile. "What's up?"

Ben was wearing his shredded Champion sweats— he thought they brought him good luck, so he wore them to every meet. He'd re-buzzed his hair over the weekend. It made his already angular face look severe. "Nothing's *up*," he answered nastily, his voice echoing off the tile walls. "I thought you were quitting."

Emily shrugged. "Yeah, well, I guess I changed my mind."

"Really? You were so into it Friday. Your girlfriend seemed so proud of you."

Emily looked away. "We were drunk."

"Right." He took a step toward her.

"Think what you want." She turned for her locker room. "And that text you sent didn't scare me."

Ben furrowed his eyebrows. "What text?"

She stopped. "The text that says you're going to tell everyone," she said, testing him.

"I didn't write you any texts." Ben tilted his chin. "But . . . I *might* tell everyone. You being a dyke is a juicy little story."

"I'm not gay," Emily said through her teeth.

"Oh yeah?" Ben took a step closer. His nostrils flared in and out. "Prove it."

Emily barked out a laugh. This was *Ben*. But then he lunged forward, wrapped his hand around Emily's wrist, and pushed her against the water fountain.

She breathed in sharply. Ben's breath was hot on her neck and smelled like grape Gatorade. "Stop it," she whispered, trying to squirm away.

Ben needed just one strong arm to hold her down. He pressed his body up against hers. "I said, *prove it*."

"Ben, stop." Frightened tears came to her eyes. She swatted at him tentatively, but his movements just became more forceful. He ran his hand up her chest. A small squeak escaped her throat.

"There a problem?"

Ben stepped back suddenly. Behind them on the far side of the hall stood a boy in a Tate Prep warm-up jacket. Emily squinted. Was that . . . ?

"It's none of your business, man," Ben said loudly.

"What isn't any of my business?" The boy stepped closer. It was.

Toby Cavanaugh.

"Dude." Ben twisted around.

Toby's eyes moved down to Ben's hand on Emily's wrist. He nudged his chin up at Ben. "What's the deal?"

Ben glared at Emily, then let go of her. She shot away from him, and Ben used his shoulder to shove open the boys' locker room door. Then, silence.

"You all right?" Toby asked.

Emily nodded, her head down. "I think so."

"You sure?"

Emily sneaked a peek at Toby. He was really tall now, and his face was no longer rodentlike and guarded but, well, high-cheekboned and dark-eyed gorgeous. It made her think of the other part of A's note. *Although most of us have totally changed . . .*

Her knees felt wobbly. It couldn't be . . . *could it?*

"I have to go," she mumbled, and ran, her arms outstretched, into the girls' locker room.

8

EVEN TYPICAL ROSEWOOD BOYS SOUL-SEARCH

Tuesday afternoon as Aria was driving home from school, she passed the lacrosse field and recognized the lone figure sprinting around the goal area, his lacrosse stick cradled in front of his face. He kept switching directions and sliding in the wet, muddy grass. Ominous gray clouds had gathered overhead, and now it was starting to sprinkle.

Aria pulled over. "Mike." She hadn't seen her brother since he'd stormed out of the Victory yesterday. A few hours afterward, he'd called home saying he was having dinner at his friend Theo's house. Then, later, he called to say he was staying overnight.

Her brother looked up from across the field and frowned. "What?"

"Come here."

Mike trudged across the close-cropped, not-a-weed-in-sight grass. "Get in," Aria commanded.

"I'm practicing."

"You can't avoid this forever. We have to talk about it."

"Talk about what?"

She raised a perfectly arched eyebrow. "Um, what we saw yesterday? At the bar?"

Mike picked at one of the rawhide straps on his lacrosse stick. Raindrops bounced off the canvas top of his Brine cap. "I don't know what you're talking about."

"What?" Aria narrowed her eyes. But Mike wouldn't even look at her.

"Fine." She shifted into reverse. "Be a wuss."

Then Mike wrapped his hand around the window frame. "I . . . I don't know what I'll do," he said quietly.

Aria pressed the brake. "What?"

"If they get divorced, I don't know what I'll do," Mike repeated. The vulnerable, embarrassed expression on his face made him look as if he were about ten years old. "Blow myself up, maybe."

Tears came to her eyes. "It's not going to happen," she said shakily. "I promise."

Mike sniffed. She reached out for him, but he jerked away and ran down the field.

Aria decided to go, slowly rolling down the twisty, wet road. Rain was her favorite kind of weather. It reminded her of rainy days, back when she was nine. She'd sneak over to her neighbor's parked sailboat, climb under the tarp, and snuggle into one of the cabins, listening to the sound of the rain hitting the canvas and writing entries in her Hello Kitty diary.

She felt like she could do her best thinking on rainy days, and she definitely needed to think now. She could have dealt with A telling Ella about Meredith if it had been in the past. Her parents could talk through it, Byron could say it would never happen again, yadda yadda yadda. But now that Meredith was back, well, that changed everything. Last night, her father hadn't come home for dinner—because of the, um, papers he had to grade—and Aria and her mom had sat on the couch in front of *Jeopardy!* with bowls of soup in their laps. They were both totally silent. The thing was, she didn't know what she'd do if her parents divorced, either.

Climbing a particularly steep hill, Aria gunned the engine—the Subaru always needed an extra push on inclines. But instead of revving forward, the interior lights flickered out. The car began to roll backward down the hill. "Shit," Aria whispered, jerking up the e-brake. When she tried the ignition again, the car wouldn't even start.

She looked down the empty, two-lane country road. Thunder broke overhead, and the rain started to hurtle down from the sky. Aria searched through her bag, figuring she needed to call a tow truck or her parents to come get her, but after rooting around the bottom, she realized she'd left her Treo at home. The rain was falling so violently, the windshield and windows blurred. "Oh God," Aria whispered, feeling claustrophobic. Spots formed in front of her eyes.

Aria knew this anxious feeling: It was a panic attack. She'd had them a few times before. One was after The Jenna Thing, one was after Ali went missing, and one was when she was walking down Laugavegur Street in Reykjavík and saw a girl on a billboard that looked exactly like Meredith.

Calm down, she told herself. *It's just rain.* She took two cleansing breaths, stuck her fingers in her ears, and started singing "Frère Jacques"—for some reason, the French version did the trick. After she went through three rounds, the spots began to disappear. The rain had let up from hurricane-force to merely torrential. What she needed to do was walk back to the farmhouse she'd passed and ask to use their phone. She thrust open the car door, held her Rosewood Day blazer over her head, and started to run. A gust of wind blew up her miniskirt, and she stepped in an enormous, muddy puddle. The water seeped right through the gauzy straps of her stacked-heel sandals. "Damn it," she muttered.

She was only a hundred feet from the farmhouse when a navy-colored Audi passed. It splashed a wave of puddle water at Aria, then stopped at the dead Subaru. It slowly backed up until it was right next to her. The driver's window glided down. "You okay?"

Aria squinted, raindrops dripping off the tip of her nose. Hanging out the driver's side was Sean Ackard, a boy in her class. He was a typical Rosewood boy: crisp polo, moisturized skin, All-American features, expensive car. Only he played soccer, not lacrosse. *Not* the kind of person she wanted to see right now. "I'm fine," she yelled.

"Actually, you're soaked. Need a ride?"

Aria was so wet, she felt like her face was pruning. Sean's car looked dry and snuggly. So she slid into the passenger seat and shut the door.

Sean told her to throw her soaked blazer into the back. Then he reached over and turned up the heat. "Where to?"

Aria pushed her matted-down, fringey black bangs off her forehead. "Actually, I'll just use your cell phone and then be out of your way."

"All right." Sean dug through his backpack to find it.

Aria sat back and looked around. Sean hadn't plastered his car with band stickers like some guys did, and the interior didn't reek of boy sweat. Instead, it smelled like some combination of bread and a freshly shampooed dog. Two books sat on the passenger-side floor: *Zen and the Art of Motorcycle Maintenance* and *The Tao of Pooh*.

"You like philosophy?" Aria moved her legs so she wouldn't get them wet.

Sean ducked his head. "Well, yeah." He sounded embarrassed.

"I read those books, too," Aria said. "I also got really into French philosophers this summer, when I was in Iceland." She paused. She'd never really spoken to Sean. Before she left, Rosewood boys terrified her—which was probably partly why she hated them. "I, um, was in Iceland for a while. My dad was on sabbatical."

"I know." Sean gave her a crooked smile.

Aria stared at her hands. "Oh." There was an awkward pause. The only sound was the hurtling rain and the windshield wipers' rhythmic *whaps*.

"So you read, like, Camus and stuff?" Sean asked. When Aria nodded, he smirked. "I read *The Stranger* this summer."

"Really?" Aria jutted her chin into the air, certain he hadn't understood it. What would a typical Rosewood boy want with deep philosophy books, anyway? If this were an SAT analogy, it would be "typical Rosewood boy: reading French philosophers :: American tourists in Iceland: eating anywhere but McDonald's." It just didn't happen.

When Sean didn't answer, she dialed her home number into his cell phone. It rang and rang, not going to voice mail—they hadn't set up the answering machine yet. Next she dialed her dad's number at school—it was almost five, and he had posted his 3:30–5:30 office hours on the refrigerator. It rang and rang too.

The spots started to flash in front of Aria's eyes again as she imagined where he could be . . . or who he could be with. She leaned forward over her bare legs, trying to breathe deeper. *Frère Jacques*, she chanted silently.

"Whoa," Sean said, his voice sounding very far away.

"I'm all right," Aria called, her voice muffled in her legs. "I just have to . . ."

She heard Sean fumbling around. Then he pressed a Burger King bag into her hands. "Breathe into this. I think there were some fries in there. Sorry about that."

Aria put the bag over her mouth and slowly inflated and deflated it. She felt Sean's warm hand on the middle of her back. Slowly, the dizziness started to fade. When she raised her head, Sean was looking at her anxiously.

"Panic attacks?" he asked. "My stepmom gets them. The bag always works."

Aria crumpled the bag in her lap. "Thanks."

"Something bothering you?"

Aria shook her head quickly. "No, I'm cool."

"C'mon," Sean said. "Isn't that, like, why people get panic attacks?"

Aria pressed her lips together. "It's complicated." *Besides,* she wanted to say, *since when are typical Rosewood boys interested in weird girls' problems?*

Sean shrugged. "You were friends with Alison DiLaurentis, right?"

Aria nodded.

"It's weird, isn't it?"

"Yeah." She cleared her throat. "Although, um, it's not weird in the way you might think. I mean, it *is* weird in that way, but it's weird in other ways, too."

"Like how?"

She shifted; her wet underwear was starting to itch. Today at school it had felt like everyone was speaking to her in babyish whispers. Did they think that if they spoke in normal-person volume, Aria would have an insta-breakdown?

"I just wish everyone would leave me alone," she managed. "Like last week."

Sean flicked the pine tree air freshener that hung from the rearview mirror, making it swing. "I know what you mean. When my mom died, everyone thought that if I had a second to myself, I'd lose it."

Aria sat up straighter. "Your mom died?"

Sean looked at her. "Yeah. It was a long time ago. Fourth grade."

"Oh." Aria tried to remember Sean from fourth grade. He had been one of the shortest kids in the class, and they'd been on the same kickball team a bunch of times, but that was it. She felt bad for being so oblivious. "I'm sorry."

A silence passed. Aria crossed and uncrossed her bare legs. The car had begun to smell like her skirt's wet wool. "It was tough," Sean said. "My dad went through all these girlfriends. I didn't even like my stepmom at first. I got used to her, though."

Aria felt her eyes well up with tears. She didn't want to get used to *her* family changing. She let out a loud sniff.

Sean leaned forward. "You sure you can't talk about it?"

Aria shrugged. "It's supposed to be a secret."

"Tell you what. How about if you tell me your secret, I'll tell you mine?"

"All right," Aria quickly agreed. The truth was, she was dying to talk about this. She would've admitted it to her old friends, but they were so tight-lipped about their own A secrets, it made Aria feel even weirder about revealing hers. "But you can't say anything."

"Absolutely."

And then Aria told him about Byron and Ella, Meredith, and what she and Mike had seen at the bar yesterday. It all just came spilling out. "I don't know what to do," she finished. "I feel like I'm the one who has to keep everyone together."

Sean was quiet, and Aria was afraid he'd stopped listening. But then he raised his head. "Your dad shouldn't be putting you in that position."

"Yeah, well." Aria glanced at Sean. If you got past his tucked-in shirt and khaki shorts, he was actually pretty cute. He had really pink lips and knobby, imperfect fingers. From the way his polo shirt fit snugly against his chest, she guessed he was in tip-top soccer boy shape. She suddenly felt incredibly self-conscious. "You're easy to talk to," Aria said shyly, staring at her naked knees. She'd missed a few hairs on her knees when shaving. It usually didn't matter, but it sort of did now. "So, um, thanks."

"Sure." When Sean smiled, his eyes got crinkly and warm.

"This definitely isn't how I imagined spending my afternoon," Aria added. The rain was still pelting the windshield, but the car had gotten really warm while she'd been talking.

"Me neither." Sean looked out the window. The rain had started to subside. "But . . . I don't know. It's kind of cool, right?"

Aria shrugged. Then she remembered. "Hey, you promised me a secret! It better be good."

"Well, I don't know if it's *good*." Sean leaned toward Aria, and she scooted closer. For a crazy second, she thought they might kiss.

"So, I'm in this thing called V Club," Sean whispered. His breath smelled like Altoids. "Do you know what that is?"

"I guess." Aria tried to keep her lips from wriggling into a smirk. "It's the no-sex-till-marriage thing, right?"

"Right." Sean leaned back. "So . . . I'm a virgin. Except . . . I don't know if I want to be one anymore."

9

SOMEONE'S ALLOWANCE JUST GOT A WHOLE LOT SMALLER

On Wednesday afternoon, Mr. McAdam, Spencer's AP economics teacher, strolled up and down the aisles, peeling papers off a stack and putting them facedown on each student's desk. He was a tall man with bulging eyes, a sloped nose, and a paunchy face. A few years ago, one of his top students had remarked that he looked like Squidward from *SpongeBob SquarePants*, and the name stuck. "A lot of these quizzes were very good," he murmured.

Spencer straightened up. She did what she always did when she wasn't sure how she'd done on a test: She thought of the rock-bottom grade she could get, a grade that would still ensure she had an A for the class. Usually, the grade in her mind was so low—although low for Spencer was a B plus or, at the very worst, a B—that she ended up being pleasantly surprised. *B plus,* she told herself now, as Squidward put the test on her desk. *That's rock-bottom.* Then she turned it over.

B *minus*.

Spencer dropped the paper to her desk as if it were on fire. She scanned the quiz for answers that Squidward had graded incorrectly, but she didn't know the answers to the questions that had big red X marks next to them.

Okay, so maybe she hadn't studied enough.

When they'd taken the quizzes yesterday, all she'd been able to think about while filling in the multiple choice bubbles were a) Wren and how she could never see him, b) her parents and Melissa and how she could get them to love her again, c) Ali, and d), e), f), and g), her festering Toby secret.

The Toby torture was insane. But what could she do—go to the cops? And tell them . . . what? *Some kid said,* I'll get you, *to me four years ago, and I think he killed Ali and I think he's going to kill me? I got a text that said my friends and I were in danger?* The cops would laugh and say she'd been snorting too much Ritalin. She was afraid, too, to tell her friends what was going on. What if A was serious and something happened to them if she did?

"How'd you do?" a voice whispered.

Spencer jumped. Andrew Campbell sat next to her. He was as big an overachiever as she was. He and Spencer were ranked number one and number two in the class, and they were always switching positions. His quiz was proudly faceup on his desk. A big red A plus was at the top of it.

Spencer pulled her own quiz to her chest. "Fine."

"Cool." A lock of Andrew's long lion's mane of blond hair fell in his face.

Spencer gritted her teeth. Andrew was notoriously nosy. She'd always thought it was just a symptom of his über-competitiveness, and then last week, she wondered if he might be A. But while Andrew's earnest interest in the minutiae of Spencer's life was suspect, she didn't think he had it in him. Andrew had helped Spencer the day the workers discovered Ali's body, covering her up with a blanket when she was in shock. A wouldn't do something like that.

As Squidward gave them their homework assignment, Spencer looked at her notes. Her handwriting, which was normally squeezed neatly in the lines, had wavered all over the page. She began to quickly recopy the notes, but the bell interrupted her, and Spencer sheepishly rose to leave. B *minus*.

"Miss Hastings?"

She looked up. Squidward was gesturing her toward his desk. She walked over, straightening her navy Rosewood Day blazer and taking extra caution not to trip in her caramel-colored kidskin riding boots. "You're Melissa Hastings's sister, yes?"

Spencer felt her insides wilt. "Uh-huh." It was obvious what was coming next.

"This is quite a treat for me, then." He tapped his mechanical pencil on his desk. "It was such a pleasure to have Melissa in class."

I'm sure, Spencer growled to herself.

"Where is Melissa now?"

Spencer gritted her teeth. *At home, hogging up all our parents' love and attention.* "She's at Wharton. Getting her MBA."

Squidward smiled. "I always knew she'd go to Wharton." Then he gave Spencer a long look. "The first set of essay questions is due next Monday," he said. "And I'll give you a hint: the supplemental books I've mentioned on the syllabus will help."

"Oh." Spencer felt self-conscious. Was he giving her a tip because she'd gotten a B minus and he felt sorry for her, or because she was Melissa's sister? She squared her shoulders. "I was planning to get them anyway."

Squidward looked at her evenly. "Well, good."

Spencer trudged into the hall, feeling unhinged. Normally, she could kiss ass with the best of them, but Squidward made her feel like she was at the bottom of the class.

It was the end of the day. Rosewood students were bustling around their lockers, dragging books into their bags, making plans on their cell phones, or getting their gear for sports practice. Spencer had field hockey at three, but she wanted to hit Wordsmith's for Squidward's books first. Then, after that, she had to check in with the yearbook staff, see what was up with the Habitat for

Humanity volunteer list, and say hi to the drama club advisor. She might be a couple minutes late to hockey, but what could she do?

As she pushed through the door of Wordsmith's Books, she instantly felt calmer. The store was always quiet, with no obsequious salespeople shooing you out. After Ali disappeared, Spencer used to come in here and read *Calvin and Hobbes* comic books just to be alone. The staff didn't get pissy when cell phones rang, either, which was exactly what Spencer's was doing right now. Her heart pounded . . . and then pounded in a different way when she saw who it was.

"Wren," she whispered into her phone, sinking against the travel shelf.

"Did you get my e-mail?" he asked in his sexy British accent when she answered.

"Um . . . yeah," Spencer responded. "But . . . I don't think you should be calling me."

"So you want me to hang up?"

Spencer looked around cagily, eyeing two freshman dorks giggling by the self-help sex books and an old woman who was leafing through a Philadelphia Streetwise map. "No," she whispered.

"Well, I'm dying to see you, Spence. Can we meet somewhere?"

Spencer paused. It ached how much she wanted to say yes. "I'm not sure if that's a good idea right now."

"What do you mean, you're not sure?" Wren laughed. "C'mon, Spence. It was hard enough to wait this long before calling."

Spencer shook her head. "I . . . I can't," she decided. "I'm sorry. My family . . . they hardly even look at me. I mean, maybe we could try this in . . . in a couple months?"

Wren was quiet for a moment. "You're serious."

Spencer sniffed uncertainly in response.

"I just thought . . . I don't know." Wren's voice sounded tight. "Are you sure?"

She pushed her hand through her hair and looked out Wordsmith's big front windows. Mason Byers and Penelope Waites, two kids from her class, were kissing outside Ferra's, the cheesesteak place across the street. She hated them. "I'm sure," she said to Wren, the words choked in her throat. "I'm sorry." She hung up.

She heaved a sigh. Suddenly, the bookstore felt too quiet. The classical CD had stopped. The hair on the back of her neck rose. A could have heard her conversation.

Shaking, she walked to the economics section, suspiciously eyeing a guy as he paused at the World War II shelf and a woman as she thumbed through a bulldog-of-the-month calendar. Could one of them be A? How did A know *everything*?

She quickly found the books on Squidward's list, walked to the counter, and handed over her credit card, nervously fidgeting with the silver buttons on her navy blue school blazer. She so didn't want to go to her activities and hockey after this. She just wanted to go home and hide.

"Hmm." The checkout girl, who had three eyebrow rings, held up Spencer's Visa. "Something's wrong with this card."

"That's impossible," Spencer snapped. Then she fished out her MasterCard.

The salesgirl ran it through, but the card machine made the same disapproving beep. "This one's doing the same thing."

The salesgirl made a quick phone call, nodded a few times, then hung up. "These cards have been canceled," she said quietly, her heavily lined eyes wide. "I'm supposed to cut them up, but . . ." She shrugged meekly and handed them back to Spencer.

Spencer snatched the cards from her. "Your machine must be broken. Those cards, they're . . . " She was about to say, *They're linked to my parents' bank account.*

Then it hit her. Her parents had canceled them.

"Do you want to pay with cash?" the salesgirl asked.

Her parents had *canceled* her credit cards. What was next, putting a lock on the refrigerator? Cutting off the A/C to her bedroom? Limiting her use of oxygen?

Spencer pushed her way out of the store. She'd used her Visa to buy a slice of soy-cheese pizza on her way home from Ali's memorial. It had worked then. Yesterday morning, she had apologized to her family, and now her cards were no good. It was a slap in the face.

Rage filled her body. So that was how they felt about her.

Spencer stared sadly at her two credit cards. They'd gotten so much use, the signature strip was almost worn off. Setting her jaw, she slapped her wallet shut and whipped out her Sidekick, scrolling through her received calls list for Wren's number. He answered on the first ring.

"What's your address?" she asked. "I changed my mind."

10

ABSTINENCE MAKES THE HEART GROW FONDER

That same Wednesday afternoon, Hanna stood at the entrance of the Rosewood YMCA, a restored, Colonial-style mansion. The façade was redbrick, it had two-story-high white pillars, and the moldings around the eaves and the windows looked like they belonged on a gingerbread house. The Briggses, a legendary eccentric, wealthy family, built the place in 1886, populating it with ten Briggs family members, three live-in guests, two parrots, and twelve standard poodles. Most of the building's historical details had been torn down to make way for the Y's six-lane swimming pool, fitness center, and "meeting" rooms. Hanna wondered what the Briggses would think about some of the groups that now met in their mansion. Like the Virginity Club.

Hanna threw her shoulders back and walked down the slanted wood hall to room 204, where V Club was meeting. Sean still wasn't returning her calls. All she wanted to say was that she was sorry, *God.* How were they supposed to get back together if she couldn't apologize to him? The one place she knew Sean went—and Sean thought she'd *never* be—was Virginity Club.

So maybe it was a violation of Sean's personal space, but it was for a worthy cause. She missed Sean, especially with everything that was happening with A.

"Hanna?"

Hanna whirled around. Naomi Zeigler was on an elliptical trainer in the exercise room. She was dressed in dark red Adidas terry-cloth short-shorts, a tight-fitting pink sports bra, and matching pink socks. A coordinated red hair tie held her perfect blond ponytail in place.

Hanna fake-smiled, but inside she was wincing. Naomi and her best friend, Riley Wolfe, hated Hanna and Mona. Last spring, Naomi stole Mona's crush, Jason Ryder, and then dumped him two weeks later. At last year's prom, Riley learned that Hanna was wearing a sea-foam-green Calvin Klein dress . . . and bought the exact same dress, except in lipstick red.

"What are you doing here?" Naomi yelled, still cycling. Hanna noticed that the elliptical's LED screen said Naomi had burned 876 calories. Bitch.

"I'm just meeting someone," Hanna mumbled. She pressed her hand against room 204's door, trying to seem casual, only she didn't realize the door was ajar. It tipped open, and Hanna lost her balance and toppled halfway over. Everyone inside turned to look at her.

"Yoo-hoo?" A woman in a hideous plaid knockoff Burberry jacket called. She stuck her head out the door and noticed Hanna. "Are you here for the meeting?"

"Uh," Hanna sputtered. When she glanced back at the elliptical, Naomi was gone.

"Don't be afraid." Hanna didn't know what else to do, so she followed the woman inside and took a seat.

The room was wood-paneled, dark, and airless. Kids sat on high-backed wooden chairs. Most of them looked normal, if a bit on the goody-goody side. The boys were either too pudgy or too scrawny. She didn't recognize anyone from Rosewood Day except for Sean. He was sitting across the room next to two wholesome-looking blond girls, staring at Hanna in alarm. She gave him a tiny wave, but he didn't react.

"I'm Candace," the woman who'd come to the door said. "And you are . . ."

"Hanna. Hanna Marin."

"Well! Welcome, Hanna," Candace said. She was in her mid-forties, had short blondish hair, and had drowned herself in Chloé Narcisse perfume—ironic, since Hanna had spritzed herself with Narcisse last Friday night, when she was supposed to do it with Sean. "What brings you here?"

Hanna paused. "I guess I've come to . . . to hear more about it."

"Well, the first thing I want you to know is, this is a safe space." Candace curled her hands around the back of a blond girl's chair. "Whatever you tell us is in the strictest confidence, so feel free to say anything. But you have to promise not to repeat anything anyone else says, too."

"Oh, I promise," Hanna said quickly. There was no way she'd repeat what anyone said. That would mean telling someone she'd come here in the first place.

"Is there anything you'd like to know?" Candace asked.

"Well, um, I'm not sure," Hanna stuttered.

"Is there anything you'd like to say?"

Hanna sneaked a peek at Sean. He gave her a look that seemed to say, *Yes, what* would *you like to say?*

She straightened up. "I've been thinking a lot about sex. Um, I mean, I was really curious about it. But now . . . I don't know." She took a deep breath and tried to imagine what Sean would want to hear. "I think it should be with the right person."

"The right person you *love*," Candace corrected. "And marry."

"Yes," Hanna added quickly.

"It's hard, though." Candace strolled around the room. "Does anyone have any thoughts for Hanna? Any experiences they want to share?"

A blond boy in camo cargo pants who was almost cute—if you squinted—raised his hand, then changed his mind and put it down. A brown-haired girl who wore a pink Dubble Bubble T-shirt raised two tentative fingers in the air and said, "I thought a lot about sex, too. My boyfriend threatened to break up with me if I wouldn't do it. For a while, I was considering giving in, but I'm glad I didn't."

Hanna nodded, trying to look thoughtful. Who were these people kidding? She wondered if they were secretly dying to get some.

"Sean, how about you?" Candace asked. "You were saying last week that you and your girlfriend had differing opinions about sex. How's that going?"

Hanna felt heat rise to her cheeks. She. Could. *Not.* Believe. It.

"Fine," Sean mumbled.

"Are you sure? Did you have a talk with her, like we discussed?"

"Yes," Sean said curtly.

A long silence followed. Hanna wondered if they knew that "her" was . . . her.

Candace went around the room asking the others to speak about their temptations: Had anyone gotten horizontal with a boyfriend or girlfriend? Had anyone made out? Had anyone watched Skinamax? *Yes, yes, yes!* Hanna ticked off in her head—even though she knew they were all V Club no-no's.

A few other kids asked sex questions—most were trying to figure out what counted as "a sexual experience," and what they should avoid. "All of it," Candace deadpanned. Hanna was flabbergasted—she'd figured V Club banned intercourse, but not the whole sexual menu. Finally, the meeting adjourned, and the V Club kids got out of their chairs to stretch. Cans of soda, paper cups, a plate of Oreos, and a bag of Terra Yukon Golds were on a table off to the side. Hanna stood up, slid the straps of her purple wedges back around her ankles, and stretched her arms in the air. She couldn't help but notice that Sean was staring at her exposed abs. She gave him a flirty smile, then walked over.

"Hey," she said.

"Hanna . . ." He ran his hand through his close-cropped hair, looking uncomfortable. When he cut it last spring, Hanna said it made him look a little like Justin Timberlake, only less skanky. In response, Sean had done an awful but also cute rendition of "Cry Me a River." That was back when he was fun. "What are you doing?" he asked.

She fluttered her hand to her throat. "What do you mean?"

"I just . . . I don't know if you should be here."

"Why?" she fumed. "I have every right to be here, just like everyone. I just wanted to apologize, all right? I've been trying to chase you down in school, but you keep running away from me."

"Well, it's complicated, Hanna," Sean said.

Hanna was about to ask what was so complicated when Candace put her hands on both their shoulders. "I see you two know each other!"

"That's right," Hanna chirped, momentarily burying her irritation.

"We're so happy to have you, Hanna." Candace beamed. "You'd be a very positive role model for us."

"Thanks." Hanna felt a little thrill. Even if it was V Club, she wasn't often embraced like this. Not by her third-grade tennis coach, not by her friends, not by her teachers, certainly not by her parents. Perhaps V Club was her calling. She pictured herself as the spokeswoman of V Club. Maybe it was like being Miss America, except instead of a crown, she'd get a fabulous V Club ring. Or maybe a V Club bag. A cherry-monogrammed Louis Vuitton clutch with a hand-painted *V*.

"So, do you think you'll join us next week?" Candace asked.

Hanna looked at Sean. "Probably."

"Wonderful!" Candace cried.

She left Hanna and Sean alone again. Hanna sucked in her stomach, wishing she hadn't hogged down a Good Humor chocolate éclair bar she'd impetuously bought from the Y's ice cream truck before the meeting. "So, you talked about me here, huh?"

Sean shut his eyes. "I'm sorry she mentioned that."

"No, it's all right," Hanna interrupted. "I didn't realize how much all this . . . meant to you. And I really like some of the stuff they were saying. About, um, the person being someone you love. I'm all for that. And everyone seems really sweet." She felt surprised the words were coming out of her mouth. She actually kind of meant them.

Sean shrugged. "Yeah, it's okay."

Hanna frowned, surprised by his apathy. Then she sighed and raised her eyes. "Sean, I'm really sorry about what happened. About . . . about the car. I just . . . I don't really know how to apologize. I just feel so stupid. But I can't deal with you hating me."

Sean was quiet. "I don't hate you. Things came out kind of harsh on Friday. I think we were both in weird places. I mean, I don't think you should've done what you did, but . . ." He shrugged. "You're volunteering at the clinic, right?"

"Uh-huh." She hoped her nose didn't wrinkle up in disgust.

He nodded a few times. "I think that's really good. I'm sure you'll brighten the patients' day."

Hanna felt her cheeks flush with gratitude, but his sweetness didn't surprise her. Sean was a textbook good, compassionate guy—he gave money to homeless people in Philly, recycled his old cell phones, and never badmouthed anyone, even celebrities who existed to be made fun of. It had been one of the reasons she'd first come to love Sean back in sixth grade when she still was a chubby loser.

But just last week, Sean *had* been hers. She'd come a long way from being a loserish girl who did Ali's gossipy dirty work, and she couldn't let a little drunken error in judgment at a field party ruin their relationship. Although . . . there was something—or *someone*—else that might ruin their relationship.

I can RUIN you.

"Sean?" Hanna's heart pounded. "Have you gotten any weird texts about me?"

"Texts?" Sean repeated. He cocked his head. "No . . ."

Hanna bit her fingernail. "If you do," she said, "don't believe them."

"All right." Sean smiled at her. Hanna felt electric.

"So," she said after a pause. "Are you still going to Foxy?"

Sean looked away. "I guess. Probably with a bunch of guys or whatever."

"Save me a dance," she purred, and squeezed his hand. She loved the way his hands felt—solid, warm, and masculine. It made her so happy to touch him that maybe she *could* give up sex until marriage. She and Sean would stay constantly vertical, cover their eyes at sex scenes, and avoid Victoria's Secret in the mall. If that was what it took to be with the only boy she'd ever kind of, well, *loved*, then maybe Hanna could make that sacrifice.

Or maybe, if the way Sean was eyeing her midriff again was any indication, she could talk him out of it.

11

DIDN'T EMILY'S MOTHER EVER TEACH HER NOT TO GET IN STRANGERS' CARS?

Emily twisted the dial on the Fresh Fields' gumball machine. It was Wednesday after swim practice, and she was picking up stuff for dinner for her mom. She hit the gumball machine every time she came into Fresh Fields, and had made a game out of it: if she got a yellow gumball, something good would happen to her. She looked at the gumball in her palm. It was green.

"Hey." Someone stood over her.

Emily looked up. "Aria. Hey."

As usual, Aria clearly wasn't afraid to stand out with her outfit. She wore a neon blue puffy vest that accentuated her arresting, ice-blue eyes. And although she wore the school's standard-issue uniform skirt, she'd hiked it up well above her knees and paired it with black leggings and funky royal blue ballet flats. Her black hair was up in a high, cheerleader-style ponytail. It completely worked, and most of the guys in the Fresh Fields parking lot under seventy-five were staring at her.

Aria leaned closer. "You holding up okay?"

"Yeah. You?"

Aria shrugged. She gave a surreptitious glance around the parking lot, which was full of eager cart boys pushing stray carts into the corral. "You haven't gotten any—"

"Nope." Emily avoided Aria's eyes. She'd deleted Monday's text from A—the one about her new love—so it was *almost* as if it hadn't happened. "You?"

"Nada." Aria shrugged. "Maybe we're in the clear."

We're not, Emily wanted to say. She chewed on the inside of her cheek.

"Well, you can call me anytime." Aria took a step toward the soda cases.

Emily left the store, a cold sweat covering her body. Why was she the only one who'd heard from A, anyway? Was A singling her out?

She put the grocery bag into her backpack, unlocked her bike, and pedaled out of the parking lot. As she turned onto a side street that was nothing but miles of white-picket farm fencing, she felt the teensiest hint of fall in the air. Fall in Rosewood always reminded Emily that it was the start of swimming season. That was usually a good thing, but this year, Emily felt uneasy. Coach Lauren had made the captain announcement yesterday after the Rosewood Tank ended. All the girls had mobbed Emily to congratulate her, and when she'd told her parents, her mom had gotten teary-eyed. Emily knew she should feel happy—things were back to normal. Except she felt like *she'd* already irrevocably changed.

"Emily!" someone called behind her.

She twisted around to see who was calling her, and her bike's front wheel skidded on a wet patch of leaves. All of a sudden, she found herself on the ground.

"Oh my God, are you okay?" a voice called.

Emily opened her eyes. Standing over her was Toby Cavanaugh. He had the hood of his parka up, so his face looked shadowed and hollow.

She yelped. Yesterday's incident in the locker room hallway kept coming back to her. Toby's face, his frustrated expression. How he'd just *looked* at Ben, and Ben had backed off. And was it a coincidence that he'd been coming through the hall at that moment, or had he been following her? She thought of A's note. *Although most of us have totally changed . . .* Well, Toby certainly had.

Toby crouched down. "Let me help you."

Emily pushed the bike off herself, cautiously moved her legs, then pulled up her pant leg to inspect the long, harsh scrape on her shin. "I'm fine."

"You dropped this back there." Toby handed Emily her lucky change purse. It was made of pink patent leather and had a monogrammed *E* on the front; Ali had given it to Emily a month before she went missing.

"Um, thanks." Emily took it from him, feeling uneasy.

Toby frowned at the scrape. "That looks kind of bad.

You want to get into my car? I think I have some
Band-Aids. . . ."

Emily's heart pounded. First she'd gotten that note
from A, then Toby had rescued her in the locker room,
now this. Why was he at Tate, anyway? Wasn't he supposed to be in Maine? And she'd always wondered if
Toby knew about The Jenna Thing and why he'd confessed. "Really. I'm okay," she said, her voice rising.

"Can I at least drive you somewhere?"

"No!" Emily yelped. Then she noticed how much
blood was gushing out of her leg. She despised seeing
blood. Her arms started to feel limp.

"Emily?" Toby asked her. "Are you . . . ?"

Emily's vision warped. She couldn't faint right now.
She had to get away from Toby. *Although most of us have
totally changed* . . . And then everything went black.

When she woke up, she was lying in the backseat of a
small car. A bunch of mini Band-Aids crisscrossed the
scrape on her leg. She looked around woozily, trying to
get her bearings, when she noticed who was driving.

Toby twisted around. "Boo."

Emily screamed.

"Whoa!" Toby paused at a stoplight and held his
hands in the air, a gesture that said, *Don't shoot!* "Sorry. I
was just playing."

Emily sat up. The backseat was filled with stuff: empty
Gatorade bottles, spiral-bound notebooks, textbooks,

beat-up sneakers, and a pair of gray sweats. Toby's seat cushion had worn off in places, revealing a core of ratty blue foam. A Grateful Dead dancing bear air freshener hung from the rearview mirror. The car didn't smell fresh, though. It smelled sharp and acrid. "What are you doing?" Emily screeched. "Where are we going?"

"You passed out," Toby said calmly. "From the blood, maybe. I didn't know what to do, so I lifted you up and put you in my car. I stuck your bike in my trunk."

Emily glanced at her feet; there was her backpack. Toby picked her up? Like, in his arms? She felt so freaked, she felt like she was going to faint again. Looking around, she didn't recognize the woodsy road they were on. They could be *anywhere.*

"Let me out," Emily cried. "I can bike from here."

"But there isn't a shoulder. . . ."

"Seriously. Pull over."

Toby pulled over to the grassy hump and faced her. The corners of his mouth drooped down and his eyes widened in concern. "I didn't mean . . ." He ran his hand over his chin. "What was I supposed to do? Leave you there?"

"Yes," Emily said.

"Well, um, I'm sorry then." Toby got out of the car, walked to her side, and opened her door. A lock of dark hair fell over his eyes. "At school, I volunteered for the EMS unit. I kind of want to rescue everything now. Even, like, roadkill."

Emily looked down the country road and noticed the

giant Applegate Horse Farm waterwheel. They weren't in the middle of nowhere. They were a mile from her house.

"C'mon," Toby said. "I'll help you out."

Maybe she was overreacting. There were a lot of people who'd really changed—take any of Emily's old friends, for instance. It didn't mean Toby was definitely A. She unclenched her grip on the seat cushion. "Um, you can drive me. If you want."

He stared at her for a minute. One side of his mouth curled up into an almost-smile. The expression on his face said, *Um, okay, crazy girl,* but he didn't say it.

He got back in the driver's seat, and Emily quietly inspected him. Toby really *had* transformed. His formerly creepy-looking dark eyes now just looked deep and brooding. And he actually spoke. Coherently. The summer after sixth grade, Emily and Toby went to the same swim camp, and Toby would stare at Emily unashamedly, then pull his cap over his eyes and hum. Even then, Emily wished she could ask him the billion-dollar question: Why had he taken the blame for blinding his stepsister, when he hadn't?

The night it happened, Ali came inside the house and told them that everything was fine, that no one had seen her. Everyone was too scared to sleep at first, but Ali scratched everyone's backs, calming them down. The next day, when Toby confessed, Aria asked Ali if she'd known he was going to do that all along—how else could she have been so chill? "I just had this vibe we'd be okay," Ali explained.

Over time, Toby's confession had just become one of those life mysteries they'd never understand—like why Brad and Jen *really* got divorced, what was on the Rosewood Day girls' bathroom floor the day the janitorial worker screamed, why Imogen Smith missed so much school in sixth grade (because it definitely wasn't mono), or like . . . who killed Ali. Maybe Toby felt guilty about something else, or wanted to get out of Rosewood? Or maybe he did have a firework in the tree house and shot it by mistake.

Toby steered into Emily's street. A rambling, bluesy song played on his stereo, and he drummed the steering wheel with his palms. She thought of how he'd saved her from Ben yesterday. She wanted to thank him, but what if he asked more about it? What would Emily say? *Oh, he was pissed because I was French-kissing a girl.*

Emily finally thought of a safe question. "So, you're at Tate now?"

"Yep," he answered. "My parents said if I got in, I could go. And I did. It's nice being close to home. I get to see my sister—she's at school in Philadelphia."

Jenna. Emily's whole body, including her toes, tensed. She tried not to show any reaction, and Toby stared straight ahead, seemingly unaware that she was nervous. "And, um, where were you before? Maine?" Emily asked, making it sound like she didn't know he'd been at the

Manning Academy for Boys, which, according to her Google research, was on Fryeburg Road in Portland.

"Yup." Toby slowed down to let two little kids on Rollerblades cross the street. "Maine was pretty cool. The best thing about it was EMS."

"Did you . . . did you see anyone die?"

Toby met her eyes in the rearview mirror again. Emily had never noticed they were actually dark blue. "Nope. But this old lady willed me her dog."

"Her *dog*?" Emily couldn't help but laugh.

"Yep. I was with her in the ambulance and visited her in the ICU. We talked about her dog, and I said I loved dogs. When she died, her lawyer found me."

"So . . . did you keep the dog?"

"She's at my house now. She's really sweet, but about as old as the lady was."

Emily giggled, and something inside her began to thaw. Toby seemed sort of . . . normal. And *nice*. Before she could say anything else, they were at her house.

Toby parked the car and pulled Emily's bike out of the trunk. As she took the handlebars from him, their fingers touched. A little spark went through her. Toby looked at Emily for a moment, and she looked down at the sidewalk. Eons ago, she'd pressed her hand into the freshly poured concrete. Now, the handprint looked way too small ever to have been hers.

Toby climbed into the driver's seat. "So I'll see you tomorrow?"

Emily's head shot up. "W-Why?"

Toby turned the ignition. "It's the Rosewood-Tate meet. Remember?"

"Oh," Emily answered. "Of course."

As Toby pulled away, she felt her heart slow down. For some crazy reason, she'd thought Toby wanted to ask her out on a date. *But c'mon,* she told herself as she walked up the front steps to her house. This was Toby. The two of them together was about as likely as . . . as, well, Ali still being alive. And for the first time since she'd disappeared, Emily had finally given up hoping for that.

12

NEXT TIME, STASH EMERGENCY COVER-UP IN YOUR PURSE

"¿Cuándo es?" a voice said in her ear. *"What time is it? Time for Spencer to die!"*

Spencer shot up. The dark, familiar figure that had been looming over her face had vanished. Instead, she was in a clean, white bedroom. There were Rembrandt etchings and a poster of the human musculature system on the bedroom wall. On TV, Elmo was teaching kids how to tell time in Spanish. The cable box said 6:04, and she assumed it was A.M.: out the window, she saw that the sun was just coming up, and she could smell fresh bagels and scrambled eggs wafting up from the street.

She looked next to her, and it all made sense. Wren slept on his back, one arm thrown over his face, his chest bare. Wren's father was Korean and his mother was British, so his skin was this perfect, golden shade. There was a scar above his lip; he had freckles across his nose, and shaggy blue-black hair, and smelled like Adidas deodorant and Tide. The thick silver ring he wore on his right pointer finger glinted in the morning sun. He pulled his arm off his face and opened his gorgeous almond-shaped eyes.

"Hey." He slowly grabbed Spencer around her waist and pulled her toward him.

"Hey," she whispered, hanging back. She could still hear the voice from her dream: *It's time for Spencer to die!* It was Toby's voice.

Wren frowned. "What's wrong?"

"Nothing," Spencer said quietly. She pressed her fingers to the base of her neck and felt her pulse race. "Just . . . bad dream."

"You want to share?"

Spencer hesitated. She wished she could. Then she shook her head.

"Well, then. C'mere."

They spent a few minutes kissing, and Spencer got a relieved, grateful rush. Everything was going to be all right. She was safe.

This was the first time Spencer had slept—*and* stayed over—in a guy's bed. Last night, she'd sped into Philly, parked on the street, and hadn't even bothered with the Club; her parents were probably planning on repossessing her car, anyway. She and Wren had fallen into bed immediately and hadn't gotten up since except to answer the door for the Chinese takeout delivery boy. Later on, she called and left a message on her parents' machine that she was staying the night at her hockey friend Kirsten's house. She felt silly, trying to be all responsible when she was really being so *irresponsible*, but whatever.

For the first time since her first A note, she'd slept like a baby. It was partly because she was in Philadelphia and not Rosewood, *next door* to Toby, but it was also because of Wren. Before they went to sleep, they'd talked about Ali—their friendship, what it had been like when Ali went missing, that someone had killed her—for an hour. He'd also let her choose the "crickets chirping" sound on the sound machine, even though it was his second–least favorite noise, after "babbling brook."

Spencer began kissing him more forcefully now, and slid out of his oversize Penn T-shirt, which she was wearing as a nightgown. Wren traced her naked collarbone, then pushed himself up onto his hands and knees. "Do you want to . . . ?" he asked.

"I think so," Spencer whispered.

"Are you *sure*?"

"Uh-huh." She wriggled out of her underwear. Wren pulled his shirt over his head. Spencer's heart pounded. She was a virgin, and was as discriminating about sex as she was about everything else in her life—she had to do it with the perfect person.

But Wren *was* the right person. She knew she was passing the Point of No Return—if her parents found out, they'd never pay for anything ever, ever, ever again. Or pay attention to her. Or send her to college. Or feed her, possibly. So what? Wren made her feel safe.

One *Sesame Street*, one *Dragon Tales*, and a half an *Arthur* later, Spencer rolled onto her back, staring blissfully at the ceiling. So much for going slow. Then she propped herself up on her elbows and looked at the clock. "Shit," she whispered. It was seven-twenty. School started at eight; she was going to miss first period at the very least.

"I have to go." She leaped out of bed and surveyed her plaid skirt, blazer, undies, cami, and boots, all in a haphazard pile on the floor. "*And* I'm going to have to go home."

Wren sat on the bed, watching her. "Why?"

"I can't wear the same outfit two days in a row."

Wren was obviously trying not to laugh at her. "But it's a uniform, right?"

"Yes, but I wore this *camisole* yesterday. And these boots."

Wren chuckled. "You're so lovably anal."

Spencer ducked her head at the word *love*.

She quickly showered, rinsing her head and body. Her heart was still pounding. She felt overcome with nerves, anxious that she was late for school, troubled by the Toby nightmare, but totally blissed about Wren. When she came out of the shower, Wren was sitting on the bed. The apartment smelled like hazelnut coffee. Spencer reached for Wren's hand and slowly slid his silver ring off his

finger and put it on her thumb. "It looks good on me."
When she looked at him, Wren wore a small, unreadable
smile. "What?" Spencer asked.

"You're just . . ." Wren shook his head and shrugged.
"It's hard for me to remember you're still in high school.
You're just so . . . together."

Spencer blushed. "I'm really not."

"No, you are. It's like . . . you actually seem more
together than—"

Wren stopped, but Spencer knew he'd been going to
say, *More together than Melissa.* She felt herself swell with
satisfaction. Melissa might have won the fight for their
parents, but Spencer had won the battle for Wren. And
that was the one that mattered.

Spencer strode up her house's long, brick-paved driveway. It was now 9:10 A.M., and second period at
Rosewood Day had already started. Her father would be
long gone to work by now, and with any luck, her mom
would be at the stables.

She opened the front door. The only sound was the
hum of the refrigerator. She tiptoed up to her room,
reminding herself that she'd have to forge a tardy slip
from her mother—and then realizing that she'd never
had to forge a tardy slip before. Every year, Spencer
earned Rosewood Day's perfect-attendance and punc-
tuality awards.

"Hey."

Spencer screamed and whirled around, her schoolbag slipping from her hands.

"Jesus." Melissa stood in the doorway. "Calm down."

"W-Why aren't you in class?" Spencer asked, her nerves vibrating.

Melissa wore dark pink velour sweatpants and a faded Penn T-shirt, but her blunt-cut, chin-length blond hair was held back by a navy blue headband. Even when Melissa relaxed, she still managed to look uptight. "Why aren't *you* in class?"

Spencer ran her hand along the back of her neck, finding it sweaty. "I . . . I forgot something. I had to come back."

"Ah." Melissa gave her a mysterious smile. Chills ran up Spencer's spine. She felt like she was on the edge of a cliff, about to topple over. "Well, I'm actually glad you're here. I've thought about what you said on Monday. I'm sorry about everything too."

"Oh," was all Spencer could think to say.

Melissa lowered her voice. "I mean, we really should be nicer to each other. Both of us. Who knows what might happen in this crazy world? Look at what happened to Alison DiLaurentis. It makes what we're fighting about seem sort of petty."

"Yeah," Spencer murmured. It was sort of an odd comparison to make.

"Anyway, I talked to Mom and Dad about it, too. I think they're coming around."

"Oh." Spencer ran her tongue over her teeth. "Wow. Thanks. That means a lot."

Melissa beamed at her in response. There was a long pause, and then Melissa took another step into Spencer's bedroom, leaning up against a cherry highboy dresser. "Sooooo . . . what's going on with you? You going to Foxy? Ian asked me, but I don't think I'm going to go. I'm probably too old."

Spencer paused, completely thrown off guard. Was Melissa up to something? These weren't the types of things they usually talked about. "I . . . uh . . . I don't know."

"Damn." Melissa smirked. "I hope you're going with the guy who gave you *that*." She pointed at Spencer's neck.

Spencer ran to her mirror and saw a huge, purple hickey near her collarbone. Her hands fluttered frantically to her neck. Then she noticed she was still wearing Wren's thick silver ring.

Melissa used to *live* with Wren—had she recognized it? Spencer yanked the ring off her finger and shoved it into her underwear drawer. Her pulse raged at her temples.

The phone rang, and Melissa picked it up in the hall. Within seconds, her head was back inside Spencer's room. "It's for you," she whispered. "A boy!"

"A . . . *boy*?" Was Wren stupid enough to call? Who else would it be, at nine-fifteen on a Thursday morning? Spencer's mind scattered in twenty directions. She took the phone. "Hello?"

"Spencer? It's Andrew. Campbell." He let out a nervous laugh. "From school."

Spencer glanced at Melissa. "Um, hey," she croaked. For a split second, she couldn't even recall who Andrew Campbell *was*. "What's up?"

"Just wanted to see if you have that flu going around. I didn't see you at the student council meeting this morning. You're never, um, not in student council."

"Oh." Spencer swallowed hard. She glanced at Melissa, who stood expectantly in the doorway. "Well, yeah, but I . . . I'm better now."

"I just wanted to say that I offered to pick up your homework for your classes," Andrew said. "Since we're in all the same ones." His voice echoed; it sounded like he was calling from the gym locker room. Andrew would be just the type to duck out of gym. "For calc, we have a bunch of end-of-chapter problem sets."

"Oh. Well, thanks."

"And do you maybe want to go over some notes for the essays? McAdam says it's a huge percentage of our grade."

"Um, sure," Spencer answered. Melissa caught Spencer's eye and gave her a hopeful, excited look. *Hickey?* she mouthed, pointing at Spencer's neck and then at the phone.

Spencer's brain felt like it was plodding through yogurt. Then, suddenly, she had an idea. She cleared her throat. "Actually, Andrew . . . do you have a date for Foxy?"

"Foxy?" Andrew repeated. "Um, I don't know. I guess I didn't have any pla—"

"Do you want to come with me?" Spencer interrupted.

Andrew laughed; it sounded like a hiccup. "Seriously?"

"Um, yeah," Spencer said, her eyes on her sister.

"Well, yeah!" Andrew said. "That'd be great! What time? What should I wear? Are you going out with any friends beforehand? Are there any after-parties?"

Spencer rolled her eyes. Leave it to Andrew to ask questions, like he was going to be quizzed on it. "We'll figure it out," Spencer said, turning to the window.

Then she hung up, feeling winded, as if she'd sprinted miles and miles for field hockey. When she turned back to her door, Melissa was gone.

13

A CERTAIN ENGLISH TEACHER IS SUCH AN UNRELIABLE NARRATOR

On Thursday, Aria hesitated in the AP English classroom doorway when Spencer walked by. "Hey." Aria grabbed her arm. "Have you gotten any . . . ?"

Spencer's eyes darted back and forth, sort of like those of the big lizards Aria had seen on display at the Paris Zoo. "Um, no," she said. "But I'm really late, so . . . " She ran down the hall. Aria bit down hard on her lip. *Okay.*

Someone put a hand on her shoulder. She let out a little shriek and dropped her water bottle. It clunked to the floor and started rolling.

"Whoa. Just trying to get by."

Ezra stood behind her. He'd been absent from school on Tuesday and Wednesday, and Aria had wondered if he'd resigned. "Sorry," she mumbled, her cheeks bright red.

Ezra had on the same rumpled corduroys he'd worn last week, a tweedy jacket with a tiny hole in the elbow, and Merrill lace-ups. Up close, he smelled faintly like the

Seda France ylang-ylang and saffron-scented "man candle" Aria remembered from his living room mantel. She'd visited his apartment just six days ago, but it felt like two lifetimes had passed since then.

Aria tiptoed into the classroom behind him. "So, were you sick?" she asked.

"Yes," Ezra aswered. "I had the flu."

"Sorry to hear that." Aria wondered if she was going to get the flu too.

Ezra looked at the empty classroom and walked closer to her. "So. Listen. How about a fresh start?" His face was businesslike.

"Um, okay," Aria croaked.

"We have a year to get through," Ezra added. "So we'll forget this happened?"

Aria swallowed. She knew their relationship was wrong, but she still had feelings for Ezra. She'd bared her soul to him, and she couldn't do that with just anyone. And he was so different. "Of course," she said, although she didn't entirely believe it. They'd had a real . . . connection.

Ezra nodded slightly. Then, ever so slowly, he reached out and put his hand on the back of Aria's neck. Tingles ran up her spine. She held her breath until he brought his hand back to his side and walked away.

Aria took a seat at her desk, her mind churning. Was that some sort of sign? He had *said* forget it, but it hadn't *felt* that way.

Before she could decide if she should say anything to Ezra, Noel Kahn slid into the seat across from Aria and poked her with his Montblanc pen. "So, I hear you're cheating on me, Finland."

"What?" Aria sat up, alert. Her hand fluttered to her neck.

"Sean Ackard was asking about you. You know he's with Hanna though, right?"

Aria poked the backs of her teeth with her tongue. "Sean . . . Ackard?"

"He's not with Hanna anymore," James Freed interrupted, sliding into his seat in front of Noel. "Mona told me Hanna dumped him."

"So, you like Sean?" Noel pushed his wavy black hair out of his eyes.

"No," Aria said automatically. Although she kept coming back to the conversation she'd had with Sean in his car on Tuesday. It had felt good to talk to someone about things.

"Good," Noel said, brushing a hand across his forehead. "I was worried."

Aria rolled her eyes.

Hanna sauntered into the room just as the bell rang, putting her oversize Prada bag on her desk and sinking dramatically into her chair. She gave Aria a tight smile.

"Hey." Aria felt a little shy. In school, Hanna seemed awfully closed off.

"Hey, Hanna, are you with Sean Ackard anymore?" Noel asked loudly.

Hanna stared at him. Her eyelid twitched. "It wasn't working between us. Why?"

"No reason," Aria butted in quickly. Although she wondered why Hanna had broken up with him. They were two peas in a typical Rosewood pod.

Ezra clapped his hands. "All right," he said. "In addition to the books we're reading as a class, I want to do an extra side project on unreliable narrators."

Devon Arliss raised her hand. "What does *that* mean?"

Ezra strode around the room. "Well, the narrator tells us the story in a book, right? But what if . . . the narrator isn't telling us the truth? Maybe he's telling his skewed version of the story to get you on his side. Or to scare you. Or maybe he's crazy!"

Aria shivered. That made her think of A.

"I'm going to assign each of you a book," Ezra said. "In a ten-page paper, you are to make the case for and against its narrator being unreliable."

The class groaned. Aria rested her head in her palm. Maybe A wasn't entirely reliable? Maybe A didn't really know anything but was just *trying* to convince them otherwise. Who was A, anyway? She looked around the classroom, at Amber Billings, poking her finger through a tiny hole in her stockings; at Mason Byers, secretly checking the Phillies scores on his cell phone, using his notebook as a shield; and at Hanna, writing down what

Ezra was saying with her purple-ink feather pen. Could any of these people be A? Who could know about Ezra, her parents . . . *and* The Jenna Thing?

A groundskeeper zoomed by on a John Deere mower outside the window, and Aria jumped. Ezra was still talking about lying narrators, pausing to take a sip out of his mug. He shot Aria the tiniest smile, and her heart began to thrum.

James Freed leaned over, poked Hanna, and gestured to Ezra. "So, I hear Fitz gets some serious ass," he whispered, loud enough for Aria—and the rest of her row—to hear.

Hanna looked at Ezra and wrinkled her nose. "Him? Ew."

"Apparently he's got this girlfriend in New York, but he's on a different Hollis girl every week," James went on.

Aria straightened up. *Girlfriend?*

"Where'd you hear that?" Noel asked James.

James grinned. "You know Ms. Polanski? The bio student teacher? She told me. She hangs out with us at the smoking corner sometimes."

Noel gave James a high five. "Dude, Ms. Polanski is *hot.*"

"Seriously," James answered. "You think I could take her to Foxy?"

Aria felt like someone had just thrown her into a bonfire. A *girlfriend?* Friday night, he'd said he hadn't dated anybody in a long time. Aria remembered noticing his bachelorish frozen dinners for one, his eight thousand books but one drinking glass, and his sad, dead spider plants. It didn't *look* like he had a girlfriend.

James could have his facts wrong, but she doubted it. Aria bubbled with anger. Years ago, she might've thought only typical Rosewood boys were players, but she'd learned a lot about boys in Iceland. Sometimes the most unassuming boys were the sketchiest. No girl would look at Ezra—sensitive, rumpled, sweet, caring Ezra—and distrust him. He reminded Aria of someone. Her father.

Aria suddenly felt sick. She stood up, grabbed the hall pass from the peg, and strode out the door.

"Aria?" Ezra called, sounding concerned.

She didn't stop. In the girls' room, she rushed to the sink, dispensed pink soap into her hands, and scrubbed the spot on her neck Ezra had touched. She was walking back to class when her cell phone chimed. She pulled it out of her bag and pressed *read*.

Naughty, naughty Aria! You should know better than to go after a teacher, anyway. It's girls like you who break up perfectly happy families. —A

Aria froze. She was in the middle of the empty front hallway. When she heard a noise, she whirled around. She was facing the glass trophy case, which had been transformed into an Alison DiLaurentis temple. Inside were various candids from Rosewood Day classes—teachers always took tons of pictures throughout the year, and the school typically presented them to parents when their child graduated. There was Ali as a gap-toothed kindergartner; there she was dressed up as a pilgrim for their fourth-grade play. There was even some of her schoolwork, like an Under the Sea diorama from third grade and an illustration of the circulatory system from fifth.

A square of hot pink caught Aria's eye. Someone had stuck a Post-it note on the memorial's glass. Aria's eyes widened.

> P.S. Wondering who I am, aren't you? I'm closer than
> you think. —A

14

EMILY'S PERFECTLY FINE WITH TAKING ALI'S SLOPPY SECONDS

"Say *butterfly*!" crowed Scott Chin, Rosewood Day's yearbook photographer. It was Thursday afternoon, and the swim team was in the natatorium for team photos before the Tate meet started. Emily had been on swim teams for so long, she didn't even think about having her picture taken in a bathing suit.

She posed with her hands on the starting block and tried to smile. "Gorgeous!" Scott cried, pursing his pink lips. A lot of kids at school speculated about whether Scott was gay. Scott never outwardly admitted it, but he didn't do anything to dispel the rumors, either.

As Emily maneuvered across the deck to her duffel bag, she noticed Tate Prep's team strolling to their bleachers. Toby was in the middle of the pack, wearing a blue Champion sweatshirt and rolling his shoulders back and forth to warm up.

Emily held her breath. She'd been thinking about

Toby ever since he rescued her yesterday. She couldn't imagine Ben ever having picked her up like that—he'd have worried that lifting her might pull his shoulder muscles and compromise his race today. And thinking about Toby had triggered something else, too: a memory of Ali that Emily had nearly forgotten.

It was one of the last times Emily was ever alone with Ali. She'd never forget that day—clear blue sky, all the flowers had bloomed, there were bees everywhere. Ali's tree house smelled like Kool-Aid, sap, and cigarette smoke—Ali had pilfered a Parliament from her older brother's pack. She grabbed Emily's hands. "You *can't* tell the others this," she said. "I've started secretly seeing this older guy, and it's a-*maz*-ing."

Emily's smile drooped. Every time Ali told her about a guy she liked, a little piece of her heart cracked off.

"He's *so* hot," Ali went on. "I almost want to go sort of far with him."

"What do you mean?" Emily had never heard anything so horrifying in her life. "Who is he?"

"I can't tell." Ali smiled slyly. "You guys would *freak*."

And then, because Emily couldn't stand it any longer, she leaned forward and kissed Ali. There was a singular, wonderful moment; then Ali pulled away and laughed. Emily tried to pass it off like she was just playing . . . and then they went to their separate houses to have dinner.

She'd thought about the kiss so many times, she'd hardly remembered what had come before it. But now that Toby was back and he was so cute . . . it got Emily thinking that maybe Ali's guy had been Toby? Who else would've made them freak?

Ali liking Toby sort of made sense. At the end of seventh grade, she'd been on a bad-boy kick, talking about how she wanted to go out with someone who was "like, *bad*." Being sent to reform school qualified as bad, and maybe Ali saw something in Toby that no one else did. Emily thought maybe she could see that same something, now. And, slightly bizarre as it was, the possibility that Ali had liked Toby made Toby seem that much more attractive to Emily. What was good enough for Ali was certainly good enough for her.

As soon as the swim meet broke for the diving competition, Emily pulled her flip-flops out of her Rosewood Day swimming tote, preparing to walk over to Toby. Her fingers bumped against her cell phone, tucked under her towel. It was blinking; she'd missed seven calls from Maya.

Emily's throat tightened. Maya had called, IM'ed, texted, and e-mailed her all week, and Emily hadn't responded. With every new missed phone call, she felt more confused. Part of her wanted to find Maya in school and run her hand through her soft, curly hair. To climb on the back of her bike and ditch school. Kissing Maya had felt dangerously good. But part of her wished Maya would just . . . disappear.

Emily stared at her cell phone window, a lump in her

throat. Then, slowly, she snapped it shut. It kind of felt like the time when she was eight and decided to throw away Bee-Bee, her security blanket. *Big girls don't need blankies,* she'd told herself, but it had been awful to close the trash can's lid with Bee-Bee inside.

She took a deep breath and headed for Tate's bleachers. On her way there, she glanced over her shoulder, looking for Ben. He was over on Rosewood Day's side, slapping Seth's shoulder with his Sammy towel. Since the Tank on Tuesday, Ben had stayed out of Emily's way, acting like she didn't exist. It was certainly better than attacking her, but it made her paranoid that he was saying stuff about her behind her back. She kind of wanted Ben to see her right now, just as she approached Toby. *Look! I'm talking to a guy!*

Toby had laid his towel on the natatorium tile and had headphones over his ears and an iPod on his lap. His hair was slicked back from his face, and the royal blue sweats he wore over his Speedo—which Emily hadn't been brave enough to peek at during his first event—made his eyes look even bluer.

When he saw Emily, he brightened. "Hey. Told you I'd see you here, didn't I?"

"Yeah." Emily smiled shyly. "So, um, I just wanted to say thanks. For helping me yesterday. *And* the day before."

"Oh. Well, it was nothing."

Just then, Scott appeared with his yearbook camera. "Gotcha!" he cried, and snapped a picture. "I can see the caption now: 'Emily Fields, flirting with the enemy!'" Then he said to Emily in a lower voice, "Although I thought he wasn't your type."

Emily looked at Scott questioningly. What was *that* supposed to mean? But he fluttered away. When she turned to Toby again, he was playing with his iPod, so she started back for her team's side. She'd taken three steps when Toby called out, "Hey, you want to get some air?"

Emily paused. Quickly, she glanced at Ben. Still not paying any attention. "Um, all right," she decided.

They walked through the Rosewood Day natatorium's double doors, past a bunch of kids waiting for the late buses, and sat down on the edge of the Founder's Day fountain. Water gushed out of the top in a long, shimmering plume. It was cloudy out, though, so the water just looked dull and white instead of sparkly. Emily stared at a bunch of pennies on the fountain's shallow, shiny bottom. "On the last day of school, seniors push their favorite teacher into this fountain," she told him.

"I know," Toby said. "I used to go here, remember?"

"Oh." Emily felt like a moron. Of course he did. And then they sent him away.

Toby pulled a package of chocolate chip cookies out of his bag. He held them out to Emily. "Want one? Pre-race snack?"

Emily shrugged. "Maybe half."

"Good for you," Toby said, handing her one. He

looked away. "It's funny how it's totally different between guys and girls. Guys want to out-eat each other. Even guys I know that are older. Like my shrink, in Maine? One time, at his house, we had a shrimp-eating contest. He beat me by six shrimp. And he's, like, at least thirty-five."

"Shrimp." Emily shuddered. Because she didn't want to ask the obvious—*You had a shrink?*—she asked, "What happened after your, um, shrink ate all that?"

"He threw up." Toby skimmed the surface of the water with his fingertips. The fountain water smelled even more like chlorine than the pool did.

Emily ran her hands over her knees. She wondered if he had a shrink for the same reason he'd taken the blame for The Jenna Thing.

A luxury bus pulled into the Rosewood Day parking lot. Slowly, members of the Rosewood Day band trooped off, still in their uniforms—red jackets with braided trim, flared tuxedo pants, the drum major in a goofy furry hat that looked like it would be really hot and uncomfortable to wear. "You, um, talk a lot about Maine," Emily said. "Are you happy to be in Rosewood again?"

Toby raised an eyebrow. "Are *you* happy to be in Rosewood?"

Emily frowned. She watched as a squirrel ran circles around one of the oak trees. "I don't know," she said quietly. "Sometimes I feel kind of wrong here. I used to be normal, but now . . . I don't know. I feel like I should be one way, but I'm not."

Toby stared at her. "I hear that." He sighed. "There are all these perfect people here. And . . . it's like, if you're not one of them, then you're messed up. But I think, inside, the flawless-looking people are just as messed up as we are."

He turned his gaze to Emily, and her insides turned over. She felt like her thoughts and secrets were 72-point-font newspaper headlines, and Toby could read all of them. But Toby was also the first person who'd expressed something close to how she felt about things. "I feel pretty messed up most of the time," she said quietly.

Toby looked like he didn't believe her. "How are you messed up?"

A clap of thunder exploded overhead. Emily slid her hands inside her warm-up jacket sleeves. *I'm messed up because I don't know who I am or what I want,* she wanted to say. But instead, she looked directly at him and blurted, "I love storms."

"Me too," he answered.

And then, slowly, Toby leaned forward and kissed her. It was very soft and tentative, just a little whisper across her mouth. When he pulled back, Emily touched her lips with her fingers, like the kiss might still be on her lips.

"What was that for?" she whispered.

"I don't know," Toby said. "Should I not have . . . ?"

"No," Emily whispered. "It was nice." Her first thought was, *I just kissed a boy Ali might have kissed.* Her second was that maybe it was messed up of her to have even thought that.

"Toby?" a voice interrupted them. A man in a leather jacket stood under the natatorium awning, hands on his hips. It was Mr. Cavanaugh. Emily recognized him from summer swim team, years ago . . . and from the night Jenna got hurt. Her shoulder muscles tightened. If Mr. Cavanaugh was here, was Jenna? Then she remembered that Jenna was at school in Philadelphia. Hopefully.

"What are you doing out here?" Mr. Cavanaugh put his hand outside the awning, feeling the rain, which had just begun to fall. "Your relay's soon."

"Oh." Toby jumped off the wall. He smiled at Emily. "You going back in too?"

"In a sec," Emily said weakly. If she tried to use her legs right now, they might not work. "Good luck with your race."

"Okay." Toby's eyes lingered on her for another moment. He looked ready to say something else, but he broke away, falling into step with his dad.

Emily sat on the stone wall for a few minutes, the rain soaking through her jacket. She felt strangely fizzy, like she was carbonated. What had just happened? When her Nokia announced that she had a text, she flinched and dug it out of her jacket pocket. Her heart sank. It was who she thought it was.

Emily, how about this picture of you for the yearbook
instead?

She clicked on the attachment. It was a shot of Emily
and Maya from Noel's photo booth. They were looking
into each other's eyes longingly, inches from kissing.
Emily's mouth fell open. She remembered hitting the
button in the booth to start the photos—but hadn't Maya
taken them when they left?

You wouldn't want this to get around, would you? said the
line of text under the photo.

And—of course—it was signed, *A*.

15

SHE STEALS FOR YOU, AND
THIS IS HOW YOU REPAY HER

Mona emerged from the Saks dressing room in a square-necked, sheer green Calvin Klein dress. Its full skirt fanned out as she twirled. "What do you think?" she asked Hanna, who was standing at the racks right outside.

"Gorgeous," Hanna murmured. Under the dressing room's fluorescent lights, she could tell Mona wasn't wearing a bra.

Mona posed in the three-way mirror. She was so skinny, sometimes she dipped down to an enviable size zero. "I think this might be better with your coloring." She pulled at one of the straps. "You want to try?"

"I don't know," Hanna said. "It's kind of see-through."

Mona frowned. "Since when do you care?"

Hanna shrugged and looked through a rack of Marc Jacobs blazers. It was Thursday evening, and they were at the designer department of Saks in the King James Mall, frantically searching for Foxy dresses. A lot of prep school and out-of-college-but-living-in-the-estate-with-the-'rents girls attended, and it was important to find a dress that five other girls wouldn't be wearing.

"I want to look classy," Hanna answered. "Like Scarlett Johansson."

"Why?" Mona asked. "She's got a big ass."

Hanna pursed her lips. When she said *classy*, she meant *subtle*. Like those girls in those diamond ads who looked sweet but had the words *fuck me* airbrushed into a strand of their hair. Sean needed to be so entranced by Hanna's virtue, he'd reject his V Club vows and tear her underwear off.

Hanna picked up a pair of peep-toe, camel-colored Miu Miu shoes from the sale shelf just outside the dressing room. "I love these." She held one up for Mona to see.

"Why don't you . . . ?" Mona nudged her chin down to Hanna's bag.

Hanna dropped them back on the shelf. "No way."

"Why not?" Mona whispered. "Shoes are the easiest. You know that." When Hanna hesitated, Mona clucked her tongue. "You're still freaked about Tiffany?"

Instead of answering, Hanna pretended to be interested in a pair of metallic Marc Jacobs sling-backs.

Mona pulled a few more things off the racks and went back into the changing room. Seconds later, she emerged empty-handed. "This place blows. Let's try Prada."

They walked through the mall, Mona typing on her

Sidekick. "I'm asking Eric what color flowers he's getting me," she explained. "Maybe I'll match my dress to them."

Mona had decided to go to Foxy with Noel Kahn's brother, Eric, who she'd hung out with a few times this week already. The Kahn boys were always a safe Foxy date—they were good-looking and rich, and society photographers loved them. Mona tried to coax Hanna into asking Noel, but she'd waited too long. Noel had asked Celeste Richards, who went to the Quaker boarding school—a surprise, since everyone thought Noel had a thing for Aria Montgomery. Hanna didn't care, though. If she wasn't going with Sean, she wasn't going with anyone.

Mona looked up from her texting. "Which spray-on tan place do you think is better, Sun Land or Dalia's? Celeste and I might go to Sun Land tomorrow, but I think they make you look orange."

Hanna shrugged, feeling a pang of jealousy. Mona should've been going tanning with her, not Celeste. She was about to answer, when her own phone rang. Her heart sped up a little. Whenever her phone rang, she thought of A.

"Hanna?" It was her mom. "Where are you?"

"I'm out shopping," Hanna answered. Since when did her mom care?

"Well, you need to go home. Your father is stopping over."

"What? Why?" Hanna glanced at Mona, who was checking out the cheapo sunglasses at an esplanade kiosk.

She hadn't told Mona that her dad had visited on Monday. It was too weird to talk about.

"He just . . . He needs to pick something up," her mom said.

"Like what?"

Ms. Marin let out a flustered snort. "He's coming over to get some financial paperwork we need to settle before he gets married. Is that enough explanation for you?"

A prickly sweat gathered on the back of Hanna's neck. One, because her mom had mentioned what she hated to think about—that her dad was getting *married* to Isabel, and he would be Kate's *father*. And two, she'd sort of thought her dad might be stopping by to see her, specifically. Why should she go home if he was coming for another reason? It would look like she didn't have a life. She checked her reflection in the Banana Republic window. "When's he coming?" she asked.

"He'll be here in an hour." Her mother abruptly hung up. Hanna snapped her phone closed and cradled it between her hands, feeling its warmth seep into her palms.

"Who was *that*?" Mona singsonged, linking her arm through Hanna's.

"My mom," Hanna said distractedly. She wondered if she'd have enough time to shower when she got home; she reeked of all the different perfumes she'd sampled at Neiman Marcus. "She wants me to go home."

"Why?"

"Just . . . because."

Mona stopped and eyed Hanna carefully. "Han. Your mom doesn't just randomly call to summon you home."

Hanna stopped. They were standing in front of the entrance to Year of the Rabbit, the mall's upscale Chinese bistro, and the overpowering smell of hoisin sauce wafted into her nostrils. "Well, it's because . . . my dad's coming over."

Mona frowned. "Your dad? I thought he was—"

"He's not," Hanna said quickly. When Mona and Hanna became friends, Hanna told Mona that her father was dead. She'd vowed never to speak to him again, so it wasn't exactly a lie. "We weren't in touch for a really long time," she explained. "But I saw him the other day, and he has business in Philly or whatever. He's not coming over today because of me. I don't know why my mom wants me there."

Mona put one hand on her hip. "Why didn't you tell me before?"

Hanna shrugged.

"So when did this happen?"

"I don't know. Monday?"

"Monday?" Mona sounded hurt.

"Girls!" interrupted a voice. Hanna and Mona looked up. It was Naomi Zeigler. She and Riley Wolfe were coming out of Prada, black shopping bags slung over their perfectly spray-tanned shoulders.

"Are you shopping for Foxy?" Naomi asked. Her

blond hair was as lustrous as ever and her skin glowed irritatingly, but Hanna couldn't help note that her BCBG dress was last season's. Before she could answer, Naomi added, "Don't bother with Prada. We bought the only good stuff."

"Maybe we've already *got* dresses," Mona said stiffly.

"Hanna, you're going, too?" Riley widened her brown eyes and tossed her shiny red hair. "I thought maybe since you aren't with Sean . . ."

"I wouldn't miss Foxy," Hanna said haughtily.

Riley put her hand on her hip. She was wearing black leggings, a frayed denim shirt, and a fugly black-and-white striped sweater. Recently there had been a paparazzi shot of Mischa Barton wearing the exact same outfit. "Sean's so beautiful," Riley purred. "I think he got even cuter over the summer."

"He's totally gay," Mona said quickly.

Riley didn't look worried. "I bet I can get him to change his mind."

Hanna clenched her fists.

Naomi brightened. "So, hey, Hanna, the Y is awesome, huh? You'll have to take the Pilates class with me. The instructor, Oren? *Gorgeous.*"

"Hanna doesn't go to the Y," Mona interrupted. "We go to Body Tonic. The Y is a shithole."

Hanna swiveled from Mona to Naomi, her stomach fluttering.

"You don't go to the Y?" Naomi made the most

innocent face she could. "I'm confused. Didn't I see you there yesterday? Outside the elliptical room?"

Hanna grabbed Mona's arm. "We're late for something." She dragged her away from the Prada store, back in the direction of Saks.

"What was that all about?" Mona asked, skirting gracefully around a horsey woman laden with shopping bags.

"Nothing. I just can't stand her."

"Why were you at the Y yesterday? You told me you were seeing the dermatologist."

Hanna stopped. She'd known seeing Naomi before V Club was trouble. "I . . . I had something to do there."

"What?"

"I can't tell you."

Mona frowned, then whirled around. She took determined, stiff steps into Burberry. Hanna caught up with her. "Look, I just can't. I'm sorry."

"I'm sure you are." Mona started digging through her purse and pulled out the camel-colored Miu Mius from Saks. They weren't in their box, and the security tag had been ripped off them. She dangled them in front of Hanna's face. "I was *going* to give these to you as a present. But forget it."

Hanna's mouth fell open. "But . . ."

"That thing with your dad happened three days ago, and you never told me about it," Mona said. "And now you're lying to me about what you're doing after school."

"It's not like that at all . . ." Hanna stuttered.

"It looks that way to me." Mona frowned. "What else are you lying about?"

"I'm sorry," Hanna squeaked. "I just . . ." She looked down at her shoes and took a deep breath. "You want to know why I was at the Y? Fine. I went to Virginity Club."

Mona's eyes widened. Her cell phone rang in her bag, but she made no motion to get it. "Now I *hope* you're lying."

Hanna shook her head. She felt a little nauseated; Burberry smelled way too much like its new perfume.

"But . . . why?"

"I want Sean back."

Mona burst out laughing. "You told me you ended it with Sean at Noel's party."

Hanna glanced into Burberry's window and nearly had a heart attack. Was her butt really that chunky? She suddenly had the same proportions as dorky, fat Hanna of the past. She gasped, looked away, and looked again. Normal Hanna stared back. "No," she told Mona. "He ended it with me."

Mona didn't laugh, but she didn't try to comfort Hanna, either. "Is that why you were at his dad's clinic, too?"

"No," Hanna said quickly, forgetting that she'd seen Mona there. Then, realizing that she might have to tell Mona the *real* reason, she backtracked. "Well, yeah. Sort of."

Mona shrugged. "Well, I sort of heard Sean broke up with you from somewhere else, anyway."

"*What?*" Hanna hissed. "From who?"

"Maybe in gym. I don't remember." Mona shrugged. "Maybe Sean started it."

Hanna's eyesight blurred. She doubted Sean had told . . . but maybe A had.

Mona considered her. "I thought you wanted to lose your virginity, not prolong it."

"I just wanted to see what it was like," Hanna said softly.

"And?" Mona pursed her lips mischievously. "Give me the dirt. I bet it was hilarious. What did you talk about? Did you chant? Sing? What?"

Hanna frowned and then turned away. Normally, she'd have told Mona everything. Except it stung that Mona was laughing at her, and she didn't want to give her the satisfaction. Candace had so plaintively said, *This is a safe space*. Right now, Hanna didn't feel she had the right to give up anyone's secrets, not when it looked like A was giving up hers. And why, if Mona had heard a rumor about her, hadn't she said anything? Weren't they supposed to be best friends? "None of that, really," she murmured. "It was pretty boring."

Mona's face had held a look of expectation; now it wilted in disappointment. She and Hanna stared at each other. Then Mona's cell rang and she looked away.

"Celeste?" Mona said when she answered. "Hey!"

Hanna chewed nervously on her lips and looked at her Gucci bracelet watch. "I have to go," she whispered to Mona, gesturing toward the mall's east exit. "My dad . . ."

"Hold on," Mona said into her phone. She covered the receiver with her hands, rolled her eyes at the Miu Miu shoes, and shoved them at Hanna. "Just take these. I actually kind of hate them."

Hanna backed away, holding the stolen shoes by their straps. All of a sudden, she kind of hated them too.

16

NICE, NORMAL, FAMILY NIGHT
AT THE MONTGOMERYS'

That night, Aria sat on her bed, knitting a stuffed owl out of mohair yarn. The owl was brown and boyish-looking; she'd started it the week before, thinking she would give it to Ezra. Now, that obviously wasn't happening, so she wondered . . . maybe she'd give it to Sean? How weird was that?

Before Ali went missing, she kept trying to set Aria up with Rosewood boys, saying, "Just go over and *talk* to him. It's not hard." But for Aria, it *was* hard. She got around a Rosewood boy and froze, blurting out the first idiotic thing that came out of her mouth—which, for some reason, was often about math. And she *hated* math. By the time she'd finished seventh grade, only one guy had spoken to her outside of class: Toby Cavanaugh.

And that had been scary. It was just a few weeks before Ali went missing, and Aria had signed up for a weekend arts camp, and who should show up in her workshop but *Toby*. Aria was astounded—wasn't he supposed to be in boarding school . . . forever? But apparently, his school broke for summer vacation earlier than Rosewood Day's did, and there he was. He sat in the corner, hair over his face, snapping a rubber band against his wrist.

Their drama teacher, a wispy, frizzy-haired woman who wore a lot of tie-dye, made everyone do a drama exercise: They paired up and shouted a phrase to each other over and over, getting into a rhythm. The phrase was supposed to change organically. They had to go around the room, partnering with everyone, and Aria soon found herself in front of Toby. The phrase for that day was, *It never snows in the summer.*

"It never snows in the summer," Toby said.

"It never snows in the summer," Aria said back to him.

"It never snows in the summer," Toby repeated. His eyes were sunken and his nails were bitten down to the quick. Aria felt twitchy standing this close to him. She couldn't help thinking about Toby's ghoulish face in Ali's window just before they hurt Jenna. And how the paramedics pulled Jenna down the tree house ladder, nearly dropping her. And how, a few days later, when they were at the Firework Safety Benefit, she overheard her health teacher, Mrs. Iverson, say, "If I were that boy's father, I wouldn't just send him to boarding school. I'd send him to *jail.*"

And then the phrase did change. It became, *I know*

what you did last summer. Toby was the one to say it first, but Aria shouted it back a few times before she realized what it really meant.

"Oh, like the movie!" the teacher cried, clapping her hands.

"Yep," Toby said, and smiled at Aria. A real smile, too, not a sinister one, which made her feel worse. When she told Ali what had happened, Ali sighed. "Aria, Toby's, like, mentally deranged. I heard he practically drowned up in Maine, swimming in a frozen creek, trying to take a picture of a moose."

But Aria never went back to drama class.

She thought again about A's Post-it. *Wondering who I am? I'm closer than you think.*

Could A be Toby? Had he sneaked into Rosewood Day and stuck that Post-it on Ali's case? Had any of her friends seen it? Or perhaps A was in one of her classes. Her English class would make the most sense—the timing of most of her notes revolved around them. But who? Noel? James Freed? Hanna?

Aria paused on Hanna. She'd wondered about her before—Ali could have told Hanna about her parents. And Hanna was part of The Jenna Thing.

But why?

She flipped through the Rosewood Day facebook—the directory that had just come out today of all her classmates' names and phone numbers—and found Sean's picture. His hair was sportily short, and he was bronzed like he'd spent the summer on his dad's yacht. The boys Aria dated in Iceland were pale and floppy-haired, and if they had boats, they were kayaks that they used to paddle to the Snaefellsjokull glacier.

She dialed Sean's number but got his voice mail. "Hey, Sean," she said, hoping her voice wasn't too singsongish. "It's Aria Montgomery. I, um, I was just calling to say hi, and, um, I have a philosopher recommendation for you. It's Ayn Rand. She's like, super-complex but really readable. Check it out."

She gave him her cell number and IM screen name, hung up, and wanted to delete the message. Sean probably had tons of non-spastic Rosewood girls calling.

"Aria!" Ella called from the bottom of the stairs. "Dinner!"

She threw her phone on her bed and slowly walked downstairs. Her ears pricked up at a strange beeping noise coming from the kitchen. Was that . . . the oven timer? But that was impossible. Their kitchen was done in a retro-1950s style, and the stove was an authentic Magic Chef from 1956. Ella rarely used it because she was afraid it was so old, it might set the house on fire.

But to Aria's surprise, Ella did have something in the oven, and her brother and father were at the table. This was the first time since the weekend that her whole family had been together. Mike had spent the past three nights at various lacrosse boys' houses, and her dad, well, he'd been so busy "teaching."

A roast chicken, a bowl of mashed potatoes, and a
dish of green beans sat in the middle of the table. All the
plates and utensils matched, and there were even *place
mats*. Aria tensed. It seemed way too normal . . . especially
for her family. Something must be wrong. Had someone
died? Had A told?

But her parents seemed untroubled. Her mom pulled
a tray of rolls from the oven—which, miraculously, wasn't
on fire—and her dad sat quietly, flipping the op-ed pages
of the *New York Times*. He was always reading: at the
table, at Mike's sporting events, even while driving.

Aria turned to her dad, whom she'd hardly seen since
Monday at the Victory bar. "Hey, Byron," she said.

Her father gave Aria a genuine smile. "Hello, Monkey."
He sometimes called her Monkey; he used to call her
Hairy Ape, too, until she told him to stop. He always
looked like he'd just rolled out of bed: He wore holey,
thrift-store T-shirts, Philadelphia 76ers boxers or plaid
pajama pants, and old shearling-lined slippers. His dark
brown bushy hair was always crazy messy, too. Aria
thought he resembled a koala bear.

"And hey, Mike!" Aria said brightly, ruffling his hair.

Mike recoiled. "Don't freaking touch me!"

"Mike," Ella said, pointing at him with one of the
chopsticks that usually secured the bun in her brownish-
black hair.

"I was just being nice." Aria stopped herself from
shooting Mike a standard sarcastic retort. Instead, she sat

down, unfolded her embroidered floral napkin onto her lap, and picked up a Bakelite-handled fork. "The chicken smells *really* good, Ella."

Ella spooned potatoes onto everyone's plates. "It was just one of those things from the deli counter."

"Since when do you think chicken smells good?" Mike snarled. "You don't eat it."

That was true. Aria had been a vegetarian ever since her second week in Iceland, when Hallbjorn, her first boyfriend, bought her a snack from a food cart that she thought was a hot dog. It was to die for, but after she ate it, he told her it was puffin meat. Ever since then, whenever meat was in front of her, she always imagined a cute baby puffin's face. "Well, still," Aria said. "I *do* eat potatoes." She shoved a steaming hot spoonful into her mouth. "And *these* are awesome."

Ella furrowed her brow. "They're just instant. You know I can't cook."

Aria knew she was trying too hard. But if she was a model daughter instead of her sarcastic, grumbling self, Byron might realize what he was missing.

She turned again to Byron. Aria didn't want to hate her dad. There were tons of good things about him—he always listened to her problems, he was smart, he made her Get Well Soon fudge brownies when she had the flu. She'd tried to come up with logical, non-romantic reasons why the Meredith thing had happened. She didn't want to think he loved someone else, or that he was trying to break up the family. It was hard, though, not to take it personally.

As she took a spoonful of green beans, Ella's cell phone, which was sitting on the kitchen island, began to ring. Ella looked at Byron. "Should I get that?"

Byron frowned. "Would someone be calling you at dinnertime?"

"Maybe it's Oliver from the gallery."

Suddenly, Aria felt her throat constrict. *What if it's A?* The phone rang again. Aria stood up. "I'll answer it."

Ella wiped her mouth and pushed back her chair. "No, I should get it."

"No!" Aria rushed to the island. The phone rang a third time. "I . . . um . . . it's . . ."

She flailed her arms wildly, trying to think. Out of ideas, she grabbed the phone and flung it into the living room. It skidded across the floor, stopped against the couch, and stopped ringing. The Montgomerys' cat, Polo, padded up and tapped the phone with his striped paw.

When Aria turned back around, her family was staring at her. "What is the matter with you?" Ella asked.

"I just . . ." Aria was damp with sweat, and her whole body throbbed with her heartbeat. Mike crossed his hands behind his head. *Fuh-REEK*, he mouthed.

Ella swished by her to the living room and crouched to look at the phone's screen. Her crinkle skirt grazed the floor, picking up dust. "It *was* Oliver."

At the same time, Byron stood up. "I have to be going."

"Going?" Ella's voice caught. "But we just started eating."

Byron carried his empty plate to the sink. He had always been the fastest eater on the planet, even faster than Mike. "I have stuff to do in my office."

"But . . ." Ella clasped her hands at her small waist. They all watched helplessly as Byron disappeared up the stairs and then came down about a half a minute later in rumpled gray pants and a blue button-down. His hair was still completely uncombed. He grabbed his worn leather briefcase and keys. "See you in a little while."

"Can you pick up orange juice?" Ella cried, but Byron shut the front door without answering.

A second later, Mike stormed out of the kitchen without putting his plate in the sink. He grabbed his jacket and lacrosse stick and wormed his feet into his sneakers without untying them. "Now, where are *you* going?" Ella asked.

"Practice," Mike snapped. He had his head way down and was chewing on his lip, like he was trying to keep from crying. Aria wanted to run up to her brother and hug him and try to figure out what to do here, except she felt stuck, as if grouted to the checkerboard ceramic tiles on the kitchen floor.

Mike slammed the door, making the whole house

shake. A few seconds of silence passed, then Ella raised her gray eyes to Aria. "Everyone's leaving us."

"No, they're not," Aria said quickly.

Her mother went back to the table and stared at the remaining chicken on her plate. After a few seconds of pondering, she laid a napkin over it, uneaten, and turned back to Aria. "Has your father seemed strange to you?"

Aria felt her mouth go dry. "About what?"

"I don't know." Ella traced her finger around the porcelain dinner plate's edge. "It seems like something's bothering him. Maybe it's about teaching? He seems so busy. . . ."

Aria knew she should say something, but the words felt gummed up in her stomach, like she needed a toilet plunger or a vacuum to suck them out. "He hasn't said anything about that, no." It wasn't exactly a lie.

Ella stared at her. "You'd tell me if he had, right?"

Aria bent her head down, pretending she had something in her eye. "Of course."

Ella rose and cleared the rest of the stuff off the table. Aria stood there, useless. This was her chance . . . and she was just standing here. Like a sack of potatoes.

She wandered up to her room and sat down at her desk, not sure what to do with herself. Downstairs, she could hear the beginning strains of *Jeopardy!*. Perhaps she should go back down and hang out with Ella. Except what she really wanted to do was cry.

Her Instant Messenger made the bloopy noise of a

new message. Aria went over to it, wondering if maybe it was Sean. But . . . it wasn't.

A A A A A: Two choices: Make it go away or tell your mom. I'm giving you till the stroke of midnight Saturday night, Cinderella. Or else. —A

A creaking sound made her jump. Aria whirled around and saw that her cat had nosed her bedroom door open. She petted him absentmindedly, reading the IM again. And again. And again.

Or else? And *make it go away?* How was she supposed to do that?

Her computer made another *bloop*. The IM window flashed.

A A A A A: Not sure how? Here's a hint: Strawberry Ridge Yoga Studio. 7:30 a.m. Tomorrow. Be there.

17

DADDY'S LITTLE GIRL
HAS A SECRET

Hanna stood six inches from her bedroom mirror, closely inspecting herself. It must've been a freak reflection at the mall—here, she looked normal and thin. Although . . . were her pores looking a little bigger? Were her eyes slightly crossed?

Nervous, she opened her bureau drawer and pulled out a giant bag of salt-and-pepper kettle chips. She shoved a big handful into her mouth, chewed, then stopped. Last week, A's notes had led her into the horrible binge/purge cycle all over again—even though she'd refrained from the habit for years. She *wouldn't* start doing this again. And especially not in front of her father.

She rolled up the bag and looked out the window again. Where *was* he? Nearly two hours had passed since her mom called her at the mall. Then she saw a forest-green Range Rover turn into her driveway, which was a winding, wooded, quarter-mile-long road. The car easily maneuvered around the driveway's twists and turns in a way that only someone who had lived there could. When Hanna was younger, she and her dad used to sled on the driveway. He taught her how to lean into each turn so she wouldn't tip.

When the doorbell rang, she jumped. Her miniature pinscher, Dot, started to bark, and the bell rang again. Dot's barking became more high-pitched and frenzied, and the bell rang for the third time. "Coming!" Hanna growled.

"Hey," her father said as she flung open the door. Dot began to dance around his heels. "Hello there." He reached down to pick up the tiny dog.

"Dot, no!" Hanna commanded.

"No, he's fine." Mr. Marin petted the miniature pinscher's little nose. Hanna had gotten Dot shortly after her dad left.

"So." Her father lingered on the porch awkwardly. He wore a charcoal gray business suit and a red and blue tie, as if he'd just come from a meeting. Hanna wondered if he wanted to come in. She felt funny inviting her dad into his own house. "Should I . . . ?" he started.

"Do you want to . . . ?" Hanna said at the same time. Her father laughed nervously. Hanna wasn't sure if she wanted to hug him. Her father took a step toward her, and she took a step back, bumping into the door. She tried to make it look like she'd meant to do it. "Just come in," she said, the annoyance in her voice showing.

They stood in the foyer. Hanna felt her father's eyes on her. "It's really nice to see you," he said.

Hanna shrugged. She wished she had a cigarette or something to do with her hands. "Yeah, well. So do you want the financial thingie? It's right here."

He squinted, ignoring her. "I meant to ask you the other day. Your hair. You did something different with it. It's . . . Is it shorter?"

She smirked. "It's *darker*."

He pointed. "Bingo. And you don't have your glasses on!"

"I got LASIK." She stared him down. "Two years ago."

"Oh." Her father put his hands in his pockets.

"You make it sound like it's a bad thing."

"No," her father answered quickly. "You just look . . . different."

Hanna crossed her arms. When her parents decided to divorce, Hanna thought it was because she got fat. And clumsy. And ugly. Meeting Kate had just felt like more proof. He'd found his replacement daughter, and he'd traded up.

After the Annapolis disaster, her father tried to stay in touch. At first, Hanna complied, having a couple of moody, one-word phone conversations. Mr. Marin tried to tease out what was wrong, but Hanna was too embarrassed to talk about it. Eventually, the length of time between conversations became longer and longer . . . and then they stopped happening altogether.

Mr. Marin strolled down the foyer, his feet creaking on the wood floor. Hanna wondered if he was assessing what was the same and what had changed. Did he notice the black-and-white photo of Hanna and her dad that hung above the Mission-style hall table had been removed? And that the lithograph of a woman going through the yoga sun salutations—a print Hanna's father *hated*, but Hanna's mom loved—hung in its place?

Her dad flopped on the living room couch, even though no one ever used the living room. *He* never used to use the living room. It was dark, way too stuffy, had ugly Oriental rugs, and smelled like Endust. Hanna didn't know what else to do, so she followed him in and sat down on the claw-foot ottoman in the corner.

"So. How are you doing, Hanna?"

She curled her legs underneath her. "I'm all right."

"Good."

Another ocean of silence. She heard Dot's tiny toenails tick across the kitchen floor, and his little tongue lap up water from his dish. She wished for an interruption—a phone call, the fire alarm going off, even another text from A—anything to take her away from this awkwardness.

"And how are you?" she finally asked.

"Not too bad." He picked up a tasseled pillow from the couch and held it out at arm's length. "These things were always so ugly."

Hanna agreed with him, but what, were the pillows at Isabel's house *perfect*?

Her father looked up. "Remember that game you used to play? You put the pillows on the floor and jumped from one to the other, because the floor was lava?"

"Dad." Hanna wrinkled her nose and hugged her knees even tighter.

He squeezed the pillow. "You could play that for hours."

"I was six."

"Remember Cornelius Maximilian?"

She looked up. His eyes were twinkling. "Dad . . ."

He threw the pillow up in the air and caught it. "Should I not talk about him? Has it been too long?"

She stuck her chin stiffly into the air. "Probably."

Inside, though, she cracked a tiny smile. Cornelius Maximilian was this inside joke they made up after they saw *Gladiator*. It had been a big treat for Hanna to go to a gory, R-rated movie, except she'd been only ten, and all the blood traumatized her. She was positive she wouldn't be able to sleep that night, so her father made up Cornelius to make her feel better. He was the only dog—a poodle, they thought, although sometimes they changed him to a Boston terrier—mighty enough to fight in the gladiator ring. He beat the tigers, he beat the other scary gladiators. He could do anything, including bring the dead gladiators back to life.

They made up a whole Cornelius character, talking about what he did on his off days, what sorts of studded collars he liked to wear, how he needed a girlfriend. Sometimes, Hanna and her father would reference

Cornelius around her mother, and she'd say, "What? Who?" even though they'd explained the joke a thousand times. When Hanna got Dot, she considered naming him Cornelius, but it would've been too sad.

Her father sat back on the couch. "I'm sorry that things are like this."

Hanna pretended to be interested in her French manicure. "Like what?"

"Like . . . with us." He cleared his throat. "I'm sorry I haven't been in touch."

Hanna rolled her eyes. This was way too after-school special for her. "No biggie."

Mr. Marin drummed his fingers on the coffee table. It was obvious he was really squirming. Good. "So why'd you steal your boyfriend's dad's car, anyway? I asked your mom if she knew, but she didn't."

"It's complicated," Hanna said quickly. Talk about ironic: when they first divorced, Hanna tried to think of ways she could get her parents to talk again so they'd fall back in love—like Lindsay Lohan's twin characters did in *The Parent Trap*. Turned out all she'd needed to do was get arrested a few times.

"Come on," Mr. Marin coaxed. "Did you guys break up? Were you upset?"

"I guess."

"He ended things?"

Hanna gulped miserably. "How'd you know?"

"If he's giving you up, maybe he wasn't worth it."

Hanna couldn't believe he just said that. In fact, she didn't believe it. Maybe she'd misheard. Maybe she'd been listening to her iPod too loud.

"Have you been thinking about Alison?" her father asked.

Hanna looked at her hands. "I guess. Yeah."

"It's pretty unbelievable."

Hanna gulped again. All of a sudden, she felt like she was going to cry. "I know."

Mr. Marin leaned back. The couch made a strange farting sound. It was something her dad might have commented on years ago, but now he kept quiet. "You know what my favorite memory of Alison is?"

"What?" Hanna asked quietly. She prayed he wasn't going to say, *That time you girls came to Annapolis and she bonded with Kate.*

"It was summer. I guess you guys were going into seventh grade or so. I took you and Alison to Avalon for the day. Do you remember that?"

"Vaguely," Hanna said. She recalled that she'd eaten too much saltwater taffy, that she looked fat in her bikini and Ali looked perfectly skinny in hers, and that a surfer boy invited Ali to a bonfire party, but she ditched him at the last minute.

"We were sitting on the beach; there were a girl and a boy a few blankets over. You guys knew the girl from school—but she wasn't anyone you typically hung around with. She had some sort of water bottle contraption strapped to her back that she sucked through with a straw. Ali talked to her brother and ignored her."

Suddenly, Hanna remembered it perfectly. It was common to run into people from Rosewood at the Jersey Shore—and that girl had actually been *Mona.* The boy was Mona's cousin. Ali thought he was cute, so she went over to talk to him. Mona seemed ecstatic that Ali was even in her vicinity, but all Ali did was turn to Mona and say, "Hey, my guinea pig drinks water from a bottle like that."

"*That's* your favorite memory?" Hanna blurted. She'd blocked it out; she was pretty sure Mona had too.

"I'm not done," her father said. "Alison walked down to the edge of the beach with the boy, but you stayed behind and talked to the girl, who looked just crushed that Alison had left. I don't know what you said, but you were nice to her. I was really proud of you."

Hanna wrinkled her nose. She doubted she was nice—she just probably wasn't straight-up mean. After The Jenna Thing happened, Hanna didn't savor teasing quite as much.

"You were always so nice to everyone," her father said.

"No, I wasn't," she said quietly.

She remembered how she used to talk about Jenna: *You wouldn't believe this girl, Dad,* she said. *She tried out for the same part Ali wants in the musical, and you should've heard her sing. She was like a* cow. Or, *Jenna Cavanaugh might've gotten every question right on the health test and done twelve pull-ups in gym for the Presidential Fitness test, but she's* still *a loser.*

Her father had always been a good listener, as long as he knew she didn't say mean things to people's faces. Which had made what he asked a few days after Jenna's accident, as they were driving to the store, that much more devastating. He'd turned to her and said, out of no where, *Wait. That girl that was blinded? She's the one who sings like a cow, right?* He looked as if he'd made the connection. Hanna, too terrified to answer, faked a coughing fit and then changed the subject.

Her father stood up and walked over to the living room's baby grand piano. He lifted the lid, and dust sifted into the air. When he pressed down a key, a tinny sound came out. "I guess your mother told you that Isabel and I are getting married?"

Hanna's heart sank. "Yeah, she said something like that."

"We were thinking next summer, except that Kate won't be able to make it then. She's going to a pre-college summer program in Spain."

Hanna bristled at Kate's name. *Poor baby has to go to Spain.*

"We'd like you to be at the wedding as well," her father added. When Hanna didn't respond, her dad kept talking. "If you could. I know it's kind of weird. If it is, we should talk about it. I'd rather have you talk to me than steal cars."

Hanna sniffed. How dare her father think stealing

stuff boiled down to him and his stupid marriage! But then she stopped. *Did* it? "I'll think about it," she said.

Her father ran his hands along the edge of the piano bench. "I'm staying in Philly all weekend, and Saturday, I've booked us for dinner at Le Bec-Fin."

"Really?" Hanna cried, despite herself. Le Bec-Fin was a famous French restaurant in downtown Philadelphia that she'd wanted to eat at for years. Spencer's and Ali's families used to drag them there, and they'd whine about it. It was so snotty, they said, the menu wasn't even in English, and it was full of old ladies in hideous furs that had heads and faces. But to Hanna, Le Bec-Fin sounded totally glamorous.

"And I booked you a suite at the Four Seasons," her father went on. "I know you're supposed to be in trouble, but your mother said it was okay."

"Seriously?" Hanna clapped her hands. She adored staying in fancy hotels.

"It has a pool." He smiled coyly. Hanna used to get really excited when they stayed in hotels with pools. "You could come early Saturday afternoon for a swim."

Suddenly, Hanna's face fell. Saturday was . . . Foxy. "Can we do Sunday instead?"

"Well, no. It has to be Saturday."

Hanna chewed on her lip. "Then I can't."

"Why?"

"I just . . . there's this dance thing. It's sort of . . . important."

Her father folded his hands. "Your mom's letting you go to a dance after . . . after what you did? I thought you were grounded."

Hanna shrugged. "I bought the tickets way in advance. They were expensive."

"It would mean a lot to me if you came," her father said softly. "I'd love a weekend with you."

Her dad looked genuinely *upset*. Almost like he was going to cry. She wanted a weekend with him, too. He'd remembered the molten lava floor, how she used to talk about Le Bec-Fin, and how much she adored ritzy hotels with pools. She wondered if he shared inside jokes like that with Kate. She didn't want him to. She wanted to be special.

"I guess I can blow it off," she finally answered.

"Great." Her father smiled back.

"For Cornelius Maximilian's sake," she added, giving him a shy look.

"Even better."

Hanna watched as her father got into his car and drove slowly down the driveway. A warm, buzzing feeling filled her body. She was so happy, she didn't even think about digging out the bag of kettle chips that she'd thrown back into the pantry. Instead, she felt like dancing through the house.

When she heard her BlackBerry buzzing upstairs, she snapped back to attention. There was so much to do. She had to tell Sean she wasn't going to Foxy. She had to call and tell Mona, too. She had to dig up a fabulous outfit to wear to Le Bec-Fin—maybe that pretty Theory belted dress she hadn't had a chance to wear yet?

She ran upstairs, opened the BlackBerry, and frowned. It was . . . a text.

> Four simple words:
> Hanna. Marin. Blinded. Jenna.
> What would Daddy think about you if he knew that?
> I'm watching you, Hanna, and you'd better do what I say. —A

18

SURROUND YOURSELF WITH NORMAL, AND MAYBE YOU'LL BE NORMAL TOO

"You're so lucky you get to go to Foxy for free," Emily's older sister Carolyn said. "You really should take advantage of it."

It was Friday morning, and Emily and Carolyn were outside on the driveway, waiting for their mom to drive them to early-morning swim practice. Emily turned to her sister, running her hand through her hair. As captain, she got free Foxy tickets, but it seemed weird to party so soon after Ali's funeral. "It's not like I'm going to go. I have no one to go with. Ben and I aren't together anymore, so . . ."

"Go with a friend." Carolyn smeared ChapStick over her thin, naturally pink lips. "Topher and I would love to go, but I'd have to spend all my baby-sitting money just on a ticket. So we're going to have movie night at his house instead."

Emily glanced at her sister. Carolyn was a senior and

looked just like Emily, with reddish-blond, chlorine-dried hair, freckles across her cheeks, pale eyelashes, and a strong, compact, swimmer's body. When Emily was named captain, she worried that Carolyn would be jealous—she *was* older. But Carolyn seemed completely fine with the whole thing. Secretly, Emily would have loved to see her wig out about something. Just once.

"Oh hey!" Carolyn perked up. "I saw a funny picture of you yesterday!"

Emily's field of vision narrowed. "Picture?" she repeated hoarsely. She thought of the photo booth picture A had texted her yesterday. A had spread it around. It was starting.

"Yeah, it's from the Tate meet yesterday?" Carolyn reminded her. "You look . . . I don't know. Ambushed. You have this funny expression on your face."

Emily blinked. The picture Scott took. With Toby. Her muscles relaxed. "Oh," she said.

"Emily?"

Emily looked up and made a tiny, inaudible gasp. Maya stood a few feet away from them on the street, straddling her blue Trek mountain bike. Her curly, brownish-black hair was clipped out of her face, and she'd rolled up the sleeves of her white denim jacket. There were dark circles under her eyes. It seemed weird, seeing her at such an early hour of the morning.

"Hey," Emily squeaked. "Um, what's up?"

"This was the only place I thought I could actually

catch you." Maya gestured to Emily's house. "You haven't said a word to me since, like, Monday."

Emily glanced over her shoulder at Carolyn, who was now rooting through the front pocket of her purple North Face backpack. She thought again of A's note. *How* could A have gotten those pictures? Didn't Maya have them . . . or had there been others?

"I'm sorry," Emily said to Maya. She didn't know what to do with her hands, so she placed them on top of her mailbox, which was a miniaturized version of her house. "I've been sort of busy."

"Yep, sure looks that way."

The bitterness in Maya's voice made the hair on the back of Emily's neck rise. "W-What do you mean?" Emily snapped.

But Maya merely looked blank and sad. "I . . . I just mean you haven't called me back."

Emily pulled the strings of her red hoodie. "Let's go over here," she murmured, walking to the edge of her property under a weeping willow tree. All she wanted was some simple privacy, so Carolyn wouldn't listen in, but unfortunately, it was kind of sexy under the tree's thick, concealing branches. The light was a very pale green, and Maya's skin looked so . . . dewy. She looked like a wood sprite.

"I have a question for you, actually," Emily whispered, trying to block out all sexy-wood-sprite thoughts. "You know those pictures of us, from the photo booth?"

"Uh-huh." Maya was leaning so close, Emily could almost feel the tips of her hair grazing her cheek. It felt, suddenly, like she'd grown a billion extra nerve endings, and they were all tingling.

"Has anyone seen them?" Emily whispered.

It took Maya a minute to respond. "No . . ."

"Are you sure?"

Maya cocked her head, birdlike, and grinned. "But I'll show them around, if you want. . . ." When she saw Emily cringe, the teasing sparkle in her eyes dimmed. "Wait. Is this why you're avoiding me? You thought I actually *did* show them around?"

"I don't know," Emily mumbled, running her foot along one of the willow's big exposed roots. Her heart was beating so fast, she was pretty sure it was setting some sort of new world record.

Maya reached out and took Emily's chin in her hand, tilting it up so that Emily would look at her. "I wouldn't do that. I want to keep them for myself."

Emily jerked her chin away. This could *not* happen in her front yard. "There's something else you should know. I've . . . I've met someone."

Maya tilted her head. "What kind of someone?"

"His name's Toby. He's really nice. And . . . and I think I like him."

Maya blinked in disbelief, as if Emily had told her she'd fallen in love with a goat.

"And I think I might ask him to Foxy," Emily went on.

The idea had just occurred to Emily, but it felt okay. She liked that Toby wasn't perfect and didn't bother to try. And if she tried hard enough, she could almost forget the complication that he was Jenna's stepbrother. And if she took a boy to Foxy, it would negate those photos from Noel's party and prove to everyone she wasn't gay.

Er, right?

Maya clucked her tongue. "But isn't Foxy tomorrow? What if he has plans?"

Emily shrugged. She was pretty sure Toby didn't.

"And anyway," Maya went on. "I thought you said Foxy was too expensive."

"I was, um, named the captain of the swim team. So I get to go for free."

"Wow," Maya said, after a pause. It was as if Emily could *smell* Maya's disappointment, like it was a pheromone. Maya had been the person to convince Emily to quit swimming. "Well, congrats, I guess."

Emily stared at her burgundy Vans. "Thanks," she said, even though Maya clearly hadn't meant it nicely. She could feel Maya waiting for her to look up and say, *Silly. I'm just kidding.* Emily felt a surge of irritation. Why did Maya have to make this so difficult? Why couldn't they just be normal friends?

Maya sniffed loudly, then pushed through the tree's branches, back into Emily's yard. Emily followed, only to realize that her mother was at the front door. Mrs. Fields's close-cropped hair was stiff and blown out, and she had her *Don't mess with me, I'm in a hurry* look on her face.

When she noticed Maya, she paled. "Emily, time to go," she barked.

"Sure thing," Emily chirped. She had *not* wanted her mom to see this. She turned back to Maya, who now stood next to her bike at the curb.

Maya was staring at her. "You can't change who you are, Emily," she said in a loud voice. "I hope you know that."

Emily felt her mother and Carolyn staring at her. "I don't know what you're talking about," she cried just as loudly.

"Emily, you're going to be late," Mrs. Fields warned.

Maya gave Emily a parting look, then pedaled furiously down the street. Emily swallowed hard. She felt so ambivalent. On one hand, she was angry at Maya for confronting her—here, in her yard, in front of Carolyn and her mom. On the other, she had the same feeling she did when she was seven years old and had accidentally let go of the Mickey Mouse–shaped balloon she'd begged her parents to buy her at Disney World. She'd watched it float into the sky until it was no longer visible. She'd thought about it for the rest of the trip until her mom said, *It's just a balloon, sweetie! And it's your fault you let go of it!*

She trudged back to the Volvo and gave Carolyn the front seat without a fight. As they pulled out of the driveway, Emily glanced at Maya, now a tiny dot in the distance, then took a deep breath and put her hands on the back of her mother's seat.

"Guess what, Mom. I'm going to ask a boy to the charity thing tomorrow."

"What charity thing?" Mrs. Fields murmured, in a voice that said, *I'm not happy with you right now.*

"Foxy." Carolyn announced, fiddling with the radio. "The annual thing that the news covers. It's so big, some girls get plastic surgery for it."

Mrs. Fields pursed her lips. "I'm not sure I want you going to that."

"But I get to go for free. Because I'm captain."

"You *have* to let her go, Mom," Carolyn urged. "It's *soooo* glamorous."

Mrs. Fields glanced at Emily in the rearview mirror. "Who's the boy?"

"Well, his name is Toby. He used to go to our school, but now he goes to Tate," Emily explained, leaving out where Toby had been for the past three years—and *why.* Luckily, her mother didn't memorize every detail about every Rosewood kid Emily's age, like some mothers did. Carolyn didn't appear to remember the name, either—Carolyn never remembered scandals, not even juicy Hollywood ones. "He's really sweet, and he's a really good swimmer. Way faster than Ben."

"That Ben was nice," Mrs. Fields murmured.

Emily gritted her teeth. "Yeah, but Toby is much,

much nicer." She also wanted to add, *And don't worry, he's white,* but she didn't have the nerve.

Carolyn twisted around in her seat. "Is it the boy in that picture I saw of you?"

"Yeah." Emily said quietly.

Carolyn turned to their mother. "He's *good*. He beat Topher in the 200 free."

Mrs. Fields gave Emily a little smile. "You're supposed to be grounded, but after all the circumstances of this week, I suppose you can go. But no plastic surgery."

Emily frowned. It was just the sort of ridiculous, over-the-top thing her mother would worry about. Last year, Mrs. Fields saw a *20/20* program on crystal meth and how it was everywhere, even in private schools, and she banned Sudafed from the house, as if Emily and Carolyn were going to start up a mini meth lab in their bedroom. She let out a half-laugh. "I'm not going to get—"

But Mrs. Fields started chuckling and caught Emily's eye in the mirror. "I'm only kidding." She nodded to Maya's receding figure, now at the opposite end of their street, and added, "It's nice to see you making new friends."

19

WATCH OUT FOR GIRLS
WITH BRANDING IRONS

The Strawberry Ridge Yoga Studio was in a converted barn on the other side of Rosewood. On her bike ride there, Aria passed a tobacco-colored covered bridge and the row of Hollis art department houses, charmingly ramshackle Colonials that were spatter-painted various shades of purple, pink, and blue. She crammed her bike into the rack in front of the yoga studio; it was already full of other bikes, all bearing MEAT IS MURDER and PETA stickers on their frames.

She paused in the yoga studio's lobby and looked at the scruffy, makeupless girls and hairy, limber boys. Was she crazy to take A's instructions—*Strawberry Ridge Yoga Studio. Be there*—literally? And was she ready to see Meredith? Perhaps A was baiting her. Perhaps A was *here*.

Aria had seen Meredith only three times before: first when Meredith came over to her dad's student-teacher cocktail party, then when she caught Meredith and her dad in the car together, and finally the other day at the Victory, but she'd have recognized her anywhere. Now Meredith was paused in front of the studio's closet, dragging down mats, blankets, blocks, and straps. Her brown hair was up in a messy ponytail and there was that pink spiderweb tattoo on the inside of her wrist.

Meredith noticed Aria and smiled. "You're new, right?" She met Aria's eyes, and for a terrifying second Aria was certain Meredith knew who she was. But then she broke eye contact, leaning over to pop a CD into the portable stereo. Indian sitar music swam out. "Have you done Ashtanga before?"

"Um, yes," Aria answered. She noticed a big sign on the table that said INDIVIDUAL CLASSES $15, and fished out a ten and a five and laid them on the desk, wondering how A knew Meredith was here—and if A really was here.

Meredith smirked. "And I guess you know the secret, huh?"

"W-What?" Aria whispered, her heart pounding. "*Secret?*"

"You brought your own mat." Meredith pointed to the red yoga mat under Aria's arm. "So many new people come here and use the studio's mats. You didn't hear it from me, but you could scrape off the foot fungus on our mats and make cheese."

Aria tried to smile. She'd brought her own yoga mat to classes ever since she first went with Ali in seventh grade. Ali always used to tell her that community yoga mats gave you STDs.

Meredith squinted at her. "You look familiar. Are you in my drawing class?"

Aria shook her head, suddenly aware that the place smelled like a mixture of feet and incense. This was the sort of yoga studio Ella would go to. In fact, perhaps Ella already *had*.

"What's your name?"

"Um, Alison," Aria said quickly. It wasn't as if she had the most common name in the world, and she was afraid Byron might have mentioned it to Meredith. Which made her pause. *Would* Byron talk about Aria to Meredith?

"You look like this girl in the drawing class I TA for," Meredith said. "But class just started. I get everyone confused."

Aria picked up a leaflet for a seminar on Getting to Know Your Chakras. "So, you're a grad student?"

Meredith nodded. "Getting my MFA."

"What is your, um, medium?"

"Well, I do all sorts of stuff. Painting. Drawing." Meredith looked behind Aria and waved at someone else coming in. "But I recently got into branding."

"What?"

"Branding. I weld these custom-made branding irons together to make words, and then I burn the words on big blocks of wood."

"Wait, so the brands are like cattle brands?"

Meredith ducked her head. "I try to explain it, but most people think I'm crazy."

"No," Aria said quickly. "It's cool."

Meredith glanced at the clock on the wall. "We have a couple minutes. I can show you some photos." She reached into a striped cloth bag that sat next to her and pulled out her cell phone. "Just scroll through these, here. . . ."

The photos were of blond slabs of wood. A few just had single letters on them, and a few said short things, like *catch me* and *control freak*. The letters were a little strangely shaped, but looked really cool charred into the wood. Aria flipped to the next photo. It was a longer slab that said, *To err is human, but it feels divine.*

Aria looked up. "Mae West."

Meredith brightened. "It's one of my favorite quotes."

"Same." Aria handed her back the phone. "These are really cool."

Meredith smiled. "Glad you like 'em. I might have a show in a couple months."

"I'm sur . . ." Aria clamped her lips together. She was about to say, *I'm surprised.* She hadn't expected Meredith to be like this. When Aria imagined Meredith, only uncool attributes had come to mind. Imaginary Meredith #1 studied art history and worked for a stuffy, stale gallery somewhere on the Main Line that sold Hudson River School landscapes to rich old ladies. Imaginary

Meredith #2 listened to Kelly Clarkson, loved *Laguna Beach*, and, if encouraged, would lift her shirt to get on *Girls Gone Wild*. Never did Aria think she'd be arty. Why would Byron need an artist? He had Ella.

As Meredith greeted another yoga student, Aria moved into the main studio room. It had high ceilings, exposing the barn's wooden rafters; shiny, caramel-colored wood floors; and large, Indian-print sheets hanging everywhere. Most people had already sat down on their mats and were lying on their backs. It was weirdly silent.

Aria looked around the room. A girl with a brown ponytail and large thighs was doing a backbend. A lanky guy moved from downward dog into child's pose, breathing forcefully through his nose. A blond girl in the corner did a seated twist. When she faced forward, Aria's stomach dropped. "*Spencer?*" she blurted.

Spencer paled and pushed herself onto her knees. "Oh," she said. "Aria. Hey."

Aria swallowed hard. "What are you doing here?"

Spencer looked at her crazily. "Yoga?"

"No, I know that, but . . ." Aria shook her head. "I mean, did someone tell you to come here, or . . . ?"

"No . . ." Spencer narrowed her eyes suspiciously. "Wait. What do you mean?"

Aria blinked. *Wondering who I am? I'm closer than you think.*

She looked from Spencer to Meredith, who was chatting with someone in the lobby, then back to Spencer.

The wheels in her head started to turn. Something about this felt really, really messed up.

Her heart pounded as she backed out of the main room. She rushed to the door, bumping up against a tall, bearded guy in a leotard. Outside, the world was maddeningly impassive to her panic—the birds chirped, the pines swayed, a woman walked by with a baby carriage, talking on her cell phone.

As Aria flung herself toward the bike rack and unlocked her bike, a hand squeezed down on her arm. Hard. Meredith was standing next to her, giving her a very fixed stare. Aria's mouth fell open. She gasped loudly.

"You aren't staying?" Meredith asked.

Aria shook her head. "I . . . um . . . family emergency." She jerked her bike free and started pedaling away.

"Wait!" Meredith screamed. "Let me give you your money back!"

But Aria was already halfway down the block.

20

LAISSEZ-FAIRE MEANS "HANDS OFF," BTW

Friday in AP econ, Andrew Campbell leaned across the aisle and tapped the top of Spencer's notebook. "So, I can't remember. Limo or car to Foxy?"

Spencer rolled her pencil between her fingers. "Um, car, I guess."

It was a tough one. Normally, Promzilla that she was, Spencer always insisted on a limo. And she wanted her family to think she was taking tomorrow's date with Andrew seriously. Only, she felt so tired. Having a brand-new boyfriend was wonderful, but it was tough to try to see him *and* remain Rosewood Day's most ambitious student. Last night, she'd done homework until 2:30 A.M. She'd fallen asleep this morning at yoga—after Aria had so bizarrely run out. Maybe Spencer should have mentioned her note from A, but Aria bolted before she could. She'd dozed off again in study hall. Maybe she could go to the nurse's office and sleep on the little cot for a bit?

Andrew didn't have time to ask any more questions. Mr. McAdam had given up on his battle with the overhead projector—it happened every class—and was now standing at the board. "I'm looking forward to reading everyone's essay questions on Monday," he boomed. "And I have a surprise. If you can e-mail your essays to me by tomorrow, you'll get five points extra credit to reward you for beginning them early."

Spencer blinked, puzzled. She pulled out her Sidekick and checked the date. When had it become Friday? She scrolled to Monday. There it was. Econ essays due.

She hadn't started on them. She hadn't even *thought* about them. After the credit card fiasco Tuesday, Spencer had meant to get McAdam's supplemental books at the library. Except then Wren happened, and the B minus didn't matter as much. Nothing did.

She'd spent Wednesday night at Wren's house. Yesterday, after sneaking into school after third period, she ditched hockey and sneaked into Philly again, taking SEPTA this time instead of driving, because she figured it would be quicker. Except . . . her train stalled. By the time she got into Thirtieth Street station, she only had forty-five minutes before she had to turn around to get home for dinner. So Wren had met her there and they'd made out on a secluded bench behind the concourse's flower stand, emerging flushed with kisses and smelling like lilacs.

She noticed that the first ten cantos of *The Inferno* translated for Italian VI were also due Monday. And a three-page English paper on Plato. A calculus exam. Auditions for *The Tempest*, Rosewood Day's first play of the year, were Monday. She put her head on her desk.

"Ms. Hastings?"

Startled, Spencer looked up. The bell had rung, everyone else had filed out, and she was alone. Squidward stood over her. "Sorry to wake you," he said icily.

"No . . . I really wasn't . . ." Spencer mustered, gathering up her things. But it was too late. Squidward was already erasing notes off the board. She noticed he was slowly shaking his head, as if she were hopeless.

"All right," Spencer whispered. She was sitting at her computer, books and papers around her. Slowly, she mouthed the first essay question again.

Explain Adam Smith's concept of an "invisible hand" in a laissez-faire economy, and give a modern-day example.

Okaaay.

Normally, Spencer would have read the AP econ assignment *and* Adam Smith's book cover to cover, marked the appropriate pages, and made an outline for the answer. But she hadn't. She had no idea what laissez-faire even meant. Was it something to do with supply and demand? What was invisible about it? She typed a few key words into Wikipedia, but the theories were complex and unfamiliar. So were her pages of class notes; she didn't remember writing any of them down.

She'd slaved over school for eleven long, arduous years—twelve, if you counted Montessori school before kindergarten. Just this once, couldn't she write some lame, B-minus paper and make up the grade later in the semester?

But grades were more important than ever. Yesterday, as she and Wren were wrenched from each other at the train station, he suggested she should graduate at the end of this year and apply to Penn. Spencer immediately warmed to the idea, and in the last few minutes before her train pulled up, they'd fantasized about the apartment they'd share, how they'd have separate corners of the room for studying, and how they would get a cat—Wren had never had one when he was young, because his brother was allergic.

The idea had blossomed in Spencer's head on the train ride home, and as soon as she was back in her bedroom, she checked to see if she had enough credits to graduate from Rosewood and downloaded an application to Penn. It was kind of sticky since Melissa went to Penn too, but it was a big school, and Spencer figured they'd never run into each other.

She sighed and glanced at her Sidekick. Wren had told her he'd call today between five and six, and it was now six-thirty. It bothered Spencer when people didn't do what they said they would. She skimmed her phone's missed-calls log, to see if his number was there. She called her voice mail to see if her phone wasn't getting reception. No new messages.

Finally, she tried Wren's number. Voice mail again. Spencer threw her phone over on her bed and looked at her questions again. Adam Smith. Laissez-faire. Invisible hands. Big, strong, doctorly, British hands. All over her body.

She fought the temptation to try Wren again. It seemed too high school—ever since Wren remarked that Spencer seemed so grown-up, she'd started to question her every action. Her cell phone's default ringtone was "My Humps" by Black Eyed Peas; did Wren see it as ironic, as she did, or simply adolescent? What about the lucky stuffed monkey key chain she'd pinned on her backpack? And would an older girl have paused when Wren plucked a single tulip from the flower stand when the florist wasn't looking and handed it to Spencer without paying, thinking they were going to get in trouble?

The sun started to sink into the trees. When her dad poked his head into her room, Spencer jumped. "We're eating soon," he told her. "Melissa's not joining us tonight."

"All right," Spencer answered. These were the first non-hostile words he'd said to her in days.

Light reflected off her dad's platinum Rolex. His face looked almost . . . repentant. "I picked up some of those cinnamon buns you like. I'm heating them up a little."

Spencer blinked. As soon as he said it, she could smell them in the oven. Her dad knew the cinnamon rolls from the Struble Bakery were Spencer's favorite food in the world. The bakery was a hike from his law office and he rarely had time to get them. It was clearly a sticky-bun olive branch.

"Melissa tells us you're taking someone to Foxy," he said. "Anyone we know?"

"Andrew Campbell," Spencer answered.

Mr. Hastings raised an eyebrow. "Class president Andrew Campbell?"

"Yes." It was a touchy subject. Andrew had beat out Spencer for the post; her parents had seemed devastated that she'd lost. Melissa had been class president, after all.

Mr. Hastings looked pleased. Then he lowered his eyes. "Well, it's good that you're . . . I mean, I'm glad this mess is over."

Spencer hoped her cheeks weren't bright red. "Um . . . what does Mom think?"

Her dad gave her a little smile. "She'll come around." He patted the door frame, then continued down the hall. Spencer felt guilty and weird. The cinnamon buns baking downstairs almost smelled like they were burning.

Her cell phone rang, startling her. She dove for it.

"Hey there." Wren sounded happy and boisterous when she picked up, which instantly irritated Spencer. "What's up?"

"Where have you been?" Spencer demanded.

Wren paused. "Some school friends and I are hanging out before our shift today."

"Why didn't you call earlier?"

Wren paused. "It was loud in the bar." His voice became distant, annoyed.

Spencer clenched up her fists. "I'm sorry," she said. "I think I'm a little stressed."

"Spencer Hastings, stressed?" She could tell Wren was smiling. "Why?"

"Econ paper," she sighed. "It's impossible."

"Ugh," Wren said. "Blow it off. Come meet me."

Spencer paused. Her notes were scattered haphazardly across her desk. On the floor was this week's quiz. The B minus glowed like a neon sign. "I can't."

"All right," Wren groaned. "So tomorrow, then? Can I have you all day?"

Spencer bit the inside of her cheek. "I can't tomorrow, either. I . . . I have to go to this benefit thing. I'm going with this boy from school."

"A *date*?"

"Not really."

"Why didn't you ask me?"

Spencer frowned. "It's not like I *like* him. He's just this kid from school. But, I mean, I won't, if you don't want me to."

Wren chuckled. "I'm just giving you a hard time. Go to your charity thing. Have a blast. We can hang out on Sunday." Then he said he had to run—he needed to get to his shift at the hospital. "Good luck with your work," he added. "I'm sure you'll figure it out."

Spencer stared wistfully at the CALL ENDED window on her phone's screen. Their conversation had lasted a whopping one minute and forty-six seconds. "Of course I'll figure it out," she whispered to the phone. With about a week's extension.

As she passed her computer, she noticed a new e-mail at the top of her inbox. It had come in about five minutes ago, while she was talking to her father.

Want the easy A? I think you know where to find it. —A

Spencer's stomach tightened. She glanced out the window, but there was no one on her lawn. Then she stuck her head outside, checking to see if someone had installed a surveillance camera or put in a mini microphone. But all she saw was her house's grayish-brown stone exterior.

Melissa kept her high school papers on the family computer. She was as anal as Spencer, and saved everything. Spencer wouldn't even have to ask Melissa for permission to look at the papers—they were on the shared drive.

But how the hell did A know that?

It *was* tempting. Except . . . no. Anyway, Spencer doubted A wanted to help her. Was this an elaborate trap? Could A *be* Melissa?

"Spencer?" her mother called from downstairs. "Dinner!"

Spencer minimized the e-mail and walked absent-mindedly to the door. The thing was, if she took Melissa's paper, she'd have time to finish her other homework *and* see Wren. She could switch some words . . . use the thesaurus. . . . She'd never do it again.

Her computer made another *ting*, and she turned back.

P.S. You hurt me, so I'm going to hurt you. Or maybe I should hurt a certain new boyfriend instead? You guys better watch out—I'll show up when you least expect it.

—A

21

SOME SECRET ADMIRER . . .

Friday afternoon, Hanna sat on the soccer bleachers, watching the Rosewood Day boys' team battle Lansing Prep. Only she couldn't really focus. Her normally manicured fingernails were ragged, the skin around her thumbs was bleeding from nervous picking, and her eyes had become so red from sleeplessness, it looked like she had pinkeye. She should have been hiding at home. Sitting on the bleachers was way too public.

I'm watching you, A had said. *You'd better do what I say.*

But maybe it was like what politicians said about terrorist attacks: If you holed up in your house, afraid they were going to strike, it would mean the terrorists had won. She would sit here and watch soccer, like she had all last year and the year before that.

But then Hanna looked around. That someone really, truly knew about The Jenna Thing—and was poised to blame *her*—terrified her. And what if A really did tell her dad? Not now. Not when things might be getting better.

She craned her neck for the millionth time toward the commons, looking for Mona. Watching the boys' games was a little Hanna-Mona tradition; they mixed SoCo with syrupy Diet Dr Peppers from the concession stand and yelled sexy insults at the away team. But Mona was AWOL. Since their weird fight at the mall yesterday, Hanna and Mona hadn't spoken.

Hanna caught a glimpse of a blond ponytail and a loose red braid and cringed. Riley and Naomi had arrived, and had climbed up to a spot not that far away from Hanna. Today, both girls carried matching patent leather Chanel bags and wore obviously brand-spanking-new swingy tweed coats, as if it were actually a chilly fall day and not still a summery seventy-five degrees. When they looked in Hanna's direction, Hanna quickly pretended to be fascinated with the soccer game, even though she had no idea what the score was.

"Hanna looks fat in that outfit," she overheard Riley whisper.

Hanna felt her cheeks heat up. She stared at the way her cotton C&C California top gently stretched against her midsection. She probably was getting fatter, with all the nervous eating she'd been doing this week. It was just that she was really trying to resist the urge to throw it all up—although, that was what she wanted to do right now.

The teams broke for halftime, and the Rosewood

Day boys trotted to their bench. Sean flopped down on the grass and started massaging his calf. Hanna saw her chance and clomped down the bleacher's metallic seats. Yesterday, after A texted her, she hadn't called Sean to tell him she wasn't going to Foxy. She'd been too shell-shocked.

"Hanna," Sean said, seeing her standing over him. "Hey." He looked beautiful today as usual, despite his shirt being sweat-stained and his face a teensy bit unshaven. "How are you?"

Hanna sat down next to him, tucking her legs under her and arranging her pleated uniform skirt around her so all the soccer players couldn't see her undies. "I'm . . ." She swallowed hard, trying not to burst into tears. *Losing my mind. Being tortured by A.* "So, um, listen." She clasped her hands together. "I'm not going to Foxy."

"Really?" Sean cocked his head. "Why not? Are you okay?"

Hanna ran her hands through the closely cropped, sweet-smelling soccer field grass. She'd told Sean the same story she'd told Mona—that her father had died. "It's . . . complicated. But, um, I thought I should tell you."

Sean unfastened the Velcro on his shin guard and then tightened it up again. For a brief second, Hanna got a glimpse of his perfect, sinewy calves. For whatever reason, she thought they were the sexiest part of his body. "I might not go, either," he said.

"Really?" she asked, startled.

Sean shrugged. "All my friends are going with dates. I'd be the odd guy out."

"Oh." Hanna moved her legs out of the way so the soccer coach, who was staring at his clipboard, could pass by. She resisted smacking herself. Did that mean Sean had thought of her as his date?

Sean shaded his eyes and stared at her. "Are you all right? You seem . . . sad."

Hanna cupped her hands over her bare knees. She needed to talk to someone about A. Except there was no way. "I'm just tired." She sighed.

Sean touched Hanna's wrist lightly. "Listen. Maybe some night next week, let's get dinner. I don't know. . . . We probably should talk about stuff."

Hanna's heart did a tiny leap. "Sure. That sounds nice."

"Cool." Sean smiled, standing up. "See you later, then."

The band started playing the Rosewood Day fight song, signaling that the team's break was over. Hanna climbed back to the top of the bleachers, feeling a little better. As she returned to her seat, Riley and Naomi were looking at her curiously.

"Hanna!" Naomi cried, when Hanna met her gaze. "Hi!"

"Hey," Hanna said, mustering up as much fake-sweetness as she could.

"Were you talking to Sean?" Naomi ran her hand through her blond ponytail. She was always obsessively petting her hair. "I thought you guys had a bad breakup."

"It wasn't a bad breakup," Hanna said. "We're still friends . . . and whatever."

Riley let out a little laugh. "And *you* broke up with him, right?"

Hanna's stomach lurched. Had someone said something? "That's right."

Naomi and Riley exchanged a look. Then Naomi said, "Are you going to Foxy?"

"Actually, no," Hanna said haughtily. "I'm meeting my father at Le Bec-Fin."

"Ooh." Naomi winced. "I heard Le Bec-Fin was, like, the place people take people when they don't want to be seen."

"No, it's not." Heat rose to Hanna's face. "It's, like, the best restaurant in Philly." She started to panic. Had Le Bec-Fin changed?

Naomi shrugged, her face impassive. "It's just what I've heard, is all."

"Yeah." Riley widened her brown eyes. "Everyone knows that."

Suddenly, Hanna noticed a piece of paper sitting next to her on the bleachers. It was folded in the shape of an airplane and weighed down with a rock.

"What's that?" Naomi called. "Origami?"

Hanna unfolded the airplane and turned it over.

Hi again, Hanna! I want you to read Naomi and Riley the sentences below just as they're written. No cheating! And if you don't, everyone will know the truth about you-know-what. That includes Daddy. —A

Hanna stared at the paragraph below, written in rounded, unfamiliar handwriting. "No," she whispered, her heart starting to pound. What A had written would ruin her flawless rep forever:

I tried to get in Sean's pants at Noel's party, but he dumped me instead. And, oh yeah, I make myself throw up at least three times a day.

"Hanna, did you get a *luuuuve* letter?" Riley cooed. "Is it from a secret admirer?"

Hanna glanced at Naomi and Riley, in their shortened pleated skirts and wedge heels. They both stared at her like wolves, as if they could smell her weakness. "Did you see who put this here?" she asked, but they looked at her blankly and shrugged.

Next she looked around the soccer bleachers, at every clump of kids, every parent, even at Lansing's bus driver in the parking lot, leaning against the back of the bus smoking a cigarette. Whoever was doing this to her had to be *here*, right? They would have to know Riley and Naomi were sitting near her.

She looked at the note again. She couldn't say this to them. There was no way.

But then she thought about the final time her dad asked her about Jenna's accident. He'd sat down on her bed and spent a long time staring at the knitted sockto-pus Aria had made for her. "Hanna," he finally said. "I'm worried about you. Promise me you guys weren't playing with fireworks the night that girl was blinded."

"I . . . I didn't touch the fireworks," Hanna whispered. It wasn't a lie.

Down on the soccer field, two Lansing boys were giving each other high fives. Somewhere under the bleachers, someone lit up a joint; its skunky, mossy smell wafted into Hanna's nostrils. She crumpled up the piece of paper, stood up, and, stomach churning, walked over to Naomi and Riley. They looked up at her, bemused. Riley's mouth hung open. Her breath, Hanna noticed, stunk like someone who was on Atkins.

"Itriedtogetinseanspantsatnoelspartybuthedumped-meinstead," Hanna blurted out. She took a deep breath. The part wasn't even exactly *true*, but whatever. "And-Imakemyselfbarfthreetimesaday."

The words came out in a fast, unintelligible jumble, and Hanna turned swiftly around. "*What* did she say?" she heard Riley whisper, but she certainly wasn't going to turn around and make herself clearer.

She stomped down the bleachers, ducking around someone's mother who was carrying a precarious tray of Cokes and popcorn. She looked for someone—*anyone*—who might be looking back. But nothing. Not a single person was giggling or whispering. Everyone was just watching the Rosewood Day soccer boys advance toward Lansing's goal.

But A had to be here. A had to be watching.

22

YOU CAN'T HANDLE THE TRUTH

Friday evening, Aria shut off the radio in her bedroom. For the past hour, the local DJ had gone on and on about Foxy. He made it sound as if Foxy were a shuttle launch or a presidential inauguration, not just some silly benefit.

She listened to the sounds of her parents walking around the kitchen. There wasn't the usual cacophony of noise—NPR on the radio, CNN or PBS on the kitchen TV, or a classical or experimental jazz CD playing on the kitchen stereo. All Aria heard were pots and pans clanging. Then a crash. "Sorry," Ella said curtly. "It's fine," Byron answered.

Aria turned back to her laptop, feeling more and more crazed by the second. Since her Meredith-stalk had been cut short, she was now researching her online. Once you started Web-stalking someone, it was hard to stop. Aria had Meredith's last name—Stevens—from a Strawberry Ridge Yoga schedule she found online, so she searched

Google for Meredith's phone number. She thought maybe she'd try to call to tell her, kindly, to stay away from Byron. But then she found her address and wanted to see how far away Meredith lived, so she mapped it on MapQuest. From there, it got nuts. She looked at a hypertext paper Meredith had done in her freshman year of college on William Carlos Williams. She hacked into Hollis's student portal to see Meredith's grades. Meredith was on Friendster, Facebook, *and* MySpace. Her favorite movies were *Donnie Darko*; *Paris, Texas*; and *The Princess Bride*, and her interests were quirky things like snow globes, tai chi, and magnets.

In a parallel universe, Aria and Meredith could have been *friends*. It made it even harder to do what A asked in Aria's last text message: *make it go away.*

It felt like A's threat was burning a hole in her Treo, and whenever she thought about seeing not only Meredith but *Spencer* in the yoga studio that morning, she felt uneasy. What was Spencer doing there? Did Spencer know something?

Back in seventh grade, Aria had told Ali about seeing Toby at her drama workshop while she, Ali, and Spencer were hanging out at Spencer's pool. "He doesn't know anything, Aria," Ali had answered, calmly applying more sunscreen. "Chill out."

"But how can you be sure?" Aria had protested. "What about that person I saw outside the tree house that night? Maybe they told Toby! Maybe it *was* Toby!"

Spencer frowned, then glanced at Alison. "Ali, maybe you should just—"

Ali cleared her throat loudly. "Spence," she said, sort of as a warning.

Aria looked back and forth at them, confused. Then she blurted out the question she'd wanted to ask for a while: "What were you guys whispering about the night of her accident? When I woke up and you were in the bathroom?"

Ali cocked her head. "We weren't whispering."

"Ali, we *were*," Spencer hissed.

Ali gave her another sharp look, then turned back to Aria. "Look, we weren't talking about Toby. Besides"—she gave Aria a little smile—"don't you have bigger things to worry about right now?"

Aria bristled. Just days before, Aria and Ali had caught her father with Meredith.

Spencer tugged Ali's arm. "Ali, I really think you should tell—"

Ali held up her hand. "Spence, I swear to God."

"You swear to God *what*?" Spencer shrieked. "You think this is easy?"

After Aria saw Spencer at the yoga studio this morning, she'd considered tracking her down in school and talking to her. Spencer and Ali had covered something up, and maybe it was tangled in A. But . . . she felt afraid. She thought she'd known her old friends inside and out. But now that she knew they all had dark secrets they didn't want to share . . . maybe she'd never really known them at all.

Aria's cell phone rang, breaking her out of the memory. Startled, she dropped it into a pile of dirty T-shirts she'd been meaning to wash. She grabbed it.

"Hey," said a boy's voice on the other end. "It's Sean."

"Oh!" Aria exclaimed. "What's up?"

"Not much. Just got back from a soccer game. What are you doing tonight?"

Aria wiggled with glee. "Um . . . nothing, really."

"Wanna hang out?"

She heard another clatter downstairs. Then her father's voice. "I'm going." The front door slammed. He wasn't even going to have dinner with them. *Again.*

She put her mouth back to the phone. "How about right now?"

Sean parked his Audi in a desolate lot and led Aria up an embankment. To their left was a chain-link fence, to their right a sloping path. Above them were the elevated train tracks, and below them was all of Rosewood. "My brother and I found this place years ago," Sean explained.

He spread his cashmere sweater on the grass and gestured for her to sit. Then he pulled a chrome thermos out of his backpack and handed it to her. "Want some?" Aria could smell the Captain Morgan through the little space in the lid.

She took a greedy swig, then looked at him crookedly.

His face was so chiseled and his clothes fit so perfectly, but he didn't have the same *I'm hot and I know it* air about him that other typical Rosewood boys did. "You come here a lot?" she asked.

Sean shrugged and sat down next to her. "Not a lot. But sometimes."

Aria had assumed Sean and his typical Rosewood boy crowd drove around partying all night, or sneaked their parents' beer at someone's empty house while playing Grand Theft Auto on PlayStation. And there would be a soak in a hot tub to cap off the night, of course. Pretty much everyone in Rosewood had a hot tub in their backyard.

The town lights twinkled below. Aria could see Hollis's spire, which was lit up in ivory at night. "This is amazing," she sighed. "I can't believe I've never found this place."

"Well, we used to live not far from here." Sean smiled. "My brother and I rode all over these woods on our dirt bikes. We also used to come here and play Blair Witch."

"Blair Witch?" Aria repeated.

He nodded. "After the movie came out, we were obsessed with making our own ghost movies."

"I did that too!" Aria cried, so excited she laid her hand on Sean's arm. She quickly pulled it away. "Except I did mine in my backyard."

"You still have the videos?" Sean asked.

"Yep. You?"

"Uh-huh." Sean paused. "Maybe you could come see them some time."

"I'd like that." She smiled. Sean was starting to remind her of the *croque-monsieur* she once ordered in Nice. At first glance, it looked like a plain, cookie-cutter grilled cheese, nothing special. But when she bit into it, the cheese was Brie and there were chopped-up portabello mushrooms hidden underneath. There was a lot more to it than it had appeared.

Sean leaned back on his elbows. "One time, my brother and I came here and caught this couple having sex."

"Really?" Aria giggled.

Sean took the mug from her. "Yeah. And they were so into it, they didn't see us at first. I backed up really slowly but then tripped over some rocks. They totally freaked."

"I'm sure." She shivered. "God, that would be awful."

Sean poked her in the arm. "What, you've never done it in public?"

Aria looked away. "Nah."

They were quiet for a moment. Aria wasn't sure how she felt. Uneasy, sort of. But also . . . a little buzzy. It felt like something was going to happen. "So, um, remember that secret you told me, in your car?" she asked. "The one about not wanting to be a virgin?"

"Yeah."

"Why do you . . . why do you think you feel that way?"

Sean leaned back on his elbows. "I started going to V Club because everybody was rushing to have sex, and I wanted to see why the people at V Club decided not to."

"And?"

"Well, I think they're mostly scared. But also, I think they want to find the right person. Like, someone they can be completely honest and themselves with."

He paused. Aria hugged her knees to her chest. She wished—just a little—that Sean would say, *And Aria, I think you're the right person.* She sighed. "I had sex, once."

Sean put the mug in the grass and looked at her.

"In Iceland, a year after I moved there," she admitted. It felt strange to say it out loud. "It was this boy I liked. Oskar. He wanted to, and so did I, but . . . I don't know." She pushed her hair out of her face. "I didn't love him or anything." She paused. "You're the first person I ever told."

They were quiet for a while. Aria felt her heart thumping against her chest. Someone far below was grilling; she could smell the charcoal and the burgers. She heard Sean swallow and shift his weight, moving a little closer. She moved a little closer, too, feeling nervous.

"Go to Foxy with me," Sean blurted out.

Aria cocked her head. "F-Foxy?"

"The benefit thing? You dress up? Dance?"

She blinked. "I know what Foxy is."

"Unless you're going with someone else. And we could go as friends, of course."

Aria felt a tiny twinge of disappointment when he

used the word *friends*. A second ago, she'd thought they were going to kiss. "You haven't asked anyone already?"

"No. That's why I asked you."

Aria sneaked a peek at Sean. Her eyes kept gravitating toward the little cleft in his chin. Ali used to call them "butt chins," but it was actually pretty cute. "Um, yeah, okay."

"Cool." Sean grinned. Aria grinned back. Except . . . something made her wilt. *I'm giving you till the stroke of midnight Saturday night, Cinderella. Or else.* Saturday was tomorrow.

Sean noticed her expression. "What is it?"

Aria swallowed. Her whole mouth tasted like rum. "I met the woman my dad's fooling around with yesterday. Sort of by accident." She took a deep breath. "Or not by accident at all. I wanted to ask her what was going on, but I couldn't. I'm just afraid my mom's going to . . . to catch them together." Tears came to her eyes. "I don't want my family to fall apart."

Sean held her for a while. "Couldn't you try talking to the girl again?"

"I don't know." She stared at her hands. They were shaking. "I mean, I have this whole speech for her figured out in my head. I just want her to know my side." She arched her back and looked up at the sky, as if the universe might give her the answer. "But maybe it's a stupid idea."

"It's not. I'll go with you. For moral support."

She looked up. "You . . . you *would*?"

Sean glanced out over the trees. "Right now, if you want."

Aria quickly shook her head. "I couldn't right now. I left my, um, script at home."

Sean shrugged. "Do you remember what you want to say?"

"I guess," Aria said faintly. She looked out over the trees. "It's not far, actually. . . . She lives right over this hill. In Old Hollis." She knew this from stalking Meredith on Google Earth.

"C'mon." Sean extended his hand. Before she could think too much about it, they were scampering down the grassy hill, past Sean's car.

They crossed the street into Old Hollis, the student neighborhood that was full of crumbling, spooky Victorian houses. Old VWs, Volvos, and Saabs lined the curbs. For a Friday night, the neighborhood was absolutely empty. Perhaps there was some big event in Hollis elsewhere. Aria wondered if Meredith would even be home; she sort of hoped that she wouldn't be.

Halfway down the second block, Aria stopped at a pink house that had four pairs of running shoes airing out on the porch and a chalk drawing of what looked like a penis on the driveway. It was only fitting that Meredith lived here. "I think this is it."

"You want me to wait here?" Sean whispered.

Aria pulled her sweater around her. It was suddenly

freezing. "I guess." Then she grabbed Sean's arm. "I can't do this."

"Sure you can." Sean put his hands on her shoulders. "I'll be right here, okay? Nothing's going to happen to you. I promise."

Aria felt a rush of gratitude. He was so . . . sweet. She leaned forward and gently kissed Sean on the lips; as she pulled away, he looked stunned. "Thank you," she said.

She walked up Meredith's cracked front steps slowly, the rum coursing through her veins. She'd drunk three-quarters of Sean's thermos, while he'd only taken a few gentlemanly sips. As she rang the bell, she steadied herself against one of the porch's columns for balance. Tonight was not the night to be wearing her wobbly sling-backs from Italy.

Meredith flung open the door. She wore terry-cloth short-shorts and a white T-shirt with a drawing of a banana on it—it was the cover to some old album, Aria just couldn't remember what. And she seemed bigger tonight. Less lithe and more muscular, like the ass-kicking chicks on that show, *Rollergirls*. Aria felt puny.

Meredith's eyes brightened with recognition. "Alison, right?"

"Actually, it's Aria. Aria Montgomery. I'm Byron Montgomery's daughter. I know everything that's going on. I want it to stop."

Meredith's eyes widened. She took a deep breath, then exhaled slowly through her nose. Aria almost thought dragonlike steam was going to come out. "You do, huh?"

"That's right," Aria wavered, realizing she was slurring her speech. *Thassright.* And her heart was beating so loud, she wouldn't have been surprised if her skin was pulsating.

Meredith raised an eyebrow. "It's none of your business." She stuck her head out on the porch and looked around suspiciously. "How did you find out where I lived?"

"Look, you're destroying everything," Aria protested. "And I just want it to stop. Okay? I mean . . . this is hurting everyone. He's still married . . . and he has a family."

Aria winced to herself at the pathetic edge to her voice and how her perfectly crafted speech had slipped from her grasp.

Meredith crossed her arms over her chest. "I do know all that," she answered, starting to shut the door. "And I'm sorry. I really am. But we're in love."

23

NEXT STOP, GREATER ROSEWOOD JAIL

Late Saturday afternoon, a few hours before Foxy, Spencer sat at her computer. She'd just addressed an e-mail to Squidward and attached her essays. *Just send it,* she told herself. She closed her eyes, clicked the mouse, and, when she opened them, her work had been sent.

Well, it was *sort of* her work.

She hadn't cheated. Really. Well, maybe she had. But who could blame her? After A's message came in last night, she'd spent the whole night calling Wren, but his phone kept going to voice mail. And she'd left five messages for him, each of them becoming more frantic. She'd put on her shoes twelve separate times, ready to drive into Philadelphia to see if Wren was okay, but then talked herself out of it. The one time her Sidekick chimed, she dove for it, but it was just a classwide e-mail from Squidward, reminding everyone of the proper annotation style for the essay questions.

When someone put their hand on Spencer's shoulder, she screamed.

Melissa stepped back. "Whoa! Sorry! Just me!"

Spencer righted herself, breathing hard. "I . . ." She surveyed her desk. *Shit.* There was a slip of paper that said, *Gynecologist, Tuesday, 5 P.M. Ortho Tri-Cyclen?* And she had Melissa's old history essays on her computer screen. She kicked the computer hard drive's on/off switch with her foot, and the monitor went black.

"You stressed?" Melissa asked. "Lots of homework before Foxy?"

"Kinda." Spencer quickly shoved all of her desk's random papers into neat piles.

"Wanna borrow my lavender neck pillow?" Melissa asked. "It's a stress reliever."

"That's all right," Spencer answered, not even daring to look at her sister. *I stole your paper and your boyfriend,* she thought. *You shouldn't be nice to me.*

Melissa pushed her lips together. "Well, not to make you more stressed, but there's a cop downstairs. He says he wants to ask you some questions."

"*What?*" Spencer cried.

"It's about Alison." Melissa said. She shook her head, making the ends of her hair swing. "They shouldn't make you talk about it—the *week* of her memorial. It's sick."

Spencer tried not to panic. She stared at herself in the mirror, smoothing down her blond hair and dabbing concealer under her eyes. She pulled on a white button-down blouse and skinny khaki pants. There. She looked trustworthy and innocent.

But her whole body was shaking.

Sure enough, there was a cop standing in the living room but looking into her father's second office, where he kept his vintage guitar collection. When the cop turned around, Spencer realized that he wasn't the one she'd spoken to at the funeral. This guy was young. And he looked familiar, like she might've seen him somewhere else.

"Are you Spencer?" he asked.

"Yes," she said quietly.

He stuck out his hand. "I'm Darren Wilden. I've just been assigned to Alison DiLaurentis's murder case."

"Murder," Spencer repeated.

"Yes," Officer Wilden said. "Well, we're investigating it as a murder."

"Okay." Spencer tried to sound even and mature. "Wow."

Wilden motioned for Spencer to sit down on her living room couch; then he sat opposite her on the chaise. She realized where she knew him from: Rosewood Day. He'd gone there when she was in sixth grade, and he'd earned a reputation as a badass. One of Melissa's nerdy friends, Liana, had a crush on him, and once made Spencer deliver a secret admirer note to him at the espresso bar where he worked. Spencer recalled thinking that Darren had biceps the size of Chunky Soup cans.

Now he was staring at her. Spencer felt her nose itch, and the grandfather clock made a few loud ticks. Finally, he said, "Is there anything you'd like to tell me?"

Fear shot through her chest. "Tell you?"

Wilden sat back. "About Alison."

Spencer blinked. Something about this felt wrong. "She was my best friend," she managed. Her palms felt sweaty. "I was with her the night she went missing."

"Right." Wilden looked at a notepad. "That's in our files. You talked to someone at the police station after she went missing, right?"

"Yes. Twice."

"Right." Wilden clasped his hands together. "Are you sure you told them *everything*? Was there someone who hated Alison? Maybe the officer asked you all these questions before, but since I'm new, maybe you could refresh my memory."

Spencer's brain stalled. Truthfully, lots of girls had hated Ali. *Spencer* even hated Ali sometimes, especially the way she always could manipulate her, and how she'd threatened to point the finger at Spencer for The Jenna Thing if she ever told what she knew. And secretly, it was kind of a relief when Ali disappeared. Ali gone and Toby away at school meant their secret was hidden for good.

She swallowed hard. She wasn't sure what this cop knew. A could have tipped the cops off that she was hiding something. And it was brilliant—if Spencer told him, *Yes, I* do *know someone who hated Ali,* really *hated her enough to kill her,* she'd have to confess her involvement in The Jenna Thing. If she said nothing and protected herself, A still might punish her friends . . . and Wren.

You hurt me, so I'm going to hurt you.

Sweat prickled on the back of her neck. But then there was more: What if Toby was back to hurt her? What if he and A were working together? What if he was A? But if he was—and he killed Ali—would he go to the cops and incriminate himself? "I'm pretty sure I told them everything," she finally said.

There was a long, long pause. Wilden stared at Spencer. Spencer stared at Wilden. It made Spencer think about the night after The Jenna Thing happened. She'd dozed into a fitful, paranoid sleep, her friends quietly crying around her. But all of a sudden, she was awake again. The cable box clock said 3:43 A.M., and the room was still. She felt unhinged, and found Ali, sleeping sitting up on the couch with Emily's head in her lap. "I can't do this," she said, shaking her awake. "We should turn ourselves in."

Ali got up, led Spencer into the hall bathroom, and sat down on the edge of the tub. "Get a grip, Spence," Ali said. "You can't spaz if the police ask us questions."

"The *police*?" Spencer shrieked, her heart picking up speed.

"*Shhh,*" Ali whispered. She drummed her nails against the tub's porcelain edge. "I'm not saying the police are definitely going to talk to us, but we have to make a plan in case they *do.* All we need is a solid story. An alibi."

"Why can't we just tell them the truth?" Spencer asked. "Exactly what you saw Toby do, and that it surprised you so much, you set the firework off by accident?"

Ali shook her head. "It's better my way. We keep Toby's secret, he keeps ours."

A knock on the door made them stand up. "Guys?" a voice called. It was Aria.

"Fair enough," Wilden finally said, breaking Spencer from her memory. He handed her a business card. "Call me if you think of anything, all right?"

"Of course," Spencer whimpered.

Wilden put his hands on his hips and looked around the room. At the Chippendale furniture; the exquisite stained-glass window; the heavy, framed art on the walls; and her father's prized George Washington clock that had been in the family since the 1800s. Then he canvassed Spencer, from the diamond studs in her ears to the delicate Cartier watch on her wrist to her blond highlights, which cost $300 every six weeks. The smug little smile on his face seemed to say, *You seem like a girl who has a lot to lose.*

"You going to that benefit tonight?" he asked, making her jump. "Foxy?"

"Um, yeah," Spencer said quietly.

"Well." Wilden gave her a little salute. "Have fun." His voice was totally normal, but she could've sworn the look on his face said, *I'm not through with you yet.*

24

$250 GETS YOU DINNER,
DANCING . . . AND A WARNING

Foxy was held in Kingman Hall, an old English country-side mansion built by a man who'd invented some new-fangled milking machine in the early 1900s. In fourth grade, when they learned about the hall in the All About Pennsylvania social studies unit, Emily nicknamed it "Moo Mansion."

As the check-in girl scrutinized their invites, Emily looked around. The place had a labyrinthine garden in its front yard. Gargoyles leered from the arches of the mansion's stately front. Ahead of her was the tent where the actual event was being held. It was lit up with fairy lights and full of people.

"Wow." Toby came up beside her. Beautiful girls swished by them toward the tent, wearing elaborate, custom-made dresses and carrying bejeweled bags. Emily looked down at her own dress—it was a simple, strapless pink sheath Carolyn had worn to prom last year. She'd done her hair herself, put on a lot of Carolyn's ultra-girly Lovely perfume—which made her sneeze—and was wearing earrings for the first time in a while, poking them forcefully through the holes in her ears that had almost closed up. Even with all that, she still felt plain next to everyone else.

Yesterday, when Emily called Toby to ask him to Foxy, he'd sounded so surprised—but really excited. She was psyched, too. They would go to Foxy, share another kiss, and who knew? Maybe become a couple. In time, they would visit Jenna at her school in Philadelphia, and Emily would somehow make it all up to her. She'd foster Jenna's next Seeing Eye dog. She'd read to her all the books that hadn't yet come out in Braille. Maybe, in time, Emily would confess her involvement in Jenna's accident.

Or maybe not.

Except now that she was at Foxy, something just felt . . . wrong. Emily's body kept feeling hot, then cold, and her stomach kept clenching up in pain. Toby's hands felt too scratchy, and she'd been so nervous, they'd barely said anything to each other on the way over. Foxy itself didn't seem to be very calming, either; everyone was so stiff and poised. And Emily was sure someone was watching her. As she inspected every girl's made-up, glossy face and every guy's scrubbed, handsome one, she wondered, *Are you A?*

"Smile!" A flashbulb popped in Emily's face, and she let out a little scream. When the spots faded from her eyes, a blond girl in a merlot-red dress with a press badge over her right boob and a digital camera slung over her shoulder was laughing at her. "I was just taking photos for the *Philadelphia Inquirer*," she explained. "Wanna try that again, without the freaked expression this time?" Emily clutched Toby's arm and tried to look happy, except her expression was more of a petrified grimace.

After the press girl whirled away, Toby turned to Emily. "Is something wrong? You seemed so relaxed in front of a camera before."

Emily stiffened. "When have you seen me in front of a camera?"

"The Rosewood versus Tate?" Toby reminded her. "That crazy yearbook kid?"

"Oh, right." Emily breathed out.

Toby's eyes followed a waiter scurrying around with a drink tray. "So, is this your scene?"

"God, no!" Emily said. "I've never been to anything like this in my life."

He looked around. "Everyone looks so . . . so plastic. I used to want to kill most of these people."

A sharp, startled frisson passed through Emily. It was the same sort of feeling she'd felt when she woke up in the back of Toby's car. When Toby noticed her face, he quickly smiled. "Not *literally*." He squeezed her hand. "You're much prettier than all the girls here."

Emily flushed. Only she was finding that her insides didn't turn upside down when he said it or when he touched her. They *should*. Toby looked hot. Gorgeous, actually, in his black suit and black wingtips, with his hair pushed back off his angular, square-jawed face. Every girl was checking him out. When he'd shown up on her porch, even mild-mannered Carolyn had squealed, "He's so cute!"

But when he held her hand, as much as she wanted it to feel like something, it felt like nothing. It was like holding hands with her sister.

Emily tried to relax. She and Toby made their way into the tent, got two virgin piña coladas, and joined a bunch of kids on the dance floor. There were only a handful of girls who were trying to dance in that über-sexy, hands-above-the-head, I'm getting my moves down for MTV Spring Break way. Most everyone else was just jumping around, singing along to Madonna. Technicians were setting up a karaoke machine in the corner, and girls were writing down the songs they wanted to sing.

Emily broke away to go to the bathroom, leaving the tent and walking through a sexy, candlelit hallway paved in rose petals. Girls passed her, arm and arm, whispering and giggling. Emily discreetly checked out her chest; she'd never worn a strapless dress before and was certain it was going to fall down and expose her boobs to the world.

"Want a reading?"

Emily looked over. A dark-haired woman dressed in a silky, paisley-print dress sat at a small table under a huge portrait of Horace Kingman, the milking-machine inventor himself. She wore a ton of bracelets on her left arm and a large snake brooch at her throat. A deck of cards sat next to her along with a little sign at the edge of the table: THE MAGIC OF THE TAROT.

"That's okay," Emily told her. The tarot reader was so . . . public. Out here in the open, in the middle of the hall.

The woman extended a long fingernail toward her. "You need one, though. Something's going to happen to you tonight. Something life-changing."

Emily stiffened. *"Me?"*

"Yes, you. And the date you brought? He's not the one you want. You must go to the one you really love."

Emily's mouth fell open, and her mind began to race.

The tarot reader looked as if she was about to say something else, but Naomi Zeigler pushed past Emily and sat down at the table. "I met you here last year," Naomi gushed, leaning excitedly on her elbows. "You gave me the best reading ever."

Emily slunk away, her mind churning. Something was going to happen to her tonight? Something . . . *life-changing*? Maybe Ben was going to tell everyone. Or Maya was going to tell everyone. A was going to show everyone those pictures. Or A had told Toby. . . about Jenna. It could be anything.

Emily splashed cold water on her face and exited the bathroom. As she made the turn for the tent, she bumped into someone's back. As soon as she saw who it was, her body tensed.

"Hey," Ben said in a mock-friendly tone, drawing the word out. He wore a charcoal suit and had a small white gardenia pinned to his lapel.

"H-Hey," Emily stammered. "I didn't know you were coming."

"I was going to say the same thing to you." Ben leaned down. "I like your date." He put *date* in air quotes. "I saw you with him at yesterday's Tate meet, too. How much did you have to pay him to come here with you?"

Emily pushed past him. She strode down the shadowy hall, noting that this would *not* be the best time to trip in her heels. Ben's footsteps rang out behind her. "Why are you running away?" he singsonged.

"Leave me alone." She didn't turn around.

"Is that dude your bodyguard? First he protects you at swimming, now here. Only where is he now? Or did you only rent him to walk in with you, so everybody wouldn't think you were a big lesbo?" Ben let out a little snicker.

"Ha ha." Emily whirled around to face him. "You're funny."

"Yeah?" Ben shoved her up against the wall. Just like that. He pinned her wrists back and pressed his body to hers. "Is this funny?"

Ben's actions were forceful and his body was heavy.

Just feet away, kids swept past them toward the bath-rooms. Didn't they *see*? "Stop it," Emily mustered.

His rough hand reached for the hem of her dress. He poked Emily's kneecap, then slid his hand up her leg. "Just tell me that you like this," he said in her ear. "Or I'll tell everyone you're a dyke."

Tears came to Emily's eyes. "Ben," she whispered, pressing her legs together. "I'm not a dyke."

"Then say you like it," Ben growled. His hand squeezed her bare thigh.

Ben was getting closer and closer to her underwear. When they were dating, they hadn't even gotten this far. Emily bit her lip so hard, she was certain she drew blood. She was about to give in and tell him she liked it, just so he'd stop, but fury slashed through her. Let Ben think what he wanted. Let him tell the whole school. No way could he do this to her.

She pressed her body up against the wall for leverage. Then she brought up her knee and angled it toward Ben's crotch. Hard.

"*Uff!*" Ben stepped away, holding his groin. A tiny, babyish wail came out of his mouth. "What did you . . . ?" he gasped.

Emily straightened her dress. "Stay away from me." Anger coursed through her like a drug. "I swear to God."

Ben staggered backward and hit the far wall. His knees buckled, and he slid down until he was sitting on the floor. "Bad, bad move."

"Whatever," Emily said, then turned to walk away. She took long, fast, confident strides. She wouldn't let him see how upset she was. That she was on the verge of tears.

"Hey." Someone gently grabbed Emily's arm. When Emily's eyes focused, she realized it was Maya.

"I just saw the whole thing," Maya whispered, nudging her chin to where Ben was still crouched. "Are you okay?"

"Yeah," Emily said quickly. But her voice caught. She tried to hold it together, but she couldn't. She leaned against the wall and covered her face with her hands. If she just counted to ten, she could get through this. *One . . . two . . . three . . .*

Maya touched Emily's arm. "I'm so sorry, Em."

"Don't be," Emily managed, her face still covered. *Eight . . . nine . . . ten.* She took her hands away and straightened up. "I'm fine."

She paused, looking at Maya's ivory geisha-style dress. She looked so much prettier than all of the blond, French-twisted, Chanel clones she'd seen on her way in. She ran her hands along the sides of her own dress, wondering if Maya was checking her out too. "I . . . I should probably get back to my date," Emily stammered.

Maya took a tiny step to the side. Only Emily couldn't move an inch.

"I have a secret for you before you go," Maya said.

Emily came closer and Maya leaned into Emily's ear. Her lips didn't touch it, but they were so close. Tingles

224 + SARA SHEPARD

shot up Emily's back, and she heard herself breathe in sharply. It wasn't right to respond this way, but she just . . . *couldn't* . . . help it.

Go to the one you really love.

"I'll wait for you," Maya whispered, her voice a little sad and a lot sexy. "However long it takes."

25

THE SURREAL LIFE, STARRING HANNA MARIN

Saturday night, Hanna rode the elevator up to her suite at the Philadelphia Four Seasons, feeling taut, loose, and glowing. She'd just had a lemongrass body wrap, an 80-minute massage, and a Kissed by the Sun tanning treatment, all in a row. The pampering had made her feel *slightly* less stressed. That, and being away from Rosewood . . . and A.

Hopefully she was away from A.

She unlocked the door to their two-bedroom suite and strode inside. Her father was sitting on the couch in the front room. "Hey." He stood up. "How was it?"

"Wonderful." Hanna beamed at him, overcome with both happiness and sadness at once. She wanted to tell him how grateful she felt that they were back together—and yet, she knew her future with him hung in the balance—A's balance. Hopefully, blurting out stuff to Naomi and Riley yesterday would keep her safe, but what if it didn't?

Maybe she should just tell him the truth about Jenna, before A got to him first.

She pressed her lips together and looked at the carpet bashfully. "Well, I have to shower really fast if we're going to make it to Le Bec-Fin."

"Just a sec." Her dad stood up. "I have another surprise for you."

On instinct, Hanna looked at her dad's hands, hoping he was holding a gift for her. Maybe it was something to make up for all those lame birthday cards. But the only thing in his hand was his cell phone.

Then came a knock on the door to the adjoining suite. "Tom? Is she here?"

Hanna froze, feeling the blood drain from her head. She knew that voice.

"Kate and Isabel are here," her father whispered excitedly. "They're coming to Le Bec-Fin with us, and then we're all going to see *Mamma Mia!*. Didn't you say Thursday that you wanted to see that?"

"Wait!" Hanna blocked him before he got to the door. "*You* invited them?"

"Yes." Her father looked at her crazily. "Who else would have?"

A, Hanna thought. It seemed like A's style. "But I thought it was going to just be you and me."

"I never said that."

Hanna frowned. Yes, he had. Hadn't he?

"Tom?" Kate's voice called. Hanna was relieved that

Kate called her dad Tom, and not Daddy, but she tightened her grip on her dad's wrist.

Her father hesitated at the door, his eyes flickering back and forth awkwardly. "But, I mean, Hanna, they're already here. I thought this would be nice."

"Why . . . ?" *Why would you think that?* Hanna wanted to ask. *Kate makes me feel like shit and you ignore me when she's here. This is why I haven't spoken to you in years!*

But there was so much confusion and disappointment on her father's face. He'd probably been planning this for days. Hanna stared at the tassels on the Oriental rug. Her throat felt clogged, as if she'd just swallowed something enormous.

"I guess you should let them in, then," she mumbled.

When her father opened the door, Isabel cried out with glee, as if they'd been separated by whole galaxies, not just states. She was still overly thin and too tan, and Hanna's eyes went immediately to the rock on her left hand. It was a three-carat Tiffany Legacy ring—Hanna knew the catalogue backward and forward.

And Kate. She was more beautiful than ever. Her diagonal-striped slip dress had to be a size two, and her straight chestnut hair was even longer than a few years ago. She gracefully placed her Louis Vuitton purse on the hotel room's little dining table. Hanna seethed. Kate probably never tripped in her new Jimmy Choos or slid on the hardwood floors after the cleaning lady waxed them.

Kate's face looked pinched, like she was really pissed

to be here. When she noticed Hanna, however, her puckered look softened. She looked Hanna up and down—
from her structured Chloé jacket to her strappy sling-
backs—and then she smiled.

"Hey, Hanna," Kate said, her surprise obvious.
"Wow." She put her hand on Hanna's shoulder but luckily didn't hug her. If she had, she'd have found out how
badly Hanna was trembling.

"Everything looks so good," Kate breathed, staring at her
menu.

"Indeed," Mr. Marin echoed. He flagged down the
waiter and ordered a bottle of pinot grigio. Then he
gazed warmly at Kate, Isabel, and Hanna. "I'm glad we
can all be here. Together."

"It's really lovely to see you again, Hanna,"
Isabel cooed.

"Yeah," Kate echoed. "It totally is."

Hanna stared down at her dainty silverware. It was
surreal to see them again. And not the cool, Zac-Posen-
kaleidoscopic-dress sort of surreal, but nightmarish
surreal, like when that Russian guy in the book Hanna
had to read for English last year woke up and found he'd
turned into a roach.

"Darling, what are you going to get?" Isabel asked her
with her hand over Hanna's father's. She still couldn't
believe her father was into Isabel. She was so . . . plain.
And way too tan. Cute if you were a model, fourteen

years old, or from Brazil—not if you were a middle-aged woman from Maryland.

"Hmm," Mr. Marin said. "What's *pintade*? Is it fish?"

Hanna flipped through the menu's pages. She had no idea what she could eat. Everything was either fried or in cream sauce.

"Kate, will you translate?" Isabel leaned in Hanna's direction. "Kate's fluent."

Of course she is, Hanna thought.

"We spent last summer in Paris," Isabel explained, looking at Hanna. Hanna ducked behind the wine list. They went to Paris? Her father, too? "Hanna, do you study languages?" Isabel asked.

"Um." Hanna shrugged. "I took a year of Spanish."

Isabel pursed her lips. "What's your favorite subject in school?"

"English?"

"Mine too!" Kate exclaimed.

"Kate got her school's top English prize last year," Isabel bragged, looking very proud.

"*Mom,*" Kate whined. She looked at Hanna and mouthed, *Sorry.*

Hanna still couldn't believe how Kate's pissed-off look had melted when she'd seen Hanna. Hanna had *made* that look before. Like the time in ninth grade when her English teacher volunteered her to show around Carlos, the Chilean exchange student. Hanna stormed resentfully to the front office to greet him, certain that

Carlos was going to be a dork and bring down her cool quotient. When she got to the office and saw a tall, wavy-haired, green-eyed boy who looked like he'd been playing beach volleyball since birth, she stood up a little straighter and discreetly checked her breath. Kate probably thought they shared some sort of cute-girl bond.

"Do you do any extracurriculars?" Isabel asked her. "Sports?"

Hanna shrugged. "Not really." She'd forgotten that Isabel was one of *those* mothers: All she talked about were Kate's honors classes, languages, awards, extracurriculars, and so on. It was yet another thing Hanna couldn't compete with.

"Don't be so modest." Her father poked Hanna in the shoulder. "You have plenty of extracurriculars."

Hanna looked at her dad blankly. What, like stealing?

"The burn clinic?" he prompted. "And your mom said you joined a support group?"

Hanna's mouth fell open. In a moment of weakness, she'd told her mom about going to V Club, sort of to say, *See? I actually have morals.* She couldn't believe her mom had told her dad. "I . . ." she stuttered. "It's nothing."

"It's not nothing." Mr. Marin pointed his fork at her.

"Dad," Hanna hissed.

The others looked at her expectantly. Isabel's bulgy eyes widened. Kate had the tiniest whisper of a smirk on her face, but her eyes looked sympathetic. Hanna eyed the bread basket. *Screw it,* she thought, and shoved a whole roll into her mouth.

"It's an abstinence club, okay?" she blurted out, her mouth full of dough and poppy seeds. Then she stood up. "Thanks a lot, Dad."

"Hanna!" Her father pushed his chair back and stood up halfway, but Hanna kept walking. Why had she bought into his little *I'd love a weekend with you* story? It was just like the last time, when her father called Hanna a piggy. And to think what she'd risked to be here—she'd told those bitches she puked three times a day! That wasn't even true anymore!

She shoved through the bathroom door, slammed into a stall, and knelt down in front of the toilet. Her stomach gurgled, and she felt the urge to take care of it. *Calm down,* she told herself, staring dizzily at her reflection in the toilet's water. *You can get through this.*

Hanna stood up again, her jaw trembling, tears threatening to spill from her eyes. If only she could stay in this bathroom for the rest of the night. Let them have Hanna's special weekend without her. Her cell phone rang. Hanna pulled it out of her purse to silence it. Then her stomach dropped. She had an e-mail from a familiar garbled address.

Since you followed my orders so nicely yesterday, consider this a gift: Get to Foxy, now. Sean's there with another girl.

—A

She was so startled, she nearly dropped the phone on the bathroom's marble floor.

She dialed Mona. They still weren't speaking—Hanna hadn't even told Mona she wasn't going to Foxy—and Mona didn't answer. Hanna hung up, so frustrated she threw her phone against the door. Who could Sean be with? Naomi? Some V Club bitch?

She burst noisily out of the stall, making an old lady washing her hands at the sink jump. When Hanna came around the corner for the door, she skidded to a halt. Kate was sitting on the chaise lounge, applying pale, salmon-colored lipstick. Her long, slender legs were crossed and she looked super-poised.

"Everything okay?" Kate raised her deep blue eyes to Hanna. "I came to check."

Hanna stiffened. "Yeah. I'm fine."

Kate twisted up her mouth. "No offense to your dad, but sometimes he can say the most inappropriate things. Like this one time I was going out on this date with this guy. We were leaving the house, and your dad goes, 'Kate? I see you wrote OB on the grocery list. What is that? What aisle can I find it in?' I was mortified."

"God." Hanna felt a twinge of sympathy. That sounded like her dad, all right.

"Hey, it doesn't matter," Kate said gently. "He didn't mean anything."

Hanna shook her head. "It's not that." She glanced up at Kate. Oh, what the hell. Maybe they *did* have a pretty-girl bond. "It's . . . it's my ex. I got a text that he's at this benefit thing called Foxy with another girl."

Kate frowned. "When did you break up?"

"Eight days ago." Hanna sat down on the chaise. "I'm half tempted to go back there right now and kick his ass."

"Why don't you?"

Hanna slumped back in the couch. "I wish, but . . ." She motioned toward the door leading back to the restaurant.

"Listen." Kate stood up and puckered for the mirror. "Why don't you blame that support group thing you're in? Say that one of the people in it called you and said she was feeling really 'weak,' and you're her buddy, so you have to talk her down."

Hanna raised an eyebrow. "You know an awful lot about support groups."

Kate shrugged. "I have a couple friends who've been through rehab."

Okaaay. "I don't think it's a good idea."

"I'll cover for you, if you want," Kate offered.

Hanna eyed her in the mirror. "Really?"

Kate looked back at her meaningfully. "Let's just say I owe you one."

Hanna flinched. Something told her Kate was talking about that time in Annapolis. It made her feel squirmy— that Kate remembered, and that she recognized that she'd been mean. At the same time, it gave her a certain satisfaction.

"Besides," Kate said, "your dad said we'd be seeing a lot more of each other. Might as well start it off right."

Hanna blinked. "He said he . . . he wants to see me more?"

"Well, you *are* his daughter."

Hanna played with the heart-shaped charm on her Tiffany necklace. It gave her a little thrill, hearing Kate say that. Maybe she'd overreacted at the dinner table.

"What—it'll take you two hours, tops?" Kate asked.

"Probably less than that." All she wanted to do was take SEPTA to Rosewood and curse the bitch out. She opened her hobo bag to see if she had train fare. Kate stood above her and pointed to something at the purse's bottom. "What's that?"

"This?" As soon as Hanna pulled it out, she wanted to stuff it back in. It was the Percocet she'd stolen from the burn clinic on Tuesday. She'd forgotten.

"Can I have one of those?" Kate whispered excitedly. Hanna looked at her cross-eyed. "Serious?"

Kate gave Hanna a naughty look. "I need *something* to help me get through this musical your dad's dragging us to."

Hanna handed over a packet. Kate pocketed the pills, then turned on her heel and strode confidently out of the bathroom. Hanna followed, her mouth open in awe.

That was the most surreal thing of the night. Maybe if she had to see Kate again, it wouldn't be a fate worse than death. It might even be . . . *fun.*

26

AT LEAST SHE DOESN'T
HAVE TO SING BACKUP

By the time Spencer and Andrew got to Foxy, the place was mobbed. The valet line was twenty cars long, the wanna-bes who hadn't been invited swarmed around the entrance, and the main tent was jammed with kids at tables, around the bar, and on the dance floor.

As Andrew made his way back from the drinks table, Spencer checked her cell phone again. *Still* no calls from Wren. She paced around the cross-shaped marble pattern on the dining hall's floor, wondering why she was here. Andrew had come to pick her up, and, despite all her anxiety, Spencer had put her drama club skills to use and fooled her family into thinking they were an item—giving Andrew a little kiss near the lips when she saw him, graciously accepting his flowers, posing for a picture, her cheek pressed to his. Andrew had seemed giddily flustered, which helped all the more with the ruse.

Now she had no use for him, but unfortunately he

didn't know that. He kept introducing Spencer to every-one—people they both *knew*—as his date. What she really wanted to do was to go into a quiet room and think. She needed to untangle what that cop, Wilden, knew, and what he didn't. If Toby was A *and* Ali's killer, he wouldn't be talking with the police. But what if Toby wasn't A . . . and A *had* told the police something?

"I think they're doing karaoke." Andrew pointed at the stage. Sure enough, some girl was belting out "I Will Survive." "Want to sing something?"

"I don't think so," Spencer said anxiously, fiddling with the pin of her corsage. She looked around for the fiftieth time for her old friends, hoping they would appear. She felt she had to warn them about Toby—*and* the cops. A had told her not to, but maybe she could do it in code.

"Well, maybe you'll do one with me?" Andrew coaxed.

Spencer turned to him. Andrew looked just like one of her family's labradoodles, begging for table scraps. "Didn't I just say I didn't want to?"

"Oh." Andrew fiddled with his paisley tie. "Sorry."

In the end, she agreed to sing backup for Christina Aguilera's "Dirrty"—so asinine that squeaky-clean Andrew chose to sing *that* song—because it was easier that way. Now Mona Vanderwaal and Celeste What's-her-name—she went to the Quaker school—were onstage singing "Total Eclipse of the Heart." They already seemed tipsy, holding each other's arms for balance, and repeatedly dropping their suede mini bags on the floor.

"We're going to be way better than them," Andrew said. He was standing too close. Spencer felt his hot, Orbit gum–minty breath and bristled. Wren breathing heavily on her neck was one thing, but Andrew was quite another. If she didn't get some air right now, she might pass out. "I'll be back," she murmured to Andrew, and fumbled toward the door.

As soon as she passed through the terrace's French doors, her phone vibrated. She flinched. When she looked at the LED screen, her heart lifted. *Wren.*

"Are you all right?" Spencer said as she answered. "I was so worried!"

"You've left twelve messages," Wren replied. "What's going on?"

Spencer could feel the stress seeping out of her and her shoulders relaxing. "I . . . I didn't hear from you, and I thought . . . Why didn't you check your voice mail?"

Wren cleared his throat, sounding a little uncomfortable. "I was busy. That's all."

"But I thought you were—"

"What?" Wren said, sort of laughing. "In a gutter? C'mon, Spence."

"But . . ." Spencer paused, trying to figure out how to explain. "I just had a weird feeling."

"Well, I'm fine." Wren paused. "Are *you* fine?"

"Yeah," Spencer answered, smiling a little. "I mean,

I'm here at my lame-ass dance, with my lame-ass date, and I'd rather be with you, but I'm so much better now. I'm glad you're okay."

When she hung up, she was so relieved, she wanted to run up and kiss a random person on the terrace—like Adriana Peoples, the Catholic school girl who was sitting on the Dionysus statue, smoking a clove. Or Liam Olsen, the ice hockey player who was fondling his date. Or Andrew Campbell, who was standing behind her, looking forlorn and useless. When it registered in Spencer's brain that Andrew was, well, *Andrew*, her stomach clenched.

"Um, hey," she said haltingly. "How . . . how long have you been standing there?"

But by the dejected look on Andrew's face, Spencer realized he'd been standing there just long enough. "Listen," she said, sighing. She might as well just cut this off at its nerve center. "The truth is, Andrew, I hope you don't think anything's going to happen between us. I have a boyfriend."

At first, Andrew looked stunned. Then hurt, then embarrassed, then angry. The emotions passed so quickly over his face, it was like watching a sunset in time-lapse photography. "I know," he said, pointing to her Sidekick. "I heard your conversation."

Of course you did. "I'm sorry," Spencer answered. "But I—"

Andrew held up his hand to stop her. "So why bring me and not him? Is he some guy your parents don't want you to date? So you come with me, thinking you have them totally fooled?"

"No," Spencer said quickly, feeling a twinge of discomfort. Was she that transparent, or was Andrew just a lucky guesser? "It's . . . it's hard to explain. I thought we could have fun. I didn't mean to hurt you."

A lock of hair fell over Andrew's eyes. "You could've fooled me." He turned for the door.

"Andrew!" Spencer cried. "Wait!" As she watched him disappear through the crowd of kids, a cold, uneasy feeling washed over her. She'd definitely picked the wrong boy as her fake date. It would've been better to go with Ryan Vreeland, who was in the closet, or Thayer Anderson, who was too into basketball to date girls seriously.

She ran into the main tent and looked around; she at least owed Andrew an apology. The whole place was lit by candles, however, so it was hard to find anyone. She could just make out Noel and the Quaker school girl on the dance floor, sneaking drinks out of Noel's flask. Naomi Zeigler and James Freed were now onstage, singing some Avril Lavigne song Spencer couldn't stand. Mason Byers and Devon Arliss leaned in to kiss. Kirsten Cullen and Bethany Wells whispered in the corner.

"Andrew?" she called.

Then Spencer noticed Emily across the room. She wore a strapless pink dress and had a pink pashmina thrown over her shoulders. Spencer took a few steps toward her, but then noticed her date standing next to her, his hand on her arm. Just as Spencer squinted to get a better look, the guy turned his head and noticed her. He had dark, denim-blue eyes, the same exact color they'd been in her dream.

Spencer gasped and stepped back.

I'll show up when you least expect it.

It was Toby.

27

ARIA IS AVAILABLE BY PRESCRIPTION ONLY

Aria leaned against the Foxy bar and ordered a cup of black coffee. It was so crowded in this tent that the lining of her polka-dotted dress was already drenched with sweat. And she'd only been here for twenty minutes.

"Hey." Her brother sidled up next to her. He wore the same gray suit he'd worn to the funeral and polished black shoes that belonged to Byron.

"Hey," Aria squeaked, surprised. "I . . . I didn't know you were coming." By the time she'd gotten out of the shower to get ready for Foxy, the house was empty. In a moment's confusion, she'd thought her family had abandoned her.

"Yeah. I came with . . ." Mike whirled around and pointed to a thin, pale girl Aria recognized from Noel Kahn's party the week before. "Hot, huh?"

"Yeah." Aria downed her coffee in three gulps and

noticed that her hands were shaking. This was her fourth cup in an hour.

"So where's Sean?" Mike asked. "That's who you're here with, right? Everyone's talking about it."

"They are?" Aria asked faintly.

"Yeah. You're like the new It couple."

Aria didn't know whether to laugh or cry. She could just picture some of the Rosewood Day girls gossiping about her and Sean. "I don't know where he is."

"Why? Did the It couple break up already?"

"No . . ." The truth was, Aria was sort of hiding from Sean.

Yesterday, after Meredith told Aria that she and Byron were in love, Aria had run back to Sean and burst into tears. Never in a gazillion years had she expected Meredith to say what she said. Now that Aria knew the truth, she felt helpless. Her family was doomed. For ten minutes, she'd wailed into Sean's shoulder, *What am I going to doooooo?* Sean calmed her down enough to take her home and even walked her up to her room, put her into bed, and laid her favorite stuffed animal, Pigtunia, on the pillow beside her.

As soon as Sean left, Aria threw back the covers and paced. She peeked into the bedroom. Her mom was there, sleeping peacefully . . . alone. But Aria couldn't wake her. When she woke up a few hours later, she went to her bedroom again, steeling herself to *just do it*, but this time, Byron was in bed beside Ella. He lay on his side, with his arm slung over Ella's shoulder.

Now why would you cuddle, if you were in love with someone else?

In the morning, when Aria awoke from her one big hour of sleep, her eyes were puffy and her skin had broken out in little red bumps. She felt hungover, and as she ran over the night's events, she crawled back under her duvet in shame. Sean had *tucked her in*. She'd blown *snot* on his shoulder. She'd wailed like an insane person. What better way to lose the guy you like than slobber all over him? When Sean picked her up for Foxy—amazing that he'd even shown up at all—he immediately wanted to talk about last night, but Aria shrugged him off, saying she felt much better. Sean looked at her sort of funny, but was smart enough not to ask questions. And now she was dodging him.

Mike leaned up against the wooden Foxy bar, bobbing his head when the DJ put on Franz Ferdinand. There was a self-satisfied little smile on his face—Aria knew he felt like the man for scoring a Foxy ticket, since he was only a sophomore. But she was his sister, and she could see pain and sadness underneath. It was like when they were little and hanging out at the community pool, and Mike's friends were calling him a homo because he was wearing white swim trunks that had turned pinkish in the wash. Mike tried to take it like a man, but later, during adult swim, Aria caught him secretly crying by the baby pool.

She wanted to say something to make him feel better. About how she was sorry for what she was going to have to tell Ella—Aria was going to tell her mom that night when she got home, no excuses—and that none of this was his fault, and if their family fell apart, it would still be okay. Somehow.

But she knew what would happen if she tried. Mike would just run away.

Aria grabbed her coffee and strode away from the bar. She just needed to be moving. "Aria," called a voice behind her. She turned. Sean was about six feet away, near one of the tables. He looked upset.

Panicked, Aria put her drink down and dashed toward the women's bathroom. One of her chunky wedges slid right off her foot. Jamming it back on, she kept pushing forward, only to get stuck at a wall of kids. She tried to elbow her way through, but no one was moving.

"Hey." Sean was right next to her.

"Oh," Aria yelled over the music, trying to act nonchalant. "Hi."

Sean took Aria by the arm and led her into the parking lot, which was the one place at Foxy that was empty. Sean retrieved his keys from the valet. He helped Aria into his car and drove to an empty spot farther down the driveway.

"What's going on with you?" Sean demanded.

"Nothing." Aria stared out the window. "I'm fine."

"No, you're not. You're like . . . a zombie. It's freaking me out."

"I just . . ." Aria ran the strand of pearls she'd worn as a bracelet up and down her wrist. "I don't know. I don't want to bother you."

"Why not?"

She shrugged. "Because you don't want to hear it. You must think I'm a complete freak. Like, I'm super-obsessed with my parents. It's all I've talked about."

"Well . . . it sort of has been. But I mean—"

"I wouldn't be mad," she interrupted, "if you wanted to dance with other girls and whatever. There are some really cute girls here."

Sean blinked, his face blank. "But I don't want to dance with anyone else."

They were quiet. The bass line of Kanye West's "Gold Digger" pumped out of the tent.

"You thinking about your parents?" Sean asked quietly.

She nodded. "I guess. I have to tell my mom tonight."

"Why do *you* have to tell her?"

"Because . . ." Aria couldn't tell him about A. "It has to be me. This can't go on any longer."

Sean sighed. "You put a lot of pressure on yourself. Can't you take a night off?"

At first, Aria felt defensive, but then she leaned back. "I really think you should go back in there, Sean. You shouldn't let me ruin your night."

"Aria . . ." Sean let out a frustrated sigh. "Stop it."

Aria made a face. "I just don't think it's going to work out for us."

"Why?"

"Because . . ." She paused, trying to figure out what she wanted to say. Because she wasn't the typical Rosewood girl? Because whatever Sean liked about her, there was so much else about her *not* to like? She felt like she was one of those wonder drugs that were always advertised on TV. The narrator would go through paragraphs of how the drug had helped millions of people, but at the very end of the commercial, he'd say really quietly that side effects include heart palpitations and an oily discharge. With her, it'd be like, *Cool, kooky girl . . . but family baggage may result in psycho outbursts and randomly blowing snot on your expensive shirts.*

Sean carefully put his hand over Aria's. "If you're scared that I'm freaked about last night, I'm not. I really like you. I sort of like you more *because* of last night."

Tears came to Aria's eyes. "Really?"

"Really."

He pressed his forehead to hers. Aria held her breath. Finally, their lips touched. Then again. Harder, this time.

Aria pressed her mouth to his and grabbed the back of his neck, pulling him closer. His body felt so warm and right. Sean ran his hands up Aria's waist. All at once, they were biting each other's bottom lips, their hands scratching up and down each other's backs. Then they broke away, breathing heavily and staring into each other's eyes.

They dove back for each other. Sean pulled at the zipper on Aria's dress. He flung off his jacket and threw it into the backseat, and she pawed at the buttons on his shirt. She kissed Sean's gorgeous ears and ran her hands inside his shirt, to his smooth, bare skin. He circled her waist with his hands as best he could, his body at an awkward angle on the cramped Audi seat. Sean tilted the seat back, lifted Aria up, and brought her to him. The knobs of her spine grated against the steering wheel.

She arched her neck as Sean kissed her throat. When she opened her eyes, she saw something—a yellow piece of paper under the windshield wiper. At first she thought it was some sort of flyer—maybe a kid advertising some after-Foxy party—but then she noticed the big, bulky words, written sloppily in black Sharpie marker.

Don't forget! Stroke of midnight!

She jerked away from Sean.

"What is it?" he asked.

She pointed at the note, her hands shaking. "Did you write that?" It was a stupid question, though: She already knew the answer.

28

IT'S NOT A PARTY
WITHOUT HANNA MARIN

As her taxi pulled up to Kingman Hall, Hanna threw twenty bucks at the cabdriver, an older, balding guy who seemed to have a sweating problem. "Keep it," she said. She slammed the door and ran for the entrance, her stomach roiling. She'd bought a bag of Cool Ranch Doritos at the train station in Philly and had maniacally scarfed down the whole thing in five frantic minutes. Bad move.

To her right was the Foxy check-in table. A whippet-thin girl with close-cropped blond hair and tons of eyeliner was collecting tickets and checking off names in her book. Hanna hesitated. She had no idea where her ticket was, but if she tried to bargain her way in, they'd just tell her to go home. She narrowed her eyes at the Foxy tent, which glowed like a birthday cake. There was no way she was letting Sean get away with this. She was getting into Foxy, whether Eyeliner Girl liked it or not.

Taking a deep breath, Hanna sprinted at top speed past the check-in table. "Hey!" she heard the girl call. "Wait!"

Hanna hid behind a column, her heart beating fast. A beefy bouncer in a tux ran by her, then stopped and looked around. Frustrated and confused, he shrugged and said something into his walkie-talkie. Hanna felt a little satisfied thrill. Sneaking in gave her the same rush as stealing.

Foxy was a blur of kids. She couldn't remember it ever being this packed. Most of the girls on the dance floor had taken their shoes off, and they held them in the air as they spun. There was an equally enormous crowd by the bar, and more kids were gathered in line by what looked like a karaoke booth. By the looks of the neatly set, empty tables, they hadn't served dinner yet.

Hanna grabbed the elbow of Amanda Williamson, a Rosewood Day sophomore who always tried to say hi to Hanna in the halls. Amanda's face lit up. "*Heyyy*, Hanna!"

"Have you seen Sean?" Hanna barked.

A surprised look crossed Amanda's face; then she shrugged. "I'm not sure. . . ."

Hanna pressed on, her heart pounding. Maybe he wasn't here. She switched directions, nearly colliding with a waiter carrying a huge tray of cheese. Hanna grabbed an enormous chunk of cheddar and shoved it in her mouth. She swallowed without even tasting it.

"Hanna!" Naomi Zeigler, dressed in a gold sheath and looking very faux-tanned, cried. "How fun! You're here! I thought you said you weren't coming!"

Hanna frowned. Naomi was clutching James Freed. She pointed to both of them. "You guys came together?" Hanna had thought maybe Naomi was Sean's date.

Naomi nodded. Then she leaned forward. "Are you looking for Sean?" She shook her head, awestruck. "It's all *everyone's* been talking about. I seriously can't believe it."

Hanna's heart sped up. "So Sean's here?"

"He's here, all right." James ducked, pulled a Coke bottle full of a suspicious-looking clear liquid from his inside jacket pocket, and dumped it into his orange juice. He took a sip and smiled.

"I mean, they're so *different*," Naomi mused. "You said you guys were still friends, right? Did he tell you why he asked her?"

"Lay off." James nudged Naomi. "She's sexy."

"*Who?*" Hanna screamed. Why did everyone know about this but her?

"There they are." Naomi pointed across the room.

It was as if the sea of kids parted and a huge spotlight beamed down from the ceiling. Sean was in the corner by the karaoke machine, hugging a tall girl in a black-and-white polka-dotted dress. He had his head crooked around her neck, and her hands were dangerously close to his butt. Then the girl turned her head, and Hanna saw the familiar elfin, exotic features, and that trademark blue-black hair. *Aria.*

Hanna screamed.

"Oh my God, I can't believe you didn't know." Naomi put a consoling arm around Hanna's shoulder.

Hanna shook her off and stormed across the room, right up to Aria and Sean, who were hugging. Not dancing, just hugging. *Freaks.*

After Hanna stood there for a few seconds, Aria opened one eye, then the other. She made a little gasping noise. "Um, hey, Hanna."

Hanna stood there, quivering with rage. "You . . . you *bitch.*"

Sean stepped defensively in front of Aria. "Hold up. . . ."

"Hold *up*?" Hanna's voice danced up the scale. She pointed at Sean; she was so angry, her finger was shaking. "You . . . you told me you weren't coming because your friends were all bringing dates, and you didn't want to!"

Sean shrugged. "Things changed."

Hanna's cheeks stung, as if he'd slapped her. "But we're going on a *date* this week!"

"We're going out to *dinner* this week," Sean corrected. "As friends." He smiled at her like she was a slow kindergartner. "We broke up last Friday, Hanna. Remember?"

Hanna blinked. "And, what, you're with *her*?"

"Well . . ." Sean looked at Aria. "Yeah."

Hanna clutched her hand to her stomach, certain she

was going to puke. This had to be a joke. Sean and Aria made about as much sense as a fat girl wearing skinny leggings.

Then she noticed Aria's dress. The side zipper was undone, revealing half of Aria's lacy black strapless bra. "Your boob's hanging out," she growled, pointing.

Aria quickly looked down, folded her arms over her chest, and zipped her dress up.

"Where'd you get that dress, anyway?" Hanna asked. "Luella for Target?"

Aria straightened her back. "Actually, yeah. I thought it was cute."

"God." Hanna rolled her eyes. "You're such a martyr." She looked at Sean. "Actually, I guess you guys have that in common. Did you know Sean's pledged to be a virgin till he's thirty, Aria? He might've tried to feel you up, but he's never going to go all the way. He's made a sacred *promise*."

"Hanna!" Sean shushed her.

"I personally think it's because he's gay. What do you think?"

"Hanna . . ." Now there was a pleading tone in Sean's voice.

"What?" Hanna challenged. "You're a liar, Sean. And an asshole."

When Hanna looked around, she saw that a group of kids had gathered. The ones who were always invited to the parties, the ones who were interchangeably hooking up.

The girls who weren't *quite* cool enough, the overweight boys everyone kept around only because they were funny, the rich kids who spent oodles of money on everyone because they were cute or interesting or manipulative. They were hungrily eating this up. The whispers had already started.

Hanna took a final look at Sean, but instead of saying anything else, she fled.

At the girls' bathroom, she marched straight to the front of the line. As someone was coming out of a stall, Hanna shoved her way in. "Bitch!" someone screamed, but Hanna didn't care. Once the door was shut, she leaned over the toilet and got rid of the Doritos and everything else she'd eaten that night. When she was done, she sobbed.

The looks on everyone's faces. The *pity*. And Hanna had cried in front of people. It had been one of Hanna and Mona's first rules after they reinvented themselves: Never, *ever* let anyone see you cry. And more than any of that, she just felt so naïve. Hanna had really believed Sean was going to take her back. She'd thought by going to the burn clinic and V Club, she was making a difference, but all this time . . . he'd been thinking of someone else.

When she finally pushed open the door, the bathroom was empty. It was so quiet, she could hear water dripping into the mosaic-tiled basin. Hanna glanced at herself in the mirror, to see how bad she looked. When she did, she gasped.

A very different Hanna stared back. This Hanna was chubby, with poopy brown hair and bad skin. She had braces with pink rubber bands, and her eyes were narrowed from squinting because she didn't want to wear her glasses. Her tan blazer strained against her pudgy arms, and her blouse buckled at the bra line.

Hanna covered her eyes in horror. *It's A,* she thought. *A's doing this to me.*

Then, she thought of A's note: *Get to Foxy now. Sean's there with another girl.* If A had known Sean was at Foxy with another girl, then it meant . . .

A was at Foxy.

"Hey."

Hanna jumped and whirled around. Mona stood in the doorway. She looked gorgeous in a slinky black dress Hanna didn't recognize from their shopping expedition. Her pale hair was swept back from her face, and her skin shimmered. Embarrassed—she probably had puke on her face—Hanna made a beeline back to the stall.

"Wait." Mona caught her arm. When Hanna whirled back around, Mona looked earnest and concerned. "Naomi said you weren't coming tonight."

Hanna peeked at herself in the mirror again. Her reflection showed the eleventh-grade Hanna, not the seventh-grade one. Her eyes were a bit red, but otherwise she looked fine.

"It's Sean, isn't it?" Mona asked. "I just got here

and saw him with *her*." She lowered her head. "I'm so sorry, Han."

Hanna shut her eyes. "I feel like such an ass," she admitted.

"You're not. *He's* the ass."

They looked at each other. Hanna felt a rush of regret. Mona's friendship meant so much to her, and she'd been letting everything else get in the way. She couldn't remember why they were fighting. "I'm so sorry, Mon. About everything."

"*I'm* sorry," Mona said. And then they hugged, squeezing extra hard.

"Oh my God, there you are."

Spencer Hastings strode across the bathroom's marble floor and pulled Hanna out of the hug. "I need to talk to you."

Hanna pulled away, annoyed. "What? Why?"

Spencer glanced shifty-eyed at Mona. "I can't tell you right here. You have to come with me."

"Hanna doesn't have to go anywhere." Mona took Hanna's arm and pulled her close.

"This time, she does." Spencer's voice rose. "It's an emergency."

Mona clamped down on Hanna's arm. She had the same forbidding expression from the other day, at the mall—the look that said, *If you keep one more secret from me, I swear, that's it between us.* But Spencer looked terrified. Something felt wrong. *Very* wrong.

"I'm sorry," Hanna said, touching Mona's hand. "I'll be right back."

Mona dropped her arm. "Fine," she said angrily, walking to the mirror to inspect her makeup. "Take your time."

29

LET IT ALL OUT

Spencer wordlessly led Hanna out of the bathroom and past a clump of kids. Then she noticed Aria standing near the bar, alone. "You're coming too."

Hanna dropped Spencer's hand. "I'm not going anywhere she's going."

"Hanna, you told everyone you dumped Sean!" Aria protested. "In English?"

Hanna crossed her arms over her chest. "It didn't mean I wanted you to come here with him. It didn't mean I wanted you to *steal* him."

"I'm not stealing anything!" Aria screamed, raising her fist. Spencer worried for a second that Aria might try to hit Hanna and inserted her body between the two of them.

"That's *it*," she said. "Just stop it. We have to find Emily." Before they could protest, she dragged them past the ice sculptures, the karaoke line, and the jewelry auction tables. Spencer had just seen Emily not twenty minutes ago, but now Emily was gone. She passed Andrew, sitting at a long, candlelit table with his friends. He noticed her, then quickly turned back to his friends and barked out a loud, fake laugh, obviously for her benefit. Spencer felt a twinge of remorse. But she couldn't deal with him now.

Tightening her grip on the girls' hands, she strode past the tables out to the terrace. Kids were gathered around the fountain, dipping their bare feet, but still no Emily. By the giant statue of Pan, Hanna started to moan. "I have to go."

"You can't go yet." Spencer pushed Aria and Hanna back into the dining room. "This is important for all of us. We have to find Emily."

"Why is that so important?" Hanna wailed. "Who the hell cares?"

"Because." Spencer stopped. "She's here with Toby."

"So?" Aria asked.

Spencer took a deep breath. "I think . . . I think maybe Toby's going to try to hurt her. I think he wants to hurt all of us."

The girls looked shocked. "Why?" Aria demanded, her hands on her hips.

Spencer looked at the ground. Her stomach felt tight. "I think A is Toby."

"What makes you think that?" Aria looked angry.

"A sent me a note," she admitted. "It says we're all in danger."

"You got a note?" Hanna shrieked. "I thought we were going to tell each other!"

"I know." Spencer stared at her pointy Louboutins. Back inside the tent, some of the boys were having a break-dancing contest. Noel Kahn was trying to do a kickworm, and Mason Byers was doing some sort of butt-spin. Wasn't this supposed to be a *civilized* function? "I didn't know what to do. I . . . I actually got two notes. The first one said that it would be better if I *didn't* tell you guys. But the second one really sounded like it was Toby . . . and now Toby's here with Emily, and—"

"Wait, the first note said we were in trouble, and you did nothing?" Hanna asked. She didn't sound angry, exactly, just confused.

"I wasn't sure it was for real," Spencer said. She ran her hand through her hair. "I mean, if I'd known—"

"You know, I got a note too," Aria said softly.

Spencer blinked at her. "You did? Was it about Toby too?"

"No . . ." Aria seemed to consider her words. "Spencer, why were you at that yoga studio Friday?"

"Yoga studio?" Spencer narrowed her eyes. "What does that have to do with . . . ?"

"It was a *little* too much of a coincidence," Aria went on.

"What are you talking about?" Spencer cried.

Hanna interrupted. "Aria, was your note about Sean?"

"*No.*" Aria turned to Hanna and creased her brow.

"Well, I'm *sorry!*" Hanna spat. "I got a text from A, too, and it *was* about Sean! It said that he was at Foxy with another girl . . . *you!*"

"You guys . . ." Spencer warned, not wanting to get into this argument again. Then she knit her eyebrows together. "Wait. When did you get a text, Hanna?"

"Earlier tonight."

"So, that means . . ." Aria pointed at Hanna. "If your note from A said Sean was at Foxy with me, it meant A saw us. Which means—"

"A is at Foxy. I know," Hanna finished, giving Aria a tight smile.

Spencer's heart pounded. It was really happening. A was here . . . and A was Toby.

"Come on." Spencer led them into the long, narrow hall that led to the auction room. By day, the hall was stuffy and very Philadelphia, with tons of Mission end tables, oily portraits of grumpy, rich men, and creaky wood floors, but by night, each table held an aromatherapy candle, and the wainscoting was decorated with different-colored lights. As the girls paused under a blue bulb, they looked like corpses.

"Run this by me again, Spencer," Aria said slowly. "Your first note said that you shouldn't tell us. But shouldn't tell us what? That you got a note? That A was Toby?"

"No . . ." Spencer turned to face them. "I wasn't supposed to tell you what I knew. About The Jenna Thing."

Horror crossed the girls' faces. *Here it comes,* Spencer thought. She took a deep breath. "The truth is . . . Toby saw Ali light that firework. He's known all along."

Aria stepped back and bumped into a table. A piece of pottery wavered, then fell off, shattering all over the wood floor. No one moved to clean it up.

"You're lying," Hanna whispered.

"I wish I was."

"What do you mean, *Toby saw*?" Aria's voice was quivery. "Ali said he didn't."

Spencer wrung her hands together. "He told me he saw. Me and Ali, actually."

Her friends blinked at her, stunned.

"The night Jenna got hurt, when I ran out to see what was going on, Toby came up to Ali and me. He said he saw Ali . . . do it." Spencer's voice was trembling. She'd had nightmares so many times about this very moment; it was surreal to be *in it.*

"Ali stepped in," she went on. "She told Toby she'd seen him do something . . . *awful* . . . and she was going to tell everyone. The only way she wouldn't was if Toby took the blame. Before Toby ran off he said, *I'll get you.* But the next day, he confessed."

Spencer ran her hand along the back of her neck. Saying this out loud transported her right back to that night. She could smell the sulfur from the lit firework, and the freshly mown grass. She could see Ali, her blond hair pulled back in a ponytail, wearing the pearl teardrop earrings she'd gotten for her eleventh birthday. Tears came to her eyes.

Spencer swallowed and continued. "The second note A sent me said, *You hurt me, so I'm going to hurt you*, and that he was going to show up when we least expected it. A cop came to my house this morning, too, asking me about Ali again, and this cop was *grilling* me, acting like I knew something I shouldn't. I thought Toby might've been behind it. Now he's brought Emily here. I'm afraid he might hurt her."

It took Aria and Hanna a long time to respond. Finally, Aria's hands started shaking. A deep red patch crept up her neck into her cheeks. "Why didn't you tell us before?" She squinted uncertainly at Spencer, searching for words. "I mean, there was that time, in seventh grade, when I was *alone* with Toby, at that drama thing! He could've hurt me . . . or all of us . . . and if he really hurt Ali, we could've helped save her!"

"I feel sick," Hanna moaned distantly.

Tears ran down Spencer's cheeks. "I wanted to tell you guys, but I was scared."

"What did Ali say to blackmail Toby so he wouldn't tell?" Aria demanded.

"Ali wouldn't say," Spencer lied. She felt superstitious about telling Toby's secret, as if as soon as she said it, a bolt of lightning would descend through the skylight . . . or Toby would appear, supernaturally having heard everything.

Aria stared at her hands. "Toby's known *all along*," she repeated again.

"And now he's . . . back." Hanna looked positively green.

"He's not only back," Spencer said. "He's *here*. And he's A."

Aria grabbed Hanna's arm. "Come on."

"Where are you going?" Spencer called nervously. She didn't want Aria out of her sight.

Aria turned halfway around. "We have to find Emily," she said angrily. She picked up the hem of her dress and started running.

30

CORNFIELDS ARE THE SCARIEST PLACE IN ROSEWOOD

Emily had shoved herself into a little back alcove on the Kingman Hall terrace and was quietly watching all of the Foxy smokers. The girls in their frilly, pastel dresses, the boys in their elegant suits. But who was she watching *more*? She wasn't sure. She shut her eyes tight, then opened them fast, and the first person she noticed was Tara Kelley, a Rosewood Day senior. She had bright red hair and beautiful, pale skin. Emily gritted her teeth and shut her eyes again. When she opened them, she saw Ori Case, the hot football player. A *guy*. There.

But then she couldn't help but notice Rachel Firestein's thin, giraffelike arms. Chloe Davis made a sexy, teasing face at her date, Chad Something-or-other, that made her mouth look adorable. Elle Carmichael tilted her chin just so. Emily caught a whiff of someone's Michael Kors perfume and had never smelled anything so yummy in her life. Except, maybe, for banana gum.

It couldn't be true. It *couldn't*.

"What are you doing?"

Toby stood above her. "I . . ." Emily stuttered.

"I've been looking all over for you. Are you all right?"

Emily took stock: She was hiding in an alcove on a freezing-cold balcony, using her pashmina as a cloaking device, and doing a deranged peek-a-boo to test herself whether she liked boys or girls. She turned her eyes to Toby. She wanted to explain what had just happened. With Ben, with Maya, with the tarot reader—everything. "You might hate me for asking this, but . . . do you mind if we leave?"

Toby smiled. "I was *hoping* you'd ask that." He pulled Emily up by her wrists.

On their way out, Emily noticed Spencer Hastings standing on the edge of the dance floor. Spencer's back was to Emily, and Emily considered going up and saying hello. Then Toby pulled on her hand, and she decided against it. Spencer might ask her something about A, and she was in no mood to talk about any of *that* right now.

As they pulled out of the parking lot, Emily rolled down the window. The night smelled delicious, like pine needles and oncoming rain. The moon was huge and full, and thick clouds began to roll in. It was so quiet outside, Emily could hear the car's tires slapping along the pavement.

"You sure you're okay?" Toby asked.

Emily jumped a little. "Yeah, I'm fine." She glanced at

Toby. He told her he'd bought a new suit for this, and now she was making him go home three hours early. "I'm sorry the night sucked."

"It's cool." Toby shrugged.

Emily turned over the little Tiffany box that sat in her lap. She'd plucked one off the table right before she left the tent, figuring she might as well get her parting gift.

"So nothing happened?" Toby asked. "You're so quiet."

Emily blew air out of her cheeks. She watched three different cornfields roll by before she answered. "I was accosted by a tarot card reader."

Toby frowned, not understanding.

"She just said that something was going to happen to me tonight. Something, um, life-changing." Emily tried to muster up a laugh. Toby opened his mouth to say something, then quickly shut it.

"Thing was, it kind of came true," Emily said. "I ran into that guy, Ben. The one who was in the hallway at the Tank, who was . . . you know. Anyway, he tried . . . I don't know. I guess he tried to hurt me."

"*What?*"

"It's okay. I'm all right. He just . . ." Emily's chin trembled. "I don't know. Maybe I deserved it."

"Why?" Toby clenched his teeth. "What did you do?"

Emily picked at the gift's white bow. Raindrops began to spatter the windshield. She took a deep breath. Was she really going to say this out loud? "Ben and I used to date. When we were still together, he caught me kissing someone else. A girl. He was calling me a dyke, and when I tried to tell him that I wasn't, he tried to make me prove it. Like kiss him and . . . whatever. That's what was happening when you came into the locker room hall."

Toby shifted in his seat uncomfortably.

Emily ran her hands along the white gardenia Toby had given her as a corsage. "The thing is, maybe I *am* a dyke. I mean, I did, like, *love* Alison DiLaurentis. But I thought it was only Ali I loved, not that I was a lesbian. Now . . . now I don't know. Maybe Ben's right. Maybe I *am* gay. Maybe I should just deal with it."

Emily couldn't believe all that had just spilled from her mouth. She turned to Toby. His mouth was a fixed, impassive line. She thought maybe that if there was a time to admit that he'd been Ali's boyfriend, now would be it. Instead, he said quietly, "Why are you so afraid to admit that?"

"Because!" Emily laughed. Wasn't it obvious? "Because I don't want to *be* . . . you know. Gay." And then, in a quieter voice: "Everyone would make fun of me."

They rolled up to a deserted two-way stop sign. Instead of pausing and rolling through, Toby put the car into park. Emily was puzzled. "What are we doing?"

Toby took his hands off the steering wheel and stared at Emily for a long time. So long, Emily began to feel uncomfortable. He seemed upset. She touched the back of her neck, then turned away and looked out the window. The road was silent and dead and paralleled yet another cornfield, one of Rosewood's biggest. The rain was coming down harder now, and because Toby didn't turn on the windshield wipers, everything was blurry. She wished, suddenly, for civilization. For a car to drive by. A house to appear. A gas station. Something. Was Toby upset because he liked her, and she'd just come halfway out of the closet? Was Toby *homophobic*? This was what she would have to deal with, if she really thought she was gay. People would probably do this to her every day of her life.

"You've never been on that end of it, have you?" Toby finally asked. "You've never had anyone make fun of you."

"N-No . . ." She searched Toby's face, trying to understand his question. "I guess not. Well, not until Ben, anyway." Thunder cracked overhead, and she jumped. Then she saw a zigzag of lightning, slashing across the sky a few miles ahead of them. It lit things up for a moment, and Emily could see Toby frowning, picking at a button on his jacket.

"Seeing all those people tonight just made me realize how hard it used to be, living in Rosewood," he said. "People used to really hate me. But tonight, everyone was so nice—all these people who used to make fun of me. It was sickening. It was like it had never happened." He wrinkled his nose. "Do they not realize what assholes they were?"

"I guess not," Emily said, feeling uneasy.

Toby glanced at her. "I saw one of your old friends there. Spencer Hastings." Lightning flashed again, making Emily jump. Toby smiled crookedly. "You guys were such a clique, back then. You really let people have it. Me . . . my sister . . ."

"We didn't mean to," Emily said, on instinct.

"Emily." Toby shrugged. "You did. And why not? You were the most popular girls in school. You *could*." His voice was sharply sarcastic.

Emily tried to smile, hoping that this was a joke. Only Toby didn't smile back. Why were they talking about *this*? Weren't they supposed to be talking about Emily being gay? "I'm sorry. We just . . . We were so stupid. We did what Ali wanted us to do. And I mean, I thought you were over that, since you and Ali got together that next year—"

"*What?*" Toby interrupted sharply.

Emily backed against the window. Her chest burned with adrenaline. "You . . . you weren't fooling around with Ali in, um, seventh grade?"

Toby looked horrified. "It was hard for me even to *see* her," he said quietly. "Now it's hard for me even to hear her name." He put his palms to his forehead and let out a huge breath. When he faced her again, his eyes were dark. "Especially after . . . after what she did."

Emily stared at him. Lightning flashed again, and a stiff wind kicked up, making the cornstalks sway. They looked like hands, desperately reaching out for something.

"Wait, what?" She laughed, hoping–praying–she'd heard him wrong. Praying that she'd blink, and the night would right itself and go back to being normal.

"I think you heard me," Toby said in a flat, emotionless tone. "I know you were friends and you loved her and whatever, but personally, I'm glad that bitch is dead."

Emily felt like someone had sucked all the oxygen out of her body. *Something's going to happen to you tonight. Something life-changing.*

You really let people have it. Me . . . my sister . . .

It's hard for me even to hear her name. Especially after what she did . . .

AFTER WHAT SHE DID.

I'm glad that bitch is dead.

Toby . . . *knew?*

A crack started to form in her brain. He *did* know. She was sure of it, more certain than she'd ever been of anything in her life. Emily felt as if she'd always known this, that it had been right in front of her face, but she'd been trying to just ignore it. Toby knew what they'd done to Jenna, but A hadn't told him. He'd known for a very long time. And he must have hated Ali for it. He must have hated all of them, if he knew they were all involved.

"Oh my God," Emily whispered. She pulled at the door handle, gathering her dress in her hands as she stepped out of the car. The rain hit her immediately and felt like needles. Of course there was something suspicious about Toby being friendly to her. He wanted to ruin Emily's life.

"Emily?" Toby unbuckled his seat belt. "Where are you—"

Then she heard the engine roar. Toby was driving down the road toward her, the passenger door wide open. She looked right and left, and then, hoping she knew where she was, she dove into the cornfield, not even caring that she was getting absolutely soaked.

"Emily!" Toby called again. But Emily kept running.

Toby killed Ali. Toby was A.

31

LIKE HANNA WOULD STEAL AN AIRPLANE—SHE DOESN'T EVEN KNOW HOW TO FLY!

Hanna pushed her way through crowds of kids, hoping to see Emily's familiar reddish-blond hair. She found Spencer and Aria by the oversize windows, talking to Gemma Curran, one of Emily's swimming teammates.

"She was here with that guy from Tate, right?" Gemma pursed her lips and tried to think. "I'm pretty sure I saw them leave."

Hanna exchanged uneasy glances with her friends. "What are we going to do?" Spencer whispered. "It's not like we have any idea where they're going."

"I tried calling her," Aria said. "But her phone just kept ringing."

"Oh my God," Spencer said, her eyes filling up with tears.

"Well, what did you expect?" Aria said through her

teeth. "You're the one who let this happen." Hanna couldn't remember Aria ever being this angry.

"I know," Spencer repeated. "I'm sorry."

A huge *boom* interrupted them. Everyone looked outside to see the trees blowing sideways and rain coming down in sheets. "Shit," Hanna heard a girl say next to her. "My dress is going to be ruined."

Hanna faced her friends. "I know someone who can help us. A cop." She looked around, half-expecting Officer Wilden, the guy who'd arrested Hanna for stealing a Tiffany bracelet and Mr. Ackard's car *and* who'd gotten it on with her mom—to be at Foxy tonight. But the guys guarding the exits and the jewelry auction were the Foxhunting League's private security team—only if something devastating happened would they call in the cops. Last year, a Rosewood Day senior drank too much and ran off with a David Yurman bracelet that was up for auction, and even then they'd only left a tactful message on the boy's family's voice mail, saying that they'd like it back by the next day.

"We can't go to the *cops*," Spencer hissed. "The way the one cop was acting with me this morning, I wouldn't be surprised if they thought *we* killed Ali."

Hanna stared up at the giant crystal chandelier on the ceiling. A couple kids were tossing their napkins at it, trying to get the crystals to swing. "But I mean, your note pretty much says, *I'm gonna hurt you*, right? Isn't that enough?"

"It's signed *A*. And it said that *we* hurt him. How would we explain that?"

"But how do we make sure she's all right?" Aria asked, pulling up her polka-dotted dress. Hanna noted bitterly that the side zipper was still partially down.

"Maybe we should drive by her house," Spencer suggested.

"Sean and I could go right now," Aria volunteered.

Hanna's jaw dropped. "You're telling *Sean* about this?"

"No," Aria shouted, over the swells of Natasha Bedingfield and the pounding rain. Hanna could even see it fogging up the hall's skylight, thirty feet above their heads. "I won't tell him anything. Or I don't know how I'll explain it. But he won't know."

"So are you and Sean going to any after-parties?" Hanna pried.

Aria looked at her crazily. "You think I'd go to an after-party after all this?"

"Yeah, but if this hadn't happened, would you have gone?"

"Hanna." Spencer put her cool, thin hand on Hanna's shoulder. "Let it go."

Hanna gritted her teeth, grabbed a glass of champagne from a waitress's tray, and belted it down. She *couldn't* let it go. It wasn't possible.

"You check out Emily's house," Spencer said to Aria. "I'll keep calling her."

"What if we drive by Emily's and Toby is with her?"

Aria asked. "Do we confront him? I mean . . . if he *is* A . . . ?"

Hanna exchanged an uneasy glance with the others. She wanted to kick Toby's ass—how had he found out about Kate? Her father? Her arrests? How Sean had broken up with her and that she made herself puke? How dare he try to bring her down! But she was also afraid. If Toby was A—if he knew—then he really would want to hurt them. It made . . . sense.

"We should just concentrate on making sure Emily's safe," Spencer said. "How about, if we don't hear from her soon, we call the police and leave an anonymous tip. We could say we saw Toby hurt her. We wouldn't have to get into the specifics."

"If the cops come looking for him, he'll know it was us," Hanna reasoned. "And then what if he tells them about Jenna?" She could picture herself in juvenile hall, wearing an orange jumpsuit and talking to her father through a wall of glass.

"Or what if he comes after us?" Aria asked.

"We'll have to find her before that happens," Spencer interrupted.

Hanna looked at the clock. Ten-thirty. "I'm out." She strode toward the door. "I'll call you, Spencer." She didn't say anything to Aria. She couldn't even *look* at Aria. Or the giant hickey on her neck.

As she was leaving, Naomi Zeigler grabbed her hand. "Han, about what you said to me yesterday at the soccer game." She had the large-eyed, empathetic look of a talk-show host. "There are bulimia support groups. I could help you find one."

"Fuck off," Hanna said, and brushed past her.

By the time Hanna collapsed on the Philadelphia-bound SEPTA train, totally soaked from running from the cab to the train, her head felt heavy. In every reflection, a shadowy chimera of her seventh-grade self winked back. She shut her eyes.

When she opened her eyes again, the train had stalled. All the lights were out, except for the emergency glow-in-the-dark exit signs. Only, they didn't say EXIT anymore. They said WATCH IT.

To her left, Hanna saw miles of forest. The moon shone full and clear over the treetops. But hadn't it been pouring just minutes ago? The train paralleled Route 30 on the other side. The road was usually packed with traffic, but now, not a single car waited at the intersection. As she craned her neck down the aisle to see how the others were reacting to SEPTA's breakdown, she noticed that all the passengers were asleep.

"They're not asleep," a voice said. "They're dead."

Hanna jumped. It was Toby. His face was blurry, but she knew it was him. Slowly, he rose from his seat and walked over to her.

The train blew its whistle, and Hanna was jolted awake. The fluorescent lights were as bright and unflattering as ever; the train chugged toward the city; and outside, lightning crackled and danced. When she looked out the window, she saw a tree branch snap off and careen to the ground. Two white-haired old ladies in the seat ahead of her kept commenting on the lightning, saying, "Oh, goodness! That was a big one!"

Hanna pulled her knees up to her chest. Nothing like an earth-shattering confession about Toby Cavanaugh to rock your world. And make you paranoid as hell.

She wasn't sure how to take the news. She didn't react to things right away, like Aria did; she had to mull them over. She was angry at Spencer for not telling, yes. And terrified about Toby. But at the moment, her only overwhelming thoughts were about Jenna. Did she know, too? Had she known all along? Did she know that Toby had killed Ali?

Hanna had actually seen Jenna after her accident—just once, and she'd never told the others. It was just a few weeks before Ali went missing, and she'd thrown an impromptu party in her backyard. All of Rosewood Day's popular kids came—even some older girls from Ali's field hockey team. For the first time ever, Hanna was having a real conversation with Sean; they were talking about the movie *Gladiator*. Hanna was talking about how scary the movie was when Ali sauntered up beside them.

At first Ali gave Hanna a look that said, *Hooray! You're finally talking to him!* But then, when Hanna said, "When my dad and I came out of the theater, oh my God, I was so scared, I went straight to the bathroom and threw up," Ali nudged Hanna's side. "You've had some trouble with that lately, haven't you?" she joked.

Hanna paled. "*What?*" This wasn't long after the Annapolis thing happened.

Ali made sure she had Sean's attention. "This is Hanna," she said, and stuck her finger down her throat, gagged, and then giggled. Sean didn't laugh, however; he looked back and forth at them, seeming uncomfortable and confused. "I, um, have to . . ." he muttered, and slipped away to his friends.

Hanna turned to Ali, horrified. "*Why* did you do that?"

"Oh, Hanna," Ali said, whirling away. "Can't you take a joke?"

But Hanna couldn't. Not about that. She stomped to the other side of Ali's wraparound deck, heaving deep, angry breaths. When she looked up, she found herself staring right into Jenna Cavanaugh's face.

Jenna was standing at the edge of her property, wearing big sunglasses and carrying a white cane. Hanna's throat seized up. It was like seeing a ghost. *She really is blind,* Hanna thought. She sort of thought it hadn't actually happened.

Jenna stood very still on the curb. If she could have seen, she would have been looking at the big hole in Ali's side yard that they were digging for her family's twenty-seat gazebo—the exact spot where, years later, workers would find Ali's body. Hanna stared at her for a long time, and Jenna stared blankly back. Then it hit her. Back there, with Sean, Hanna had taken Jenna's place, and Ali had taken Hanna's. There was no reason for Ali to tease Hanna except that she *could*. The realization struck Hanna so forcefully, she had to grab onto the railing for balance.

She looked at Jenna again. *I'm so sorry,* she mouthed. Jenna, of course, didn't respond. She couldn't see.

Hanna was never so happy to see the lights of Philadelphia—she was finally far away from Rosewood and Toby. She still had time to get back to the hotel before her father, Isabel, and Kate returned from *Mamma Mia!,* and perhaps she could take a bubble bath. Hopefully there was something good in the minibar, too. Something strong. Perhaps she'd even tell Kate what happened and they'd order room service and kill a big bottle of something together.

Wow. *That* was a thought Hanna never imagined would cross her mind.

She slid her room card into the door, pulled it open, slumped inside, and . . . nearly bumped into her father. He was standing in front of the door, talking on his cell phone. "Oh!" she screamed.

Her father whirled around. "She's here," he said into the phone, then slapped it shut. He eyed Hanna coolly. "Well. Welcome back."

Hanna blinked. Beyond her father were Kate and

Isabel. Just . . . sitting there, on the couch, reading the Philadelphia tourist magazines that came with the room. "Hey," she said cautiously. Everyone was staring at her. "Did Kate tell you? I had to—"

"Go to Foxy?" Isabel interrupted.

Hanna's mouth fell open. Another bolt of lightning outside made her jump. She turned desperately to Kate, who had her hands haughtily folded in her lap and her head raised high. Had she . . . had she *told*? The look on her face said yes.

Hanna felt like she'd been dropped on her head. "It . . . it was an emergency."

"I'm sure it was." Her father put his hands flat on the table. "I can't believe you even came back. We thought you were going to pull another all-nighter . . . steal another car, maybe. Or . . . or who knows? Steal someone's airplane? Assassinate the president?"

"Dad . . ." Hanna pleaded. She'd never seen her father like this. His shirt was untucked, the ends of his socks weren't taut against his toes, and there was a smudge behind his ear. And he was *raving*. He never used to yell like this. "I can explain."

Her father pressed the heels of his hands to his forehead. "Hanna . . . can you explain this, too?" He reached into his pocket for something. Slowly, he unfurled his fingers, one by one. Inside, was the little foil packet of Percocet. Unopened.

As Hanna lunged for it, he snapped his hand closed like a clamshell. "Oh, no, you don't."

Hanna pointed at Kate. "She took those from me. She wanted them!"

"You gave them to me," Kate said evenly. She had this knowing, *gotcha* look on her face, a look that said, *Don't even think you're worming your way into our lives.* Hanna hated herself for being so stupid. Kate hadn't changed. Not a bit.

"What were you doing with pills in the first place?" her father asked. Then he held up his hand. "No. Forget it. I don't want to know. I . . ." He squeezed his eyes shut. "I don't know you anymore, Hanna. I really don't."

A dam inside Hanna broke. "Well, of course you don't!" she screamed. "You haven't bothered to speak to me for almost four fucking years!"

A hush fell over the room. Everyone seemed afraid to move. Kate's hands were flat against her magazine. Isabel froze, one finger bizarrely at her earlobe. Her father opened his mouth to speak, but then shut it again.

There was a knock on the door, and everyone jumped.

Ms. Marin was on the other side, looking uncharacteristically disheveled: Her hair was wet and stringy, she didn't have much makeup on, and she was wearing a simple T-shirt and jeans, a far cry from the put-together ensembles she usually wore to Wawa.

"You're coming with me." She narrowed her eyes at Hanna but didn't even glance at Isabel or Kate. Hanna wondered fleetingly if this was the first time everyone was meeting. When her mother saw the Percocet in Mr. Marin's hand, she paled. "He told me about *that* on the way here."

Hanna looked over her shoulder at her father, but he had his head down. He didn't look disappointed exactly. He just looked . . . sad. Hopeless. Ashamed. "Dad . . ." she squeaked desperately, wrenching away from her mom. "I don't have to go, do I? I want to stay. Can't I tell you what's going on with me? I thought you wanted to know."

"It's too late," her father said mechanically. "You're going home with your mother. Maybe she can talk some sense into you."

Hanna had to laugh. "You think *she's* going to talk sense into me? She's . . . she's sleeping with the cop who arrested me last week. She's been known to come home at two A.M. on school nights. If I'm sick and have to stay home from school, she tells me it's okay to call up the front office and just pretend I'm her, because she's too busy, and—"

"Hanna!" her mother screamed, clamping her fingers around Hanna's arm.

Hanna's brain was so scrambled, she had no idea whether telling her dad this stuff was helping or hurting her. She just felt so *duped*. By everyone. She was sick of people walking all over her. "There are so many things I wanted to tell you, but I can't. Please let me stay. *Please.*"

The only thing that wavered in her father was a tiny muscle, up by his neck. Otherwise, his face was stony and impassive. He took a step closer to Isabel and Kate. Isabel took his hand.

"Good night, Ashley," he said to Hanna's mother. To Hanna, he said nothing at all.

32

EMILY GOES TO BAT

Emily sobbed with relief when she discovered her house's side door was open. She threw her soaked body into the laundry room, nearly bursting into tears at the insulated, untroubled domesticity of everything: her mother's BLESS THIS MESS! cross-stitch above the washer and dryer; the neat row of detergent, bleach, and fabric softener on the little shelf; her father's green rubber gardening boots by the door.

The phone rang; it sounded like a scream. Emily grabbed a towel from the laundry pile, wrapped it around her shoulders, and tentatively picked up the cordless extension. "Hello?" Even the sound of her own voice seemed scary.

"Emily?" came a familiar gravelly voice on the other end.

Emily frowned. "Spencer?"

"Oh my God." Spencer sighed. "We've been looking for you. Are you all right?"

"I . . . I don't know," Emily said shakily. She'd run crazily through the cornfield. The rain had created rivers of mud between the rows. One of her shoes had fallen off, but she'd kept going, and now the bottom of her dress and her legs were filthy. The field butted up to the woods behind her house, and she'd torn through those, too. She'd slid twice on wet grass, scraping up her elbow and hip, and once, lightning hit a tree just twenty feet from her, violently snapping branches to the ground. She knew it was dangerous to be out there in a storm, but she couldn't stop, afraid Toby was right behind her.

"Emily. Stay where you are," Spencer instructed. "And stay away from Toby. I'll explain everything later, but for right now, just lock your door and—"

"I think Toby's A," Emily interrupted, her voice a scratchy, trembling whisper. "And I think he killed Ali."

There was a pause. "I know. So do I."

"What?" Emily cried. A crack of thunder radiated through the sky, making Emily cower. Spencer didn't answer. The line was dead.

Emily put the phone on top of the dryer. Spencer *knew*? It made Emily's revelation even more real—and much, much scarier.

Then, she heard a voice. "Emily! Emily?"

She froze. It sounded like it was coming from the kitchen. She sprinted in there and saw Toby looking in, his hands pressed against her sliding glass door. The rain had soaked through his suit and matted down his hair, and he was shivering. His face was in the shadows.

Emily screamed.

"Emily!" Toby said again. He tried the door handle, but Emily quickly latched it.

"Go away," she hissed. He could . . . he could burn down their house. Break in. Suffocate Emily while she slept. If he could kill Ali, he was capable of anything.

"I'm getting soaked," he called to her. "Let me in."

"I . . . I can't talk to you. Please, Toby, *please*. Just leave me alone."

"Why did you run away from me?" Toby looked confused. He had to yell, too, because it was raining so hard. "I'm not sure what happened in the car. I was just . . . I was just sort of messed up from seeing all those people. But that was all years ago. I'm sorry."

The sweetness in his voice made it even worse. He tried the handle again, and Emily shouted, "No!" Toby stopped, and Emily looked around frantically for something that could be a weapon. A heavy, ceramic chicken plate. A dull kitchen knife. Perhaps she could root around in the cabinets and find the griddle. . . . "Please." Emily was trembling so badly, her legs were wobbly. "Just go away."

"Let me at least give you back your purse. It's in my car."

"Just put it in my mailbox."

"Emily, don't be ridiculous." Toby started pounding angrily on the door. "Just get over here and let me in!"

Emily picked up the heavy chicken plate on the kitchen table. She held it out in front of her with both hands, like a shield. "Go away!"

Toby pushed his soaked hair off his face. "The stuff I said to you in the car . . . it came out all wrong. I'm sorry if I said something that—"

"It's too late," Emily interrupted. She squeezed her eyes shut. All she wanted was to open her eyes again and for all this to be a dream. "I know what you did to her."

Toby stiffened. "Wait. *What?*"

"You heard me," Emily said. "I. Know. What. You. Did. To. Her."

Toby's mouth fell open. The rain fell harder, making his eyeballs look like hollow pits. "How could you know about that?" his voice wobbled. "No one . . . no one knew. It was . . . it was a long time ago, Emily."

Emily's mouth dropped open. What, did he think he was so sly that he could get *away* with it? "Well, I guess your secret's out."

Toby started to pace back and forth across her deck, running his fingers through his hair. "But, Emily, you don't understand. I was so *young*. And . . . and confused. I wish I hadn't done it. . . ."

Emily felt a huge tug of regret. She didn't want Toby to be Ali's killer. The sweet way he'd helped her out of his car, how he'd defended her in front of Ben, how lost and vulnerable he'd looked when Emily glanced at him, standing alone on the Foxy dance floor. Maybe he really was sorry for what he'd done. Maybe he'd just been confused.

But then Emily thought about the night Ali went missing. It had been so beautiful out, the perfect kickoff to what was going to be a perfect summer. They were planning to go to the Jersey Shore the following weekend, had tickets to the No Doubt concert in July, and Ali was going to throw a huge thirteenth birthday party in August. All that was gone the instant Ali stepped out of Spencer's family's barn.

Toby might have come up to her from behind. Maybe he hit her with something. Maybe he said things to her. When he threw her into the hole, he must have . . . covered her up with dirt so no one would find her. Was that how it went? And after Toby hurt her, had he just gotten on his bike and ridden home? Had he returned to Maine for the rest of the summer? Had he watched everyone searching on the news with a bowl of microwave popcorn in his lap, like it was a movie on HBO?

I'm glad that bitch is dead. Emily had never heard anything so horrible in her life.

"Please," Toby cried. "I can't go through all this again. And neither can—"

He couldn't even finish his sentence. Then, suddenly, he covered his face with his hands and ran away, back into the woods in her backyard.

All was quiet. Emily looked around. The kitchen was

spotless—her parents had gone away this weekend to Pittsburgh to visit Emily's grandmother, and her mother always cleaned maniacally before she went. Carolyn was still out with Topher.

She was all alone.

Emily sprinted to the front door. It was locked, but she pulled the chain across for extra protection. She twisted the dead bolt to make sure it was secure. Then she remembered the garage door: The mechanical part of it had broken, and her dad had been lazy about fixing it. Someone strong enough could lift up the garage door himself.

And then she realized. Toby had her purse. Which meant . . . he had her *keys*.

She picked up the phone in the kitchen and dialed 911. But the phone didn't even ring. She hung up and listened for a dial tone, but there was none. Emily felt her knees weaken. The storm must have knocked out the phone lines.

She remained frozen in the hallway for a few seconds, her jaw trembling. *Had Toby dragged Ali by her hair? Had she still been alive when he tossed her into that hole?*

She ran into the garage and looked around. In the corner was her old baseball bat. It felt strong and heavy in her hands. Satisfied, she slid out to the front porch, locked the door behind her with the spare key from the kitchen, and settled gently into the porch swing in the shadows, the bat in her lap. It was freezing outside, and she could see a giant spider building a web in the other corner of the porch. Spiders always terrified her, but she had to be brave. She wouldn't let Toby hurt her, too.

33

WHO'S THE NAUGHTY
SISTER NOW?

The next morning, Spencer came back into her bedroom after taking a shower and noticed the window was open. As in, seriously hoisted up about two feet, screen and all. The curtains fluttered in the breeze.

She ran to the window, her throat tight. Although she'd calmed down after she reached Emily last night, this was odd. The Hastingses *never* opened the screens, because moths could fly in and ruin the expensive rugs. She jerked the window down, then nervously checked under her bed and in her closet. No one.

When her Sidekick buzzed, she nearly jumped out of her silk pajama pants. She found her phone buried in her Foxy dress, which she'd stripped off last night and left in a pile on the floor—something the old Spencer Hastings would never have done. It was an e-mail from Squidward.

Dear Spencer, Thank you for turning in your essay
questions early. I've read them, and I'm very pleased.
See you Monday. —Mr. McAdam

Spencer slumped back down on her bed, her heart
beating slowly but forcefully.

Out her bedroom window, she could see that it was a
beautiful, crisp September Sunday. The aroma of apples
hung in the air. Her mother, wearing a straw hat and
rolled-up jeans, strolled to the end of the driveway with
her gardening shears to prune back the bushes.

She couldn't deal with all this . . . this pleasantness.
She grabbed her Sidekick and speed-dialed Wren's number. Perhaps they could start their date early. She needed
out of Rosewood. The phone rang a few times; then there
was a clatter and a clunk. It took a few seconds for Wren
to say hello. "It's me," Spencer sobbed.

"Spencer?" Wren sounded groggy.

"Yeah." Her mood shifted to irritation. Did he not
recognize her voice?

"Could I call you back?" Wren yawned. "I'm sort
of . . . I'm still sleeping."

"But . . . I need to talk with you."

He sighed.

Spencer softened. "I'm sorry. Can you *please* talk to
me right now?" She paced around the room. "I need to
hear a friendly voice."

Wren was quiet. Spencer even checked her Sidekick's

LED screen to make sure they were still connected. "Look," he finally said. "This isn't the easiest thing to say, but . . . I don't think this is going to work out."

Spencer rubbed her ears. "What?"

"I thought this would be okay." Wren sounded numb. Robotic, almost. "But I think you're too young for me. I just . . . I don't know. We seem to be in really different places."

The room blurred, then tilted. Spencer grasped the phone so hard, her knuckles turned white. "Wait. *What?* We were just together the other day, and it was fine then!"

"I know. But . . . God, this isn't that easy . . . I've started seeing someone else."

For a few seconds, Spencer's brain shut down. She had no idea how to respond. She was pretty sure she wasn't even breathing. "But I had sex with you," she whispered.

"I know. I'm sorry. But I think this is for the best."

The best . . . for who? In the background, Spencer heard Wren's coffeemaker beep that brewing had finished. "Wren . . ." Spencer pleaded. "Why are you doing this?"

But he had already hung up.

Her phone flashed CALL ENDED. Spencer held it at arm's length.

"Hey!"

Spencer jumped. Melissa stood in Spencer's doorway. In her yellow J. Crew tissue tee and orange Adidas shorts, she looked like a ball of sunshine. "How'd it go?"

Spencer blinked. "Huh?"

"Foxy! Was it fun?"

Spencer tried to mask her swirling emotions. "Um, yeah. It was great."

"Did they have an ugly jewelry auction this year? How was Andrew?"

Andrew. She'd meant to explain everything to Andrew, but Toby had gotten in the way. Spencer had left Foxy shortly after she found out Emily was okay, hailing one of the town cars that were chugging in Kingman Hall's circular drive. Her parents had reinstated her credit cards, so she could actually pay for the trip home.

It made her squeamish to imagine how Andrew felt today. They might even be feeling the same way—blindsided, rushed. But that was silly, really. Spencer and Wren had had something serious. . . . Andrew was delusional if he'd thought he and Spencer were honestly together.

Her eyes widened. Was *she* delusional, thinking that she was honestly with Wren? What kind of jerk dumps you over the phone, anyway?

Melissa sat next to her on her bed, expectantly awaiting an answer.

"Andrew was good." Spencer's brain felt gummy. "He was very, um, chivalrous."

"What was for dinner?"

"Um, squab," Spencer lied. She didn't have a clue.

"And was it romantic?"

Spencer quickly tried to conjure up some cute scenes

with Andrew. Sharing the appetizer. Drunkenly dancing to Shakira. She caught herself. What was the point? It didn't matter anymore.

The clouds started to move out of her brain. Melissa was sitting here, so sweetly trying to make an effort to patch things up. The way she'd taken an interest in Foxy, the way she'd urged their parents to forgive her . . . and Spencer had repaid her by stealing Wren and ripping off her old econ paper. Even Melissa didn't deserve this.

"I have something to tell you," Spencer blurted out. "I . . . I saw Wren."

Melissa barely flinched, so Spencer pressed forward. "This whole week. I've gone to his new apartment in Philly, we've talked on the phone, everything. But . . . I think it's over now." She curled into the fetal position, armoring herself for when Melissa started to hit her. "You can hate me. I mean, I wouldn't blame you. You can go tell Mom and Dad to kick me out of the house."

Melissa quietly held Spencer's preppy seersucker pillow to her chest. It took a long time for her to answer. "It's all right. I won't tell them anything." Melissa leaned back. "I actually have something to tell *you*. You remember Friday night, when you couldn't reach Wren? You left five messages?"

Spencer stared at her. "H-How do you know that?"

Melissa gave her a tight, satisfied smile. A smile that suddenly made everything all too clear. *I've been seeing someone else,* Wren had said. *It can't be,* Spencer thought.

"Because Wren wasn't in Philly," Melissa answered nonchalantly. "He was here, in Rosewood. With me." She got up off the bed and pushed her hair behind her ears, and Spencer saw the hickey on Melissa's neck, practically in the same spot where Spencer's had been. Melissa couldn't have been more deliberate if she'd circled it with a Sharpie.

"And he *told* you?" she managed. "You knew, all this time?"

"No, I only found out last night." Melissa ran her hand over her chin. "Let's just say I got an anonymous tip from a concerned individual."

Spencer gripped her bedspread. *A.*

"Anyway," Melissa lilted, "I was with Wren last night, too, when you were at Foxy." She tilted her head down at Spencer, giving her the same haughty look she used to make when they played Queen, back when they were little. The rules of Queen never changed: Melissa was always Queen, and Spencer always had to do what she said. *Make my bed, loyal subject,* Melissa would say. *Kiss my feet. You're mine forever.*

Melissa took a step toward the door. "But I decided this morning. I haven't told him yet, but Wren's really *not* for me. So I'm never going to see him again." She paused, considered her words, then smirked. "And by the looks of things, I guess you won't be seeing him ever again, either."

34

SEE? DEEP DOWN, HANNA REALLY IS A GOOD GIRL

The first thing Hanna heard on Sunday morning was someone singing that Elvis Costello song "Alison."

"ALLLLLison, I know this world is KILLING you!" It was a guy, his voice loud and grating like a lawn mower. Hanna threw her covers back. Was it the TV? Was it someone outside?

When she stood up, her head felt like it was full of cotton candy. She saw the Chloé jacket she'd worn last night thrown over her desk chair, and everything came flooding back to her.

After her mom retrieved her from the Four Seasons, they'd driven home in stony silence. When they pulled into the driveway, Ms. Marin jammed the Lexus into park and stormed crookedly into the house, drunk with anger. When Hanna got to the door, her mom slammed it in her face, and there was a loud, solid *clunk*. Hanna stood back, stunned. Okay, so she'd outed her mom's worst parenting faux pas, and that was probably a bad move. But was her mom seriously locking her out?

Hanna pounded on the door, and Ms. Marin opened it a crack. Her eyebrows were drawn together. "Oh, I'm sorry. You want to come in?"

"Y-Yes," Hanna squeaked.

Her mother guffawed. "You're completely willing to insult and disrespect me in front of your father, but you're not too proud to live here?"

Hanna had made some sort of blubbering attempt at an apology, but her mom stormed away. She did, however, leave the door open. Hanna had scooped up Dot and run to her room, too traumatized to even cry.

"Obbbbb, ALLLLLison . . . I know this world is KILLLing YOU!"

Hanna tiptoed to her door. The singing was coming from inside the house. Her legs started to shake. Only a crazy person would be stupid enough to sing that "Alison" song in Rosewood right now. The cops would probably arrest you just for humming it in public.

Was it *Toby*?

She straightened her yellow camisole and stepped into the hall. At the same moment, the hall bathroom door opened and a guy stepped out.

Hanna put her hand to her mouth. The guy had a towel—*her* white, fluffy, Pottery Barn towel—wrapped around his waist. His blackish hair stood up in peaks. A silent scream got stuck in Hanna's throat.

And then he turned around and faced her. Hanna took a step back. It was Darren Wilden. *Officer* Darren Wilden.

"Whoa." Wilden froze. "Hanna."

It was hard not to gawk at his perfectly formed abs. He was definitely not a cop who ate too many Krispy Kremes. "Why were you *singing* that?" she finally asked.

Wilden looked embarrassed. "Sometimes I don't notice I'm singing."

"I thought you were . . . " Hanna trailed off. What the hell was Wilden *doing* here? But then she realized. Of course. Her mom. She smoothed down her hair, not feeling any calmer. What if it had been Toby? What would she have done? She would probably be dead.

"Do you . . . do you need to get in here?" Wilden gestured bashfully at the steamy bathroom. "Your mom's in hers."

Hanna was too stunned to respond. Then, before she knew exactly what she was saying, she blurted out, "I have something to tell you. Something important."

"Oh?" A droplet of water fell off a strand of Wilden's hair onto the floor.

"I think I know something about . . . about who killed Alison DiLaurentis."

Wilden raised an eyebrow. "Who?"

Hanna licked her lips. "Toby Cavanaugh."

"Why do you think that?"

"I . . . I can't tell you why. You just have to take my word for it."

Wilden frowned and leaned against the doorjamb, still half-naked. "You're going to have to give me a little more than that. You could be giving me the name of some guy who broke your heart, for revenge."

In that case, I'd have told you Sean Ackard, Hanna thought bitterly. She didn't know what to do. If she told Wilden about The Jenna Thing, her dad would hate her. Everyone in Rosewood would talk. She and her friends would go to juvie.

But keeping the secret from her dad—and the rest of Rosewood—didn't really matter anymore. Her whole life was ruined, and besides, she was the one who'd really hurt Jenna. That night might've been an accident, but Hanna had hurt her plenty of times on purpose.

"I'll tell you," she said slowly, "but I don't want anyone else to get in trouble. Only . . . only me, if someone has to. Okay?"

Wilden held up his hand. "It doesn't matter. We checked out Toby when Alison first disappeared. He has an airtight alibi. Couldn't have been him."

Hanna gaped. "He has an alibi? *Who?*"

"I can't disclose that." Wilden looked stern for a moment, but then the corners of his mouth curled up into a smile. He pointed at Hanna's A&F moose-printed flannel pants. "You look cute in your jammies."

Hanna curled her toes into the carpet. She'd always hated the word *jammies.* "Wait, are you *sure* Toby's innocent?"

Wilden was about to respond, but his walkie-talkie, which was perched on the edge of the bathroom sink, made a crackling sound. He turned and grabbed it, keeping one hand on the towel around his waist. "Casey?"

"There's another body," a crackling voice answered. "And it's . . ." The transmission turned to static.

Hanna's heart started pounding again. *Another body?*

"Casey." Wilden was buttoning up his police shirt. "Can you repeat that? Hello?" Fuzz was all he got in reply. He noticed Hanna still standing there. "Go to your room."

Hanna bristled. The nerve of him, trying to speak to her like he was her father! "What about another body?" she whispered.

Wilden put the walkie-talkie back on the counter, whipped on his pants, and tore the towel off his lower half, tossing it on the bathroom floor just like Hanna often did. "Just calm down," he said, his friendliness all gone. He put his gun in his holster and clomped down the stairs.

Hanna followed him. Spencer had called last night to tell her that Emily was okay—but what if she'd been mistaken? "Is it a girl's body? Do you know?"

Wilden flung the front door open. In the driveway next to her mom's champagne-colored Lexus was his squad car. ROSEWOOD PD was printed, loud and clear, on the side panel. Hanna gawked. Had that been here all night? Could the neighbors see it from the road?

Hanna followed Wilden to his car. "Can you at least tell me where the body *is*?"

He whirled around. "I can't tell you that."

"But . . . you don't understand—"

"Hanna." Wilden didn't let her finish. "Tell your mom I'll call her later." He swung into his car and put the siren on. If the neighbors didn't know he'd been there before, they sure did now.

35

SPECIAL DELIVERY

Sunday at 11:52 A.M., Aria sat on her bed, staring at her red-painted fingernails. She felt slightly disoriented, as if she were forgetting something . . . something *huge*. Like those dreams she sometimes had where it was June, and she just realized she hadn't gone to math class the whole year and was going to flunk out.

And then she remembered. Toby was A. And today was Sunday. Her time was up.

It scared her to put a name and face to A's wrath—and that Ali and Spencer *had* been covering something up, something that could be really, *really* serious. Aria still had no idea how Toby had found out about Byron and Meredith, but if Aria caught them together twice, others could have seen them together, too—including Toby.

She'd meant to tell Ella about everything last night. When Sean dropped her off at home, he asked repeatedly if he should come in with her. But Aria told him no—she had to do what she was going to do alone. The house had been dark and still, the only sound the groaning of the dishwasher on high-scrub mode. Aria had fumbled for the foyer lights, then tiptoed into the dark, empty kitchen. Usually, her mother was up at least until 1 or 2 A.M. on Saturday nights, doing Sudoku puzzles or having discussions with Byron at the table over decaf coffee. But the table was spotless; she could see dried sponge swirls on its surface.

Aria had bounded up to her parents' bedroom, wondering if Ella had fallen asleep early. Their door was wide open. The bed was unmade, but there was no one in it. The master bathroom was empty, too. Then Aria noticed that the Honda Civic her parents shared wasn't in the driveway.

So she waited at the foot of the steps for them to come home, anxiously checking her watch every thirty seconds as it ticked to midnight. Her parents were possibly the only people in the universe who didn't have cell phones, so she couldn't call them. That meant Toby couldn't call them, either . . . or had he found another way to get in touch?

And then . . . she'd woken up here, in her bed. Someone must have carried her in, and Aria, who slept like the dead, hadn't noticed a thing.

She listened to the sounds downstairs. Drawers opening and closing. The wood floor groaning under someone's feet. Pages of the newspaper turning. Were there two parents down there, or just one? She tiptoed down the stairs, a billion different scenarios going through her head. Then she saw them: tiny red droplets, all over the entrance hall floor. They made a trail from the kitchen straight to the front door.

It looked like blood.

Aria ran for the kitchen. Toby had told her mother, and Ella, in a rage, had killed Byron. Or Meredith. Or Toby. Or everyone. Or Mike had killed them. Or . . . or Byron had killed Ella. When she got to the kitchen, she stopped.

Ella was at the table alone. She wore a wine-colored blouse, high heels, and makeup, as if she were ready to go out somewhere. The *New York Times* was folded to the crossword puzzle, but instead of letters filling in the squares, the page was scribbled over in thick, black ink. Ella stared straight ahead, sort of randomly toward the kitchen window, pushing the tines of a fork into the heel of her hand.

"*Mom?*" Aria croaked, stepping closer. Aria could see now that the blouse was wrinkled and her makeup looked smudged. It was almost like she'd slept in her clothes . . . or hadn't slept at all.

"Mom?" Aria asked again, her voice tinged with fear. Finally, her mother slowly looked over. Ella's eyes were heavy and swimming. She shoved the fork farther into her palm. Aria wanted to reach out and take it away, but she was afraid. She'd never seen her mom like this. "What's going on?"

Ella swallowed. "Oh . . . you know."

Aria swallowed hard. "What's the . . . the red stuff in the hall?"

"Red stuff?" Ella asked soullessly. "Oh. Maybe it's paint. I threw out some art supplies this morning. I threw out a lot of stuff this morning."

"Mom." Aria could feel tears come to her eyes. "Is something wrong?"

Her mother looked up. Her movements were slow, like she was underwater. "You knew for almost four years."

Aria stopped breathing. "What?" she whispered.

"Are you *friends* with her?" Ella asked, still in the same, dead voice. "She's not that much older than you. And I heard you went to her yoga studio the other day."

"*What?*" Aria whispered. *Yoga studio?* "I don't know w-what you mean!"

"Of course you do." Ella gave her the saddest smile Aria had ever seen. "I got a letter. At first I didn't believe it, but I confronted your father. And to think I thought he was distant because of work."

"*What?*" Aria backed up. Spots formed in front of her eyes. "You got a *letter*? When? Who sent it?"

But by the cold, vacant way Ella looked at her, Aria knew exactly who'd sent it. A. *Toby*. And he'd told her everything.

Aria put her hands on her forehead. "I'm so sorry," she said. "I . . . I wanted to tell you, but I was so afraid and—"

"Byron's gone," Ella said, almost flip. "He's with the girl." She let out a little snicker. "Maybe they're doing *yoga* together."

"I'm sure we could get him to come back." Aria choked on tears. "I mean, he has to, right? We're his family."

At that precise second, the cuckoo clock struck twelve. The clock had been a gift from Byron to Ella on their twentieth wedding anniversary last year in Iceland; Ella was really into it because it was rumored to have belonged to Edvard Munch, the famous Norwegian painter who painted *The Scream*. She'd carefully carried it home with her on the plane, constantly peeling back the bubble wrap to make sure it was okay. Now, they had to listen to twelve chirps and see that stupid bird pop out of his wooden house twelve times. Each chirp sounded more and more accusatory. Instead of *cuckoo*, the bird singsonged, *You knew. You knew. You knew.*

"Oh, Aria," Ella scolded. "I don't think he's coming back."

"Where's the letter?" Aria asked, snot running down her face. "Can I see it? I don't know who would do this to us . . . who would ruin things like this."

Ella stared at her. Her eyes were teary and huge, too. "I threw the letter away. But it doesn't matter who sent it. What matters is that it's *true*."

"I'm so sorry." Aria kneeled next to her, drinking in

the funny, familiar way her mom smelled—like turpentine, newspaper ink, sandalwood incense, and, strangely, scrambled eggs. She put her head on her mother's shoulder, but Ella shook her away. "Aria," she said sharply, standing up. "I can't be near you right now."

"What?" Aria cried.

Ella wasn't looking at her but instead was staring at her left hand, which, Aria abruptly noticed, didn't have a wedding ring on it anymore.

She pushed past Aria, floating, ghostlike, into the hall and tracking the red paint all the way up the stairs. "Wait!" Aria screamed, following her. She scrambled up the stairs but tripped over a muddy pair of Mike's lacrosse cleats, banged her knee, and slid two steps down. "Damn it," she spat, gripping the carpet with her fingernails. She pushed herself up and reached the landing, panting with rage. Her mother's bedroom door was closed. So was the door to the bathroom. Mike's bedroom door was open, except Mike wasn't there. *Mike*, Aria thought, her heart breaking all over again. Did he know?

Her cell phone started to ring. Dazed, she went into her bedroom to find it. Her brain felt wild. She was still panting. She almost wanted the call to be from A—Toby—just so she could chew him out. But it was just Spencer. Aria stared at the number, fuming. It didn't matter that Spencer wasn't A—she might as well be. If Spencer had turned in Toby back in seventh grade, he would never have told Ella, and her family would be intact.

She snapped her phone open but didn't speak. She just sat there, taking deep, heaving breaths. "Aria?" Spencer called cautiously.

"I have nothing to say to you," Aria ground out. "You've ruined my life."

"I know," Spencer answered quietly. "It's just . . . Aria, I'm sorry. I didn't want to keep the Toby secret from you. But I didn't know what to do. Can't you see it from my perspective?"

"No," Aria said thickly. "You don't understand. You've *ruined my life.*"

"Wait, what do you mean?" Spencer sounded worried. "What . . . what happened?"

Aria put her head in her hands. It was too exhausting to explain. And she *could* see things from Spencer's perspective. Of course she could. What Spencer was saying was hauntingly close to what Aria had said to Ella, three minutes ago. *I didn't want to keep this from you. I didn't know what to do. I didn't want to hurt you.*

She sighed and wiped her nose. "Why are you calling?"

"Well . . ." Spencer paused. "Have you heard from Emily this morning?"

"No."

"Shit," Spencer whispered.

"What's the matter?" Aria sat up straighter. "I thought you said last night that you got a hold of her, and she was at home."

"Well, she was. . . ." Aria heard Spencer swallow. "I'm sure it's nothing, but my mom was just driving by Emily's neighborhood, and there are three police cars in her driveway."

36

JUST ANOTHER SLOW
NEWS DAY IN ROSEWOOD

Emily lived in an older, modest neighborhood with a lot of retired residents, and everyone was out on their porches or in the middle of the street, concerned over the three police cars in the Fieldses' driveway and by the ambulance that had just roared away. Spencer pulled up to the curb and spotted Aria. She was still in her polka-dotted dress from Foxy.

"I just got here," Aria said as Spencer approached. "But I can't find out anything. I've asked a bunch of people what's going on, but no one knows."

Spencer looked around. There were plenty of police dogs, police officers, EMS people, and even a Channel 4 news van—it had probably just driven over from the DiLaurentis house. She felt like all the police officers were looking at her.

And then Spencer started to shake. This was her fault. Completely her fault. She felt sick. Toby had warned her that people would get hurt, yet she'd done nothing. She'd been so absorbed in Wren—and look how that had turned out. She couldn't even think about Wren right now. Or Melissa. Or them together. It made her feel like there were worms crawling through her veins. Something had happened to Emily, and she'd had the chance to stop it. The police had been sitting in her living room. Even A had warned her.

Suddenly, Spencer noticed Emily's sister Carolyn standing in the driveway, talking to some cops. One of the officers leaned down and whispered something in her ear. Carolyn's face crumpled, like she was crying. She ran back into the house.

Aria's posture wavered a little, like she was about to faint. "Oh God, Emily's . . ."

Spencer swallowed hard. "We don't know anything yet."

"I can just feel it, though," Aria said, her eyes full of tears. "A—Toby—his threats." She paused, pushing away a strand of hair that had gotten in her mouth. Her hands shook badly. "We're next, Spencer. I know it."

"Where are Emily's parents?" Spencer asked in a loud voice, trying to drown out everything Aria just said. "Wouldn't they be here if Emily were . . . " She didn't want to say the word *dead*.

A Toyota Prius barreled crookedly up the road and parked behind Spencer's Mercedes. Hanna got out. Or, it was a girl who *resembled* Hanna. She hadn't bothered changing out of a pair of flannel pajama pants, and her long, normally stick-straight dark auburn hair was kinky and stuffed into a half-up, half-down bun. Spencer hadn't seen her look so un–put together in years.

Hanna spied them and ran over. "What's going on? Is it–"

"We don't know," Spencer interrupted.

"You guys, I found something out." Hanna slipped off her sunglasses. "I talked to a cop this morning, and . . ."

Another news van pulled up and Hanna stopped talking. Spencer recognized the woman from Channel 8 news. She took a couple steps closer to the girls, her cell phone to her ear. "So the body was found out-side this morning?" she said, looking at a clipboard. "Okay, thanks."

The girls exchanged a pleading look. Then Aria took the others' hands and they strode across Emily's lawn, treading straight through a flower bed. They were a few feet from Emily's front door when a police officer stepped in their path.

"Hanna, I told you to stay out of this," the cop said.

Spencer gulped. It was Wilden, the guy who'd come by her house yesterday. Her heart started to pound.

Hanna tried to push him aside. "Don't tell me what to do!" The officer grabbed Hanna by the shoulders, and she started to squirm. "Get off me!"

Spencer quickly gripped Hanna around her tiny waist.

"Try to calm her down," Wilden said to Spencer. Then he noticed who she was. "Oh," he breathed. He looked confused, then curious. "Miss Hastings."

"We just want to know what happened to Emily," Spencer tried to explain, her insides roiling. "She's . . . she's our friend."

"You guys should all go home." Wilden crossed his arms over his chest.

Suddenly, the front door opened . . . and Emily stepped out.

She was barefoot and pale, and holding a glass of water in an old McDonald's Muppet mug. Spencer was so relieved to see her, she actually cried out. A vulnerable, pained noise escaped from her throat.

The girls rushed over to her. "Are you all right?" Hanna asked.

"What happened?" Aria said at the same time.

"What's going on?" Spencer gestured to the crowd of people.

"Emily . . ." Wilden put his hands on his hips. "Maybe you should see your friends later. Your parents said you were supposed to stay inside."

But Emily shook her head, almost irritated. "No, it's okay."

Emily led them right past the cop to her side yard. They stood practically in a rosebush up against the side of the house, so they'd have a little privacy. Spencer took a good look at Emily. She had dark circles under her eyes, and there were scratches all over her legs, but otherwise, she looked fine. "What happened?" Spencer asked.

Emily took a huge breath. "A mountain biker found Toby's body in the woods behind my house this morning. I guess . . . I guess he OD'd on pills or something."

Spencer's heart stopped. Hanna gasped. Aria went pale. "What? *When?*" she asked.

"It was sometime during the night," Emily said. "I was going to call you, except that cop's watching me like a hawk." Her jaw was trembling. "My parents are visiting my grandmother this weekend." She tried to smile, but it warped into a grimace, and then her face collapsed into a sob.

"It's all right," Hanna comforted her.

"He was acting crazy last night," Emily said, wiping her face with her shirt. "He took me home from Foxy, and one minute, it was totally normal, and the next, he was telling me how much he hated Ali. He said he couldn't forgive Ali for what she did, and that he was glad she's dead."

"Oh my God." Spencer covered her eyes. It was all true.

"That's when I realized—Toby *knew*," Emily went on, her pale, freckly hands fluttering. "He must have found out what Ali did, and . . . and I think he killed her."

"Wait a second," Hanna interrupted, holding up her hand. "I don't think he—"

"Shhh." Spencer put her hand lightly on Hanna's tiny

wrist. Hanna looked like she wanted to say something, but Spencer was afraid that if Emily stopped, she wouldn't be able to finish.

"I ran away from him—the whole way to my house," Emily said. "When I got inside, Spencer called, but we got cut off. Then . . . then Toby was at my back door. I told him that I knew what he'd done, and I was going to tell the police. He acted all amazed that I'd figured it out."

Emily seemed winded by all that talking. "You guys—how did Toby know?"

Spencer's stomach dropped. The phone lines had gone down before she could explain the truth of The Jenna Thing to Emily last night. She wished she didn't have to tell Emily now—she seemed so fragile. It had been bad enough telling Aria and Hanna—but the truth was going to shatter Emily's world.

Aria and Hanna were looking at Spencer expectantly, so Spencer steeled herself. "He always knew," she said. "He saw Ali do it. Only, Ali blackmailed him into taking the blame. She made me keep the secret." She paused for a breath and noticed that Emily wasn't reacting the way she thought she would. She was standing there, completely calm, as if she were listening to a geography lecture. It kind of put Spencer off balance. "So, um, when Ali went missing, I always thought that maybe, I don't know . . ." She looked up toward the sky, realizing that what she was about to say was true. "I thought maybe Toby had something to do with it, but I was too scared to say anything. But then he came back for her funeral . . . and my A notes referenced the Toby secret. The last one said, *You hurt me, so I'm going to hurt you.* He wanted revenge on all of us. He must have known we were all involved."

Emily was still standing there so calmly. Then, slowly, her shoulders started to shake. She shut her eyes. At first, Spencer thought she was crying, but then she realized she was laughing.

Emily threw her head back, laughing louder. Spencer glanced at Aria and Hanna uneasily. Emily had obviously lost it. "Em . . ." she prodded gently.

When Emily brought her head back down, her bottom lip was trembling. "Ali promised us that no one knew what we'd done."

"Guess she lied," Hanna said flatly.

Emily's eyes flickered searchingly back and forth. "But how could she lie to us like that? What if Toby decided to tell?" She shook her head. "This . . . this happened when we were all inside Ali's house, watching at her front door?" Emily asked. "That very same night?"

Spencer nodded solemnly.

"And Ali came back inside and said everything was fine, and when none of us could sleep except for her, she comforted us by scratching our backs?"

"Yes." Tears came to Spencer's eyes. Of course Emily remembered every detail.

Emily stared off into space. "And she gave us these." She held up her arm. The bracelet Ali had made them—to symbolize the secret—was tightly knotted around her wrist. Everyone else had taken theirs off.

Emily's legs buckled, and she fell to the grass. Then she started tearing at the bracelet around her wrist, trying get it off, but the strings were old and tough. "Damn it," Emily said, collapsing her fingers together to make her wrist smaller so she could yank the bracelet off without untying it. Then she went at it with her teeth, but it wouldn't budge.

Aria put her hand on Emily's shoulder. "It's all right."

"I just can't believe any of it." She wiped her eyes, giving up on the bracelet. Emily pulled up a fistful of grass. "And I can't believe I went to Foxy with Ali's . . . *killer.*"

"We were so scared for you," Spencer whispered.

Hanna waved her arms around. "You guys, that's what I've been trying to tell you. Toby's *not* Ali's killer."

"Huh?" Spencer frowned. "What are you talking about?"

"I . . . I spoke to that cop this morning." Hanna pointed toward Wilden, who was talking to the news team. "I told him about Toby . . . how I thought he killed Ali. He said they checked him out, like, years ago. Toby's not even a suspect."

"He definitely did it." Emily stood back up. "Last night, when I told him I knew what he'd done, he got really panicked and begged me not to tell the cops."

Everyone looked at one another, confused. "So you think the cops are just wrong?" Hanna fiddled with the heart-shaped charm on her bracelet.

"Wait a minute," Emily said slowly. "Spencer, what was Ali blackmailing him about? How did she get Toby to take the blame for . . . for Jenna?"

"Spencer said Ali wouldn't tell her," Aria answered.

Spencer felt a tight, nervous feeling come over her. *It's better my way,* Ali had said. *We keep Toby's secret, he keeps ours.*

But Toby was dead. Ali was dead. It didn't matter, now. "I do know," she said quietly.

Then Spencer noticed someone coming around the side yard, and her heart sped up. It was Jenna Cavanaugh.

She was dressed in a black T-shirt and skinny black jeans, and her black hair was piled up on her head. Her skin was still a brilliant, snowy white, but her face was half-hidden by oversized sunglasses. She held a white cane in one hand and the harness to her golden retriever in the other. He led Jenna to the edge of the group.

Spencer was pretty sure she was about to faint. Either that or start crying again.

Jenna and her dog stopped right next to Hanna. "Is Emily Fields here?"

"Yes," Emily whispered. Spencer could hear the fear in her voice. "Right here."

Jenna turned in the direction of Emily's voice. "This is yours." She held out a pink satin purse. Emily took it very carefully, as if it were made of glass. "And there's something you should read." Jenna reached in her pocket for a wrinkled piece of paper. "It's from Toby."

37

STRING BRACELETS
ARE SO OUT, ANYWAY

Emily pushed her hair behind her ears and looked at Jenna. The sunglasses she wore stretched from her cheekbones to above her eyebrows, but Emily could just make out a few pinkish, wrinkled scars—burn scars—on her forehead.

She thought of that night. The way Ali's house had smelled like an Aveda peppermint candle. The way Emily's mouth tasted like salt-and-vinegar chips. How her feet rubbed against the grooves in the DiLaurentises' living room wood floor as she stood at the window, watching Ali run across the Cavanaughs' lawn. The *boom* of the firework, the paramedics climbing up the tree house ladder, how Jenna's mouth made a rectangle, she was crying so hard.

Jenna handed her the dirty, wrinkled piece of paper. "They found this with him," she said, her voice cracking on the word *him*. "He wrote things to all of us. Your part is somewhere in the middle."

The paper was actually the Foxy auction list; Toby had scrawled something on the back. Seeing the way Toby's words didn't stay between the lines, that he'd barely used any capital letters, and that he'd signed the note *Toby* in wobbly cursive made Emily clench up inside. Although she'd never seen Toby's handwriting before, it seemed to bring him to life beside her. She could smell the soap he used, feel his big hand holding her smaller one. This morning, she'd awakened not on the porch swing but in her bed. The doorbell was ringing. She stumbled down the stairs, and there was a guy in bike shorts and a helmet at her door. "Can I use your phone?" he asked. "It's an emergency."

Emily had stared at him woozily, not awake. Carolyn appeared behind her, and the cyclist started to explain himself. "I was just riding through your woods, and I found this boy, and first I thought he was sleeping, but . . ."

He'd paused, and Carolyn's eyes had widened. She ran in to get her cell phone. Meanwhile, Emily stood on the porch, trying to make sense of what was happening. She thought about Toby at her window last night. How he'd violently banged on the sliding glass door, then bolted for the woods.

She looked at the cyclist. "This boy in the woods, was he trying to hurt you?" she whispered, her heart pounding. It was horrifying that Toby really *had* camped out in her woods all night. What if he'd come up onto her porch after Emily had dozed off?

The cyclist hugged his helmet to his chest. He looked about Emily's dad's age, with green eyes and a salt-and-pepper beard. "No," he said gently. "He was . . . *blue*."

And now, this: a letter. A suicide note.

Toby had seemed so tortured, sprinting into the woods. Had he taken the pills right then? Or could Emily have stopped him? And was Hanna right—was Toby *not* Ali's killer?

The world started spinning. She felt a strong hand on the small of her back. "Whoa," Spencer whispered. "It's okay."

Emily straightened herself and looked at the letter. Her friends leaned in, too. There, right in the middle, was her name.

Emily, three years ago, I promised Alison DiLaurentis I'd keep a secret for her if she kept a secret for me. She promised that secret would never get out, but I guess it has. I've tried to deal with it—and to forget it—and when we became friends, I thought I could. . . . I thought I'd changed—and that my life had changed. But I guess you can't ever really change who you are. What I did to Jenna was the biggest mistake I've ever made. I was young and confused and stupid, and I never meant to hurt her. And I can't live with it anymore. I'm done.

Emily folded the note back up, the paper quaking in her hands. It didn't make sense—*they* were the ones who'd hurt Jenna, not Toby—what was he talking about? She handed it back to Jenna. "Thank you."

"You're welcome."

As Jenna turned to leave, Emily cleared her throat. "Wait," she croaked. "Jenna."

Jenna stopped. Emily swallowed hard. Everything Spencer just told her about Toby knowing and Ali lying, everything Toby had said last night, all the guilt she'd carried about Jenna for so many years . . . it all bubbled over.

"Jenna, *I* should apologize to you. We were . . . we used to be so mean. The stuff we did . . . the names, whatever . . . It wasn't funny."

Hanna stepped forward. "She's totally right. It wasn't funny at all." Emily hadn't seen Hanna look so tortured in a long time. "And you didn't deserve it," she added.

Jenna stroked her dog's head. "It's okay," she answered. "I'm over it."

Emily sighed. "But it's not okay. It's not okay at all. I . . . I never knew what being . . . teased because you're different . . . felt like. But now I do." She tensed her shoulder muscles, hoping it would keep her from crying. Part of her wanted to tell everyone what she was struggling with. But she held back. This wasn't the right time. There was more she wanted to say, too, but how could she? "And I'm sorry about your accident, too. I never got to tell you."

She wanted to add, *I'm sorry for what we accidentally did,* but she was too afraid.

Jenna's chin trembled. "It's not your fault. And anyway, it's not the worst thing that happened to me." She pulled on her dog's collar and walked back to the front yard.

The girls were quiet until Jenna was out of earshot.

"What could be worse than being blinded?" Aria whispered.

"There was something worse," Spencer interrupted. "The thing that Ali knew . . ."

Spencer had that look on her face again—like she had a lot to say, but she didn't want to say any of it. She sighed. "Toby used to . . . touch . . . Jenna," she whispered. "That's what he was doing, the night of Jenna's accident. That's why Ali misaimed the firework into the tree house."

When Ali got to Toby's tree house, Spencer explained, she saw Toby in the window and lit the firework. And then . . . she saw Jenna was there, too. There was something strange about Jenna's expression, and her shirt was unbuttoned. Then Ali saw Toby go over to Jenna and put his hand on her neck. He moved his other hand under Jenna's shirt and on top of the bra. He slid a strap off her shoulder. Jenna looked terrified.

Ali said she was so shocked, she bumped the firework out of position. The spark sped rapidly up the wick, and the rocket launched. Then there was a bright, confusing flash. Glass shattered. Someone screamed . . . and Ali ran.

"When Toby came up to us and told Ali he'd seen her, Ali told Toby she'd seen *him* . . . fooling around with Jenna," Spencer said. "The only way she wouldn't tell Toby's parents was if Toby admitted to lighting the firework himself. Toby agreed." She sighed. "Ali made me promise not to tell what Toby had done, along with everything else."

"Jesus," Aria whispered. "So Jenna must've been *happy* Toby was sent away."

Emily had no idea how to respond. She turned to look at Jenna, who was standing across the lawn with her mom, talking to a reporter. What must that have felt like, having your stepbrother do that to you? It had been bad enough when Ben went at her—what if she had to live with him? What if he was part of her family?

But it tore her up inside, too. Doing that to your stepsister was horrible, but it was also . . . pathetic. Of course Toby had just wanted to get past it now, to get on with his life. And he had been . . . until Emily scared him into thinking it was all coming back to haunt him.

She felt so horrified, she covered her face with her hands and took huge, gulping breaths. *I ruined Toby's life,* she thought. *I killed him.*

Her friends let her cry for a while—they were all crying, too. When Emily was reduced to dry, shuddering sobs, she looked up. "I just can't believe it."

"I can." Hanna said. "Ali only cared about herself. She was the queen of manipulation."

Emily looked at her, surprised. Hanna shrugged. "My seventh-grade secret? The one only Ali knew? Ali tortured me with it. Any time I didn't go along with something she wanted me to do, Ali threatened to tell you guys—and everyone else."

"She did that to you, too?" Aria sounded surprised. "There were times when she'd say something about my secret that made it so . . . *obvious.*" She lowered her eyes. "Before Toby . . . took those pills, he outed that secret about me. The secret Ali knew, and the one A—*Toby*—was threatening me about."

Everyone sat up straighter. "What was it?" Hanna asked.

"It was . . . just this family thing." Aria's lip trembled. "I can't talk about it now."

Everyone was quiet for a while, thinking. Emily stared at the birds fluttering in and out of her dad's feeder. "It makes perfect sense that Toby was A," Hanna whispered. "He didn't kill Ali, but he still wanted revenge."

Spencer shrugged. "I hope you're right."

It was calm and bright back inside Emily's house. Her parents weren't home yet, but Carolyn had just made microwave popcorn, and the whole house smelled like it. To Emily, microwave popcorn always smelled better than it tasted, and despite her lack of appetite, her stomach growled. She thought, *Toby will never smell microwave popcorn again.*

Neither would Ali.

She glanced through her bedroom window toward the front yard. Just hours ago, Toby had been standing there, pleading with Emily not to tell the cops. And to think, what he'd meant was *Please don't tell them what I did to Jenna.*

Emily thought about Ali again. How Ali had lied to them about everything.

The funny but sad thing about all of it was that Emily was pretty sure she'd started loving Ali the night of Jenna's accident, after the ambulances left and Ali came back inside. Ali was so calm and protective, so self-assured and wonderful. Emily had been freaking out, but Ali was there to make her feel better.

"It's all right," Ali had cooed to her, scratching Emily's back, her fingers making large, slow circles. "I promise you. It'll be okay. You have to believe me."

"But how can it be okay?" Emily sobbed. "How do you know?"

"Because I just do."

Then Ali took Emily and laid her down on the couch, propping Emily's head in her lap. Ali's hands began to softly rake her scalp. It felt spookily good. So good, Emily forgot where she was, or how scared she felt. Instead, she was . . . transported.

Ali's movements got slower and slower, and Emily began to fall asleep. What happened next, Emily would never forget. Ali bent down and kissed Emily's cheek. Emily froze, jolted awake. Ali did it again. It felt so good.

She sat back up and started scratching Emily's head again. Emily's heart beat madly.

The rational part of Emily's brain put the incident out of her mind, figuring Ali had meant it in a comforting way. But the emotional part of her let the feeling bloom like the tiny capsules her parents put in her Christmas stocking that slowly formed big, spongy shapes in hot water. That was when Emily's love for Ali took hold, and without that night, maybe it never would have happened at all.

Emily sat down on her bed, staring abstractly out the window. She felt empty, like someone had scooped her insides right out like a jack-o'-lantern.

Her room was very quiet; the only sound was of the ceiling fan's blades whapping around. Emily opened the top drawer of her desk and found a pair of old left-handed scissors. She placed the blades between the strings of the bracelet Ali had made for her so many years ago, and in one swift chop, she cut it off. She didn't quite want to throw the bracelet away, but she didn't want to leave it on the floor where she could see it, either. In the end, she pushed it far under her bed with the edge of her foot.

"Ali," she whispered, tears running down her face. *"Why?"*

A buzzing across the room startled her. Emily had hung the pink bag Jenna returned to her on her bedroom doorknob. She could see her phone glowing through its thin fabric. Slowly, she got up and retrieved her purse. By the time she pulled her phone out, it had stopped ringing.

ONE NEW TEXT MESSAGE, her little Nokia said. Emily felt her heart speed up.

> Poor, confused Emily. I bet you could use a big warm girl hug right now, huh? Don't get too comfortable. It's not over until I say it is. —A

ACKNOWLEDGMENTS

There are a lot of people to thank for *Flawless*. First and foremost, the Alloy Entertainment crew, for all of their hard work and perseverance to make these books great: the inimitable Josh Bank, who can harness his inner teenage girl better than anyone I know. Ben Schrank, whose editorial guidance and oddly witty banter I will sorely miss. Les Morgenstein, for his "Eureka!" plot ideas . . . and because he buys us cookies. And last but not least, thanks to my editor, Sara Shandler, who can talk about dogs for hours, who makes great parrot noises, and who is a big reason this book makes sense.

My appreciation also to the extraordinary people at HarperCollins: Elise Howard, Kristin Marang, Farrin Jacobs, and the rest of the Harper team. All of your unflagging enthusiasm for the Pretty Little Liars series has been wonderful.

As always, thanks and love to Bob and Mindy Shepard, for teaching me at a young age that the most important things in life are to be silly, to be happy with what you do, and to always write fake information on restaurant comment cards. You're lovely parents and always have been—combining only the good qualities of Emily's, Spencer's, Aria's, and Hanna's. Thanks to Ali and to Ali's demonic, striped, I-love-to-bite cat, Polo.

Kisses to Grammar, Pavlov, Kitten, Sparrow, Chloe, Rover, Zelda, Riley, and Harriet. I'm so happy to have my cousin Colleen around, because she throws great parties, has friends who read my books, and comes up with the best drinking games. And, as usual, all of my love to Joel for, among other things, scratching my back, dealing with me when I make no sense, eating icing out of the can, and watching catty, girly shows on TV with me and even discussing them afterward.

I'd also like to acknowledge my late grandfather, Charles Vent. He was sort of my inspiration for Hanna—he had a little habit of "taking things without paying for them." But seriously, he was one of the most loving and creative people I was lucky enough to know, and I always thought he deserved a little bit of fame, even if it's in the acknowledgments page of a book.

WHAT HAPPENS NEXT . . .

Did you really believe I was Toby? Puh-lease. I would have killed myself too. I mean, honestly—ew. He totally had it coming. Karma's a bitch, and so am I—just ask Aria, Emily, Hanna, and Spencer. . . .

Let's start with Aria. The girl's so busy getting busy, I can barely keep track of her boyfriends. First Ezra, now Sean, and I have more than a sneaking suspicion she's not done with Ezra yet. That's the irritating thing about arty girls; they can never make up their minds. I guess I'll just have to help little Aria out and make the choice for her. I'm sure she's just going to loooove that.

Then there's Emily. Sweet, clueless Emily. Alison and Toby would probably say that kissing Emily is pretty much the kiss of death. But . . . oops . . . they can't say anything—they're dead. I guess Em should watch where she puts her poisonous little lips. She's two for two, and superstitious Emily knows better than anyone that bad things always happen in threes.

Lonely wittle Hannakins. Sean dumped her. Her dad dumped her. And her mom probably would if she could. Being unpopular kinda makes you want to throw up, huh? Or is that just Hanna? At least she has her BFF, Mona, to hold her hair back. Wait a second, no she doesn't. I wish I could tell you it couldn't get any worse for Hanna, but no one likes a liar. Least of all me.

Finally, there's Spencer: Sure, the little overachiever knows her SAT words by heart, but her memory's kinda fuzzy when it comes to the night Alison disappeared. Don't worry, she's about to get a refresher course courtesy of yours truly. Look at me—so eleemosynary! That's SAT for "nice"!

If you were as smart as me, you'd probably have figured out who I am by now. OMG, not being a genius must be so annoying. And I can't help you with that one—I've got my hands full with four pretty little liars at the moment. But since you've been so patient, I'll give you one hint: Spencer may have a 4.0, but I've got As to my name, too. Kisses! —A

READ ON FOR A PREVIEW OF
PRETTY LITTLE LIARS BOOK THREE.

FROM

Perfect

Spencer was the first to speak. "Don't you just want to *kill* her sometimes?"

The others flinched. They never bad-mouthed Ali. It was as blasphemous as burning the Rosewood Day official flag on school property, or admitting that Johnny Depp really wasn't *that* cute—that he was actually kind of old and creepy.

Of course, on the inside, they felt a little differently. This spring, Ali hadn't been around as much. She'd gotten closer with the high school girls on her JV field hockey squad and never invited Aria, Emily, Spencer, or Hanna to join them at lunch or come with them to the King James Mall.

And Ali had begun to keep secrets. Secret texts, secret phone calls, secret giggles about things she wouldn't tell them. They'd bared their souls to Ali—telling her things they hadn't told the others, things they didn't want *anyone* to know—and they expected her to reciprocate. Hadn't Ali made them all promise that they would tell one another everything, absolutely *everything*, until the end of time?

The girls hated to think of what eighth grade would be like if things kept going like this. But it didn't mean they hated *Ali.*

Aria wound a piece of long, dark hair around her fingers and laughed nervously. "Kill her because she's so cute, maybe." She hit the camera's power switch, turning it on.

"And because she wears a size zero," Hanna added.

"That's what I meant." Spencer glanced at Ali's phone, which was wedged between two couch cushions. "Want to read her texts?"

"I do," Hanna whispered.

Emily stood up from her perch on the couch's arm. "I don't know. . . ." She started inching away from Ali's phone, as if just being close to it incriminated her.

Spencer scooped up Ali's cell. "C'mon. Don't you want to know who texted her?"

"It was probably just Katy," Emily whispered, referring to one of Ali's hockey friends. "You should put it down, Spence."

Aria took the camera off the tripod and walked toward Spencer. "Let's do it."

They gathered around. Spencer opened the phone and pushed a button. "It's locked."

"Do you know her password?" Aria asked, still filming.

"Try her birthday," Hanna whispered. She took the phone from Spencer and punched in the digits. The screen didn't change. "What do I do now?"

They heard Ali's voice before they saw her. "What are you guys doing?"

Spencer dropped Ali's phone back onto the couch. Hanna stepped back so abruptly, she banged her shin against the coffee table.

Ali stomped through the door to the family room, her eyebrows knitted together. "Were you looking at my phone?"

"Of course not!" Hanna cried.

"We were," Emily admitted. Aria shot her a look and then hid behind the camera lens.

But Ali was no longer paying attention. Spencer's older sister, Melissa, a senior in high school, burst into the Hastings' kitchen from the garage. Her adorable boyfriend, Ian, was with her. Ali stood up straighter. Spencer smoothed her dirty-blond hair.

Ian stepped into the family room. "Hey, girls."

"Hi," Spencer said in a loud voice. "How are you, Ian?" She fluttered her coal-black eyelashes.

Ali rolled her eyes. "Be a little more obvious," she singsonged under her breath.

But it was hard not to crush on Ian. He had curly blond hair, perfect white teeth, and stunning blue eyes.

Ian plopped down on the edge of the couch near Ali.

"So, what are you girls doing?"

"Oh, not much," Aria said, adjusting the camera's focus. "Making a film."

"A film?" Ian looked amused. "Can I be in it?"

"Of course," Spencer said quickly. She plopped down on the other side of him.

Ian grinned into the camera. "So what are my lines?"

"It's a talk show," Spencer explained. She glanced at Ali, gauging her reaction, but Ali didn't respond. "I'm the host. You and Ali are my guests. I'll do you first."

Ali let out a sarcastic snort and Spencer's cheeks flamed as pink as her Ralph Lauren T-shirt. Ian let the reference pass by. "Okay. Interview away."

Spencer sat up straighter on the couch, crossing her muscular legs just like a talk show host. She picked up the pink microphone from Hanna's karaoke machine and held it under her chin. "Welcome to the Spencer Hastings show. For my first question–"

"Ask him who his favorite teacher at Rosewood is," Aria called out.

Ali perked up. Her blue eyes glittered. "That's a good question for you, Aria. You should ask him if he wants to *hook up* with any of his teachers. In vacant parking lots."

Aria's mouth fell open. Hanna and Emily exchanged a confused glance.

"All my teachers are dogs," Ian said slowly, not getting whatever was happening.

"Ian, can you *please* help me?" Melissa made a clattering noise in the kitchen.

"One sec," Ian called out.

"Ian." Melissa sounded annoyed.

"I got one." Spencer tossed her long blond hair behind her ears. She was loving that Ian was paying more attention to them than to Melissa. "What would your ultimate graduation gift be?"

"Ian," Melissa called through her teeth. Spencer glanced at her sister through the wide French doors to the kitchen. The light from the fridge cast a shadow across her face. "I. Need. Help."

"Easy," Ian answered, ignoring her. "I'd want a base-jumping lesson."

"Base-jumping?" Aria called. "What's that?"

"Parachuting from the top of a building," Ian explained.

As Ian told a story about Hunter Queenan, one of his friends who had base-jumped, the girls leaned forward eagerly. Aria focused the camera on Ian's jaw, which looked hewn out of stone. Her eyes flickered for a moment to Ali. She was sitting next to Ian, staring off into space. Was Ali *bored*?

Aria glanced again at Ali's cell phone, which was resting on the cushion of the couch next to her arm. What was she hiding from them? What was she up to?

Don't you sometimes want to kill her? Spencer's question floated through Aria's brain as Ian rambled on. Deep down, she knew they all felt that way. It might be better if Ali were just . . . gone, instead of leaving them behind.

"So Hunter said he got the most amazing rush when he base-jumped," Ian concluded. "Better than anything. Including sex."

"*Ian,*" Melissa warned.

"That sounds incredible." Spencer looked to Ali on the other side of Ian. "Doesn't it?"

"Yes." Ali looked sleepy, almost like she was in a trance. "Incredible."

The rest of the week had been a blur: final exams, planning parties, more get-togethers, and more tension. And then, on the evening of the last day of seventh grade, Ali went missing. Just like that.

The police scoured Rosewood for clues. They questioned the four girls separately, asking if Ali had been acting strangely or if anything unusual had happened recently. They all thought long and hard. The night she disappeared had been strange—she'd been hypnotizing them and had run out of the barn after she and Spencer had a stupid fight about the blinds and just . . . *never came back.* But had there been other strange nights? They considered the night they tried to read Ali's texts, but not for very long—after Ian and Melissa left, Ali had snapped out of her funk. They'd had a dance contest and played with Hanna's karaoke machine.

Next, the cops asked if they thought anyone close to

Ali might have wanted to hurt her. Hanna, Aria, and Emily all thought of the same thing: *Don't you sometimes want to kill her?* Spencer had snarled. But no. She'd been kidding. Hadn't she?

SUTTON MERCER HAS A LIFE
ANY GIRL WOULD KILL FOR...
**AND MAYBE
SOMEONE DID.**

A DEADLY NEW SERIES FROM
SARA SHEPARD

HARPER TEEN
An Imprint of HarperCollinsPublishers
WWW.HARPERTEEN.COM

Photo by Daniel Snyder

SARA SHEPARD graduated from New York University and has an MFA in Creative Writing from Brooklyn College. She currently lives in Tucson, Arizona, with her husband. The Pretty Little Liars series was inspired by her upbringing in Philadelphia's Main Line.

For exclusive information
on your favorite authors and artists,
visit www.authortracker.com.

EVERYONE IN ULTRA-EXCLUSIVE ROSEWOOD, PENNSYLVANIA, HAS SOMETHING TO HIDE...

FIND OUT WHAT THE PRETTY LITTLE LIARS
ARE HIDING AT **WWW.PRETTYLITTLELIARS.COM**.

CHECK OUT **WWW.PRETTYLITTLELIARSBOOKS.COM**
FOR SERIES GOSSIP, GAMES, AND GIVEAWAYS.